CASCADE

Pamela Beason

WildWing Press

Bellingham, Washington, USA

For all the ski patrol employees at our mountain resorts and all those who work to protect wildlife in the United States.

Copyright Page

WILDWING PRESS
3301 Brandywine Court
Bellingham, Washington 98226

Copyright © 2022 Pamela Beason
Cover design by Christine Savoie
ISBN-13: 978-0-9983149-6-9
https://pamelabeason.com

Notes from the Author

Although I have used real locations in this book, the story is purely fictional. Although minor earthquakes and avalanches are common in the North Cascades, to my knowledge there has never been a series of avalanches as severe as depicted in *Cascade*, and I hope there never will be. In real life, the Mt. Baker Ski Area and the Raven Hut Day Lodge are still in beautiful condition and ready to welcome skiers.

In *Cascade,* I also mention a tiny-home community in Bellingham, designed to provide temporary housing for those experiencing homelessness. In real life, the residents of tiny homes are vetted to be sure they are not criminals or dangerously mentally ill. Alcohol, drugs, and weapons are not allowed, and the communities are managed. Although I have Maya living in a tent as a temporary guest in this book, tents are not allowed in tiny-home communities, as far as I know.

Acknowledgments

All authors need the opinions and suggestions of others to improve our work, and I am so grateful that my readers and editors always do that for me. I'd like to express my gratitude to the following people who graciously took the time to read my drafts and share their comments to improve Cascade: Worldkeeper Diane Garland, Barbara Ellis, Sue Brown, Jeanine Clifford, Alison Malfatti, author Elizabeth Crowens, and author Carole T. Beers. Janet Vincent gave me the title for this book. Ron Malfatti generously shared his knowledge of the Mount Baker Ski Area topography and structures. And I could never publish a book without the careful scrutiny and clever suggestions from super-editor Karen Brown.

And last but never least, thank you to my readers for being willing to go on another adventure with Sam Westin.

Thank you all!

1

The woman hung upside down in the air as if she were skiing on the cobalt sky above her feet. Summer "Sam" Westin held her breath until the contestant in the Mount Baker Aerial Freestyle Competition finally righted herself to land neatly on her skis. The sparse crowd on the sidelines roared in approval.

The daring of these young athletes astounded Sam; they seemed to have no sense of mortality. How did they even practice these incredible stunts without breaking their necks? She would be terrified of ending up a paraplegic on her first try at a maneuver like that one.

Sam could imagine her young friend, Maya Velasquez, taking a flying leap into space like that with no hesitation. As a teenager, Maya had fearlessly tackled building hiking trails in the Olympic National Forest. Then, after aging out of the foster care system, she led troubled teens in a wilderness training school, understanding them better than an older instructor because she, too, had been a delinquent only a short time ago.

At least that had been the old Maya. Last year's Maya. Now the young woman seemed to be headed again for an aimless life.

The next contestant completed an amazing twisting double flip and nailed her landing without even a spritz of snow, sailing smoothly across the finish line to the cheers of the crowd. Sam tapped off the video Record button and then slid her cell phone into her jacket pocket. Noting the number on the girl's contest bib, she matched the number on the clipboard tucked under her arm, and checked the girl's name off her list, noting the time the contestant had finished her run.

Thank heavens this contest was nearly over. Only one more skier to go. When she'd taken this part-time gig at *Out There* magazine, she hadn't expected the reporting jobs to be so awkward. Her imagination, typically confined to all things nature-oriented, hadn't included every sport from motorcycle riding to snowboarding. When she signed up to write about "outdoor adventures," she thought she'd write about backpacking and kayaking and scuba diving and such. Adventures that included wilderness and wildlife, not people out to win competitions in front of crowds.

She also hadn't imagined the physical requirements of this job would be so uncomfortable; she really needed another arm to hold onto all the gear. Still, just to see so many outdoor lovers gathered again after all the months of quarantine made the experience worthwhile. Sam could hardly believe she was getting paid to be here.

This late-season contest was obviously a hastily thrown together affair. The launch ramp was a temporary construction that would be torn down as soon as the event was over. Now, in late April, the snow was skin-grating gravel in the morning, slush by midafternoon, and ice by midnight. A dark bank of clouds was slowly slithering in from the Salish Sea to the west, and Sam was glad that she and her friends would be off the mountain when that weather system arrived. But at the moment, the sky overhead was blue, and the mood of the crowd was celebratory. Both experienced and novice skiers and snowboarders were thrilled to taste the rush of speeding down the slopes, and observers were celebrating the freedom to hug friends and talk without the muffle of masks.

The lodges were doing a booming business today selling food and drink to happy customers.

"Sam." The sound of her name was accompanied by a sharp tug on her sleeve at the elbow.

She shifted on her snowshoes, twisting around in surprise. Gina Canfield stood at her shoulder, rocking from foot to foot, her graying ponytail askew. Gina, a fellow wildlife biologist, was dedicated to various volunteer efforts in the North Cascades, most notably to installing and monitoring cameras throughout the local wilderness areas to document the wildlife there.

"Gina!" Sam greeted her. "I'm surprised to see you here. I thought you didn't do crowds. I'd hug you if I had a free hand. *Out There* has me covering this event. Thank God it's almost done. One more contestant, and then all I have left is the award ceremony. My feet are numb from standing here."

The loudspeaker announced the last competitor, and Sam pulled out her cell phone again, raising it into position and thumbing on the video recorder to catch the stunt. A young man this time. Aerial Freestyle was a co-ed contest. But could she use that word in her story on this event? Did anyone say "co-ed" anymore? The term sounded so old-fashioned in her head. Ambi-gender? Multi-gender? Would Google know?

The kid's twisting flip was impressive, but he wiped out as he landed, his skis slipping from beneath his feet. He finished his run sliding on his butt, his board scraping up a bow wave of snow in front of him.

"Sam!"

She focused on Gina again. "Chase is skiing with Blake and Claude over at the White Salmon area, near Raven Hut." Then she added, trying not to sound bitter, "And his old FBI partner, Nicole, is with them too. Some Homeland Security meeting up in—"

Scowling, Gina flicked a mittened hand impatiently

through the air. "I don't care about your lover and your housemate and their friends! I need you."

Sam couldn't remember the last time anyone except her housemate Blake had said they *needed* her for anything, and Blake usually only wanted her to sample his latest culinary experiment.

Gina's face was tense. "We have to go now. We need to rescue Feisty."

The muscles between Sam's shoulder blades tensed at the urgency in her friend's voice. "Rescue? Why? What's going on?"

"Feisty's radio signal hasn't moved more than a foot for hours now. Something really bad has happened to her."

"Radio signal? She has a collar?" Although she was trained as a wildlife biologist and she knew the value of research from radio tracking, Sam hated to see wild animals wearing collars. It seemed so wrong to burden a wild creature with the bulky human device. In some states, hunters actually used the signals to track and kill their prey. In Africa, the codes were routinely stolen or bought by poachers to kill rhinos and other endangered species. Sometimes a collar was not only an awkward inconvenience, but also a death sentence for a wild animal.

Still frowning, Gina nodded. "Not my choice, but yes, so I could get funding to continue my study in the North Cascades."

Sam noted that her friend's hands were empty. "Where's your tracker?"

Gina tapped her pocket. "Cell phone. It's a satellite feed. Sometimes we can get photos and videos, too."

"You can do that? Set up a remote camera with a cell phone connection?"

"You've been living under a rock, haven't you?" Gina responded dryly. "In this century, some collars and tags and wildlife cameras can use cell phone networks. Some come with attached solar panels. But ours are usually hidden in the trees, so my geek squad volunteers rigged up a system to connect to a solar panel on top of a tree. Which sometimes works when the panel's not covered with snow. In between times, our cameras rely on the batteries. But right now, I'm getting the signal from her collar."

"Got it." Sam felt like a dolt. "So where is Feisty?"

"Close to my camera location. She might be in a trap."

Sam's imagination immediately delivered a nightmarish vision of a wolverine with one foot clamped between the shark-toothed jaws of an old-fashioned steel trap. Her stomach lurched. Taking a deep breath, she reminded herself that there were more benign traps. She'd read a book about studying wolverines in Glacier National Park, and the biologists working there had built traps that resembled tiny log cabins.

"Who would trap her? Another biologist?"

"An asshole, more likely," Gina growled. "Probably one of the Priests."

"A priest?" Had she heard that wrong? The clergy was trapping wild animals?

"Yeesh, Sam." Gina's expression confirmed she was a nitwit. "One of Anton Priest's clan. The Priests live near Glacier; they've set traps in this area before."

Sam checked her watch. "When did Feisty last move?"

"I checked fifteen minutes ago. She was still moving then, just not much. She's been captured by that camera quite a lot recently. We think she has a den nearby. But she's never been this stationary."

Sam caught her lower lip between her teeth. The female wolverine probably had kits secluded somewhere close to that camera. Baby wolverines, buried somewhere in a den hidden ten feet under the snow, hungrily waiting for their mother, who was now injured or imprisoned.

So-called "skunk bears" were exceedingly rare in the Lower 48. Washington State had designated wolverines a "Species of Greatest Conservation Need," which seemed to mean only that they merited farther study, and the current federal authorities stubbornly refused to put them on the national endangered list, along with a multitude of other animals that deserved protection. Sam had seen Feisty only through images captured by Gina's camera. She'd give anything to see a wolverine up close.

And now this mama wolverine, designated "F3" because she was only the third known female in the North Cascades, was in trouble. What did her trapper have in mind for her? Was she about to become a pelt auctioned off on the internet, like that rare jaguar in Arizona?

Sam quickly surveyed the contest venue. The crowd had already started to melt away toward the parking lots or the day lodge, but others gathered near the flagged area designated for the winners to accept their ribbons. The winners' names were already listed on the electronic sign above. She snapped a quick photo of that, then stuffed her clipboard into the backpack resting beside her on the hard-packed snow.

"I can catch a ride back to town with you, yes?" When Gina nodded, Sam thumbed her phone. "I'll send Chase a text message. He'll get it eventually." Cell phone communications in the Mount Baker area were iffy, but Chase had a satellite phone and a text would most likely go through here by the lodge. The message sent, she zipped her cell into her jacket pocket. It was a few minutes shy of three o'clock, and sunset was roughly eight o'clock. "It's around a two-hour hike to reach the camera location, right?"

"At least. We'll have to hustle to make it back here before dark."

Sam mentally inventoried the contents of her backpack.

She carried her usual winter collection: rain pants, hat, gloves, snow scoop, extendible avalanche pole, first aid kit, extra water, extra food, headlamp, and now, the clipboard. And a small roll of duct tape. She was a big fan of duct tape. "I'm good to go," she told Gina.

"Figured you would be. I have a pistol and tranq darts if we need 'em to grab Feisty."

"Aren't we just going to free her?" Sam couldn't quite wrap her imagination around how they'd capture, let alone transport, a pissed-off wolverine. Wolverines were renowned for their ferocity. The largest members of the weasel family, they had long claws, razor-sharp teeth, and bone-crunching jaw strength that rivaled many sharks, and had been known to battle with grizzlies.

"Let's hope we only need to let her out of a trap," Gina said. "We'll only use the tranqs if she's injured."

Sam had read that a wolverine's powerful jaws could snap the thigh bone of an elk. What kind of condition was Feisty going to be in when they sprang the door of that trap? What kind of mood? Would she attack?

The humans might need the tranquilizers more than the wolverine.

2

Leaving behind the hubbub of the ski area was a relief. Aside from their breathing and an occasional slosh from a water bottle on her back, the squeak of the hard-packed snow under their snowshoes was the only sound Sam heard after she and Gina had passed over the mountain ridge at the top of the groomed ski slopes. The silhouettes of only three die-hard backcountry skiers bound for Artists Point dotted the patchwork vista of dark evergreens and white snow on the mountainside above their position. The skiers wore climbing skins attached to their skis as they trudged up the slopes.

Sam had climbed up and skied down a few times herself, but now she'd largely given up skis, at least the downhill type, in favor of trekking more slowly through the natural areas, which increased the odds of encountering wildlife.

Thoughts of Maya again oozed into her brain. The girl—no, young woman; Maya was nearly twenty-two now—had suffered so many losses and trials in her short life. The lockdown had only been the latest challenge, with college classes retreating to Zoom, a situation for which Maya had little patience. A study buddy named Brianna had helped for a few months. But then, Brianna had died a horrible death from COVID, gasping for air even while on a ventilator. Maya had promptly dropped out of community college, which caused her, a former foster child, to lose the state funds she received for education and housing.

So, Sam had reluctantly agreed that Maya could once again put up her tent in Sam's backyard. Then Maya had lost her part-time job at REI during the pandemic and, as far as Sam knew, was not on the roster for leading wayward teens on mountain treks with the local Wilderness Challenge program this summer, either.

The pandemic and lockdown had changed everyone, but now most seemed happy to be emerging from the restrictions. Why was Maya still spiraling downward? The young woman seemed to have reverted to a wayward teen herself. And she spent way too many hours with that creepy kid, the one with long greasy hair and the cold yellow gaze of a snake. Sam was certain that he often slept in Maya's tent. She didn't like the thought of him prowling around her backyard in the dark, and she hated even more the idea that he might borrow Maya's key to take a shower or use the toilet in her cabin.

What was that kid's name? Something that rhymed with sleaze—Eaze, that was it. What the hell kind of a name was Eaze? Sam had discovered his real name was Ethan Zeran; she'd had Chase run a background check on him. He wasn't really a kid, either. He was twenty-three years old to Maya's twenty-one, with a juvie record even scarier than Maya's. Neither of them seemed to have a plan to become an adult any time in the near future.

Sam's stomach churned with the suspicion that whatever Maya and Eaze might be up to right now, it was definitely not good. Even if they were doing absolutely nothing, as all the evidence seemed to indicate, that wasn't any sort of strategy to make a better future. She really needed to put her foot down, tell Maya she could no longer camp out at her house if Eaze was present.

Sam didn't care where Eaze might end up, but where would

Maya go? The girl had no family and no money. Before the discovery of her relationship to Jade Silva last year, Maya had been showing real promise, doing well in school and even serving as a mentor to other teens. Now it seemed like Maya was incapable of recognizing any good in the world, let alone contributing to it.

Sam understood all too well that fuck-it-all mindset, although her own attitude was more a shifting fog of pessimism. In the last few years, several of her friends had died violent deaths. Two of those friends had also been Maya's co-workers. Sam had also met another earlier victim, and that girl, too, had been a colleague of Maya's on the trail building crew. Then, to her amazement, Sam discovered that her new friend in New Mexico, Jade Silva, was actually Maya's half sister. Jade and Maya and even Jade's mother, Katerina Franco, had been astounded by the connection. But Maya never got the chance to meet Jade. There was so much ugliness and sorrow everywhere.

In the last few years, the COVID pandemic and the accompanying national politics had added a layer of grime to society that might not ever be cleaned away. This world could be a truly hostile place when humans were in charge.

Her opinion of the human species typically ranked lower than her estimation of bacteria and viruses. But as long as she had wilderness to explore and wild creatures to study, the world held enough fascination to make it a satisfying place to live. Simon, her cat, had always been a loyal friend, too. Animals were trustworthy.

The last two years had been a challenge. Friends with partners and families vanished into their own "pods." Sam was thankful she had Blake as a housemate. He added humor and spice to her home life, as well as great cooking. She would have gone stark raving mad without him. If his newly reactivated affair with Claude became a permanent relationship, she hoped that she and Blake would remain close friends. Maybe the three of them could live together, add a room or two onto her cabin. Would that be weird?

Blake would remind her right now that she had Chase. Who wouldn't want a smart, handsome Latino-Lakota-FBI-agent lover living only twenty minutes away? But that was the problem, wasn't it? When Chase was in town, which was rare, he was still twenty minutes away. And for the last year, he'd had to quarantine every time he came back from one of his work trips, so he'd been off limits most of the time. With so much time spent on American Indian reservations, she fretted that he was growing closer to the tribal members he worked with than to her.

He'd wanted her to move in with him. But then, when he was working, she'd be alone at his house instead of her own. She failed to see what good that would do. She was hardly a homemaker. She had no idea what the future might hold for their relationship.

Her thoughts circled back to Maya. Sam was not at all sure that the girl, the product of a drug-addict mother, foster care, and juvie hall, cared enough about anything to plan for the future. She had no idea how to light a fire under the twenty-one-year-old. Sam had never wanted children, and she'd certainly never planned on having a teenager attach to her. Maya was like a mangy stray dog you didn't want to keep as a pet, but couldn't bring yourself to abandon.

Lost in thought, Sam nearly collided with Gina when the other woman abruptly stopped on the ridge overlooking a steep valley.

They were standing on top of what would be revealed as the Lake Ann trailhead when the snow melted. The path to Lake Ann was one of Sam's favorite trails. It was a challenging hike because the trail descended steeply, then crossed a valley, and then ascended up a long steep slope on the other side to the mountain lake below the glaciers of Mount Shuksan. Unlike the majority of mountain trails in the Cascades that wound up to a high peak and then were downhill all the way back, on the Lake Ann trail, a hiker had to climb a steep slope both on the way in and out. Sam had never attempted the route in winter, because the steepness of the surrounding slopes threatened the possibility of avalanches. The freeze and thaw cycles of spring made the risk even higher, with the likelihood of slippery ice sandwiched between unstable snow layers.

Studying the snowy bowl of the valley below them and the rise of the mountains on the other side, Sam groaned. "Tell me you're kidding, Gina."

"Not kidding," Gina told her. "My camera is in the trees on the ridge to the south of Lake Ann."

"Let's at least stick to the general trail route," Sam suggested. "Less avalanche danger through the forest."

"Agreed," Gina dug her poles into the snow and set off down the slope. "Watch out for tree wells."

Sam stuck out her tongue at the other woman's back. She'd been avoiding tree wells for more than twenty years now.

The snow under the thick cover of evergreen trees was icier than on the surrounding slopes, and the litter of fallen limbs and needles and cones made the hike down difficult. Gina stumbled and slid and grabbed onto an overhanging branch to shower both of them with skin-stinging grains of ice from above. Sam struggled with each step to jam the metal claws of her snowshoes into the ground cover, her knees and ankles painfully protesting the angle of descent.

On reaching the valley floor, they paused briefly to shake the snow out of their hair and parkas. After quick swallows of water, they were off again, crunching their way swiftly across the valley. It was already nearing four o'clock, and more clouds were gathering over the peaks to the southwest. Would she and Gina return to the ski resort before sunset? Sam tried to remember the current phase of the moon, although even a full moon would be useless hidden behind heavy clouds. She could use her headlamp if she needed to, although the beam did not extend far enough in deep darkness to be of much use. Gina would most likely have a headlamp as well.

Now that she had sufficient breath to talk again, Sam asked Gina, "So you think the trap was built by this Priest guy?"

"Possibly." Gina huffed. "Probably. He and his brothers have been caught a few times trapping a variety of animals in national forest areas."

"That's not always illegal, unfortunately." Sam shook her head at the thought.

"Depends on the area and how it's done," Gina responded, striding faster. "But the rules for most areas say that trappers have to kill the wild animals they catch. And it's illegal to trap or kill a wolverine in Washington, unless it's self-defense."

Sam snorted. Had there ever been an incident where a wolverine attacked a human out of the blue?

"But most people don't know it's illegal," Gina continued, "because most people don't even realize we have wolverines in this state. And although the state uses fancy words to say they're endangered, they aren't on the federal list, and I'm not sure that rangers would go after someone who killed only one wolverine."

Please, don't let a trapper kill Feisty. Sam sped up to match Gina's pace. "Would the Priests have access to your camera photos?"

"I hope not. Unless one of them found the camera and stole the storage card. But if they placed a trap, they could have some sort of sensor attached that sends out a signal when the trap is triggered."

"Then we need to hurry." Sam's hands fisted around her

pole grips at the thought of a killer on the way to the trapped animal.

The snow was deeper on the valley floor, softer in the treeless areas exposed to the bright sun. The muffled sound of running water alerted Sam that they were approaching the creek that zigzagged across the area, one of many that flowed into Swift Creek and down the valley toward Baker Lake. The little stream was not visible; the water would be tunneling under the snow here. She recognized its route from the gap in the brush tips emerging from the melting snow.

"One at a time," she suggested. "No way to tell how thick the snow is over this bridge."

"You go first." Gina tapped Sam on the arm, most likely because Sam was smaller and lighter. "If you fall through, I'll find another way around."

"Thanks a bunch." Clenching her jaw, Sam gingerly tromped across the area. She gasped when her left snowshoe suddenly plummeted several inches, but then the snow underneath held.

Gina crossed behind her, each step of hers sinking a few inches deeper.

3

"A thousand bucks," Eaze muttered, stroking his goatee. He sat with his back against one of the trees a few feet away from the opening of Maya's tent, his skinny legs splayed across the ground. "That's not really so much."

Maya exhaled a puff of disagreement. "Would be to me." Heck, a hundred would be a fortune right now.

What would she do with $1,000? Buy a plane ticket to somewhere sunnier, somewhere warmer. Maybe New Mexico, go see Jade's mother again. If she'd have her. Maya hadn't heard from Katerina Franco since she'd called her last October. She'd expected an invitation to visit. Katerina had originally been so nice, even after she'd discovered that Maya was her first husband's "love child," and half sister to her own daughter, Jade. But during that last conversation, Katerina had been cold. The woman had even hung up after telling Maya never to call when she was in "that condition."

Maya rubbed a hand across the frown lines on her brow, remembering. She hadn't been *that* drunk; she'd just forgotten that New Mexico clocks would be an hour later. What was wrong with these uptight people? Even Troy Johnson wouldn't commit to hiring her back again at Wilderness Challenge this summer, when he'd given her nothing but praise two years before.

That was her life these days. All the good people got killed one way or the other, and others she'd thought were her friends turned out to be scumbags. All her dreams turned to shit. She had been lucky to meet Eaze while smoking a joint in Fairhaven Park a few months ago. He'd been a foster kid, too. His parents were both in prison. He was the only person who understood how you could have the rug pulled out from beneath your feet with no notice whatsoever. Sam and Blake didn't think of much of Eaze, but they didn't really know him.

She'd wondered at first if she should invite him to sleep in her tent, but it had worked out. He wasn't there every night and he wasn't perfect. But he could be nice. He often brought food and wine and other gifts. The sex was rockin'. Eaze was the only person who hugged her these days. He understood it all—the job layoffs, the lack of home. The lack of family.

Eaze crawled into the tent beside her and laid a hand on her thigh. "I know you don't have the dough." He jerked his chin in the direction of Sam's cabin. "But she does, I'll bet."

Maya rolled her eyes. "I bet different. Sam doesn't even have a regular job. That's why she's got a roommate."

"Who also has a roommate. Another queer, right?"

"Hey!" Maya objected. "Blake and Claude are both cool, most of the time. And Claude's not a roommate. He's Canadian; he just visits sometimes. Only Sam and Blake live here." Maybe she should count herself as living here, too. Did it count that she pitched her tent in Sam's backyard?

"The Canadian dude is here now, right? Between the three of them, they could come up with a thou."

Maya was tired of this conversation. Eaze had been talking about the money ever since they rolled out of their sleeping bags this morning. "How the hell did you end up owing a thousand bucks to somebody, anyway?" she asked. Was he a secret gambler or something? Hanging out in casinos on the nights he wasn't here? "And who is that somebody?"

"JW." Eaze pushed his dark hair back off his shoulders, twisting it into a rope behind his neck. He had beautiful hair, long and silky, at least when it was clean. Today it was greasy.

Maya waited for more explanation. The only JW she knew stood for Jehovah's Witnesses, and she was fairly sure that wasn't who Eaze was talking about.

"It's for the H." Eaze snarled it like a complaint.

H. Maya had snorted heroin a few times, even a few times recently with Eaze, but she'd never spent more than a few dollars on a tiny nugget or packet of powder. Inhaling H was nice; that was the best word for it. Heroin made her feel chill. And happy, although she hated the way it made her nose ooze. Eaze spent half his life wiping his. She'd never resort to shooting up, though. Sticking a needle in your arm was disgusting, not to mention you could get some horrible disease.

Eaze swore he'd never do that, either. The bruises on the insides of his elbows were from carrying heavy crates when he volunteered at the food bank.

"You bought a thousand dollars of H off this JW?" she asked him. She'd heard there were a lot of car prowls going on around town, but she didn't think Eaze was into that. And who kept hundreds of dollars in their car, anyway? "Where the fuck did you get a thousand bucks?"

He shrugged. "I didn't."

Maya put it together. "OMG, you were supposed to sell it, weren't you?" She stared at him. She and Eaze might drink a little too much and use once in a while, but that was all just for fun, something to pass the time. Selling drugs was sinking into the abyss. Drugs had killed her mother. "You used it all yourself?"

His amber gaze blazed into hers. "You helped."

"Only twice. You offered!"

"Like that's gonna matter to JW," he explained. "I gotta get the H somehow. *We* gotta get it." He pulled her hand out of her lap, intertwined his fingers with hers. "See, he'll be looking for you, too. He knows who I hang with."

"I never heard of anyone named JW," she protested, jerking her hand away. "How would he know me?"

"Ah, babe." Eaze reached for her hand again, but when Maya pulled it back, he settled for slipping a finger through the rip in her jeans to stroke her thigh. "I mighta shown him your picture. You're so beautiful, I like to show you off. I'm proud of you."

Sam and Blake had sometimes said things like that when she studied or worked hard, but nobody had ever really been proud of her. Not her mother. She'd never even met her father. And now, apparently not even her boss at Wilderness Challenge was proud of her accomplishments. *Former boss*, she bitterly corrected her thoughts.

"I always said you were smart as well as hot," Eaze murmured, a smile gliding onto his lips. "You could sweet-talk JW." Moving his fingers away from the rip, he slid his hand up the inside of her thigh.

She slapped his fingers away and scooted back farther into the tent. "Not on your life."

"Babe." Eaze sighed heavily. "We gotta get it somehow." He frowned at a brown smear that extended from his big toe around the edge of his sandal. "Is that dog shit?"

"*Ewww.*" Maya jerked her chin toward the hose spigot on the side of Sam's cabin. "Go outside and clean it off."

Leaning back, Eaze snagged a piece of fabric from the pile of clothing at the rear of the tent and began to scrub at the smear.

Maya screeched and grabbed his arm. "That's a quilt square! That's *my* quilt square!" She pulled the fabric out of his hands. "I embroidered it! Sam taught me how. I told you! It's me, see?" She stretched it out in front of him, pointing to the figure's flaming, spiky hair. "I had red hair then." She'd let it grow out to her original black.

"You . . . with an axe?" Eaze laughed. "An axe and a pile of shit!"

Tears stung her eyes. "I told you. That's me, with a Pulaski. When I worked on the trail crew in Olympic National Park for my community service time. It was hard work, but it was kinda cool, being out in the woods all the time. We saw deer and elk and owls almost every day. I'm gonna do it again." She would, she promised herself. She could easily get strong again, be the outdoor expert people looked up to again. She just needed someone to give her a chance.

Eaze was still smirking, still staring at the quilt square. "Bet they made you shit in the woods, too."

"So?" Why was he attaching the word "shit" to everything? "That's when I met Sam. One day she brought a bear to our dorm."

Eaze frowned. "Why the fuck would anyone shoot a bear?"

"He wasn't dead. She had him in a cage. She was saving that bear, taking him somewhere safe. And then Sam and I got together later, after I was done with trail work, and we were making picture quilts, making different squares about our lives. And now you ruined my first one!"

He put his hand on her thigh again. "Sorry. At least it's still good for wiping off shit."

"You're such a bastard." Maya swiped at the tear that ran down her cheek. That wasn't just her first quilt square, it was her *only* quilt square. She had sketched out another that depicted her leading the Wilderness Challenge group last year, and a third that was supposed to be about going to college. But she hadn't started embroidering either one.

She didn't have a clue where her embroidery stuff was. Did

she even have it anymore?

"Aw, you're not gonna cry, are you?" Eaze leaned close. "You still love me, don't you, babe?"

She twisted away from his hot breath, folding the quilt square and tucking it beside her sleeping bag. She'd wash it; maybe the stain would come out. Sniffling, she wiped her wet eyes with her fingers.

Sam's cat, Simon, peered into the tent. Maya stretched out a hand to pet him, but when the cat spied Eaze next to her, he pivoted away toward the trees at the back of Sam's lot. Spying a robin hopping among the trees, he lowered his belly toward the ground and began to stalk the bird.

Eaze slid a hand into his jacket pocket. Maya expected him to pull out his usual pack of cigarettes, rubber-banded together with his lighter. Eaze always smoked when he was pissed off or worried. But when his hand emerged, it was clutching a pistol.

Her heartbeat sped up. "What's that for?"

"Dunno yet." Grinning, he slapped the gun from one hand to the other like a hot potato. Then he pointed the barrel toward the cat. "Leverage, maybe."

4

The clouds she'd witnessed earlier in the west were scudding across the sky to pile up over North Cascades National Park just a few miles to the east, slowly blurring the heavens from the startling clear blue to a gray wool coverlet that boded snow in the near future. Sam hoped that she and Gina would not be hiking back to the resort in a whiteout.

After crossing the valley, Gina led her halfway up the next mountain, rounding the slope into a steep wooded area Sam had never explored before, well away from the Lake Ann trail. "Isn't this where those two ..." she wasn't sure she wanted to finish the sentence.

"Bodies were found?" Gina guessed, finishing for her. "Yep, the two snowboarders. Somewhere around here."

The snow in this steep, rugged terrain was often unstable. They were miles away from the safer, groomed slopes of the ski resort. The two college students had been missing for most of a year before a hiker stumbled onto the grim remains of one of them. Sam struggled to pull her imagination away from what those remains must have looked like after eleven months of snow and thaw. Not to mention hungry animals. Would a wolverine dine on a human corpse?

The first icy crystals of snow stung her cheeks. "Oh, crap, it's starting to snow."

Gina didn't bother to turn her head. Her voice was muffled as she responded, "Yep."

"Are we getting close?" Sam puffed, clomping up the mountainside as Gina climbed toward a clearing that was more vertical than any sane woman should scale in snowshoes.

"*Shhh!*" Gina hissed, stopping at the edge of the trees. "We're there." She scanned the clearing above. "Shit!"

Then she took off, galloping on her snowshoes up the sheer slope, her poles raised, losing her stocking cap as she floundered in the snow. Startled by Gina's abrupt shout, Sam barely had time to take in the scene. A hundred yards above them, near the top of the clearing, next to a log trap, stood a figure dressed in a black parka and camouflage pants. Beside him was a large blue plastic dog carrier. The top of a log trap was propped open with a stick.

"Stop!" Gina bellowed.

The figure twisted to gaze downhill. The black shade of beard along his jawline proved he was male, but with a parka bunched around his neck and a stocking cap pulled low on his brow and with a slow curtain of snow blurring the details, it was hard to guess anything more. Reaching into the trap, the man hefted out a bulky bundle of dark fur, clutching it tightly to his chest.

That mass of fur had to be a wolverine. Feisty. Tranquilized. Or dead. Bending over the carrier, the guy hastily shoved his burden inside. The radio collar around the limp neck scratched against the plastic as the wolverine slid through the opening.

Sam's temper flared. She raced into the snow of the slope, adding her tracks and her voice to Gina's. "Stop, you bastard! You won't get away with this!"

The mountainside was steep, and the snow in the clearing was softer and deeper than it had been in the woods. Each step punched a hole into the drifts, forcing Sam to lift a heavy clump of snow every time she raised a snowshoe. She wanted to sprint upward, but this was more like stomping in place. A few yards upslope, Gina was making only slightly better progress, yelling epithets with every step.

The man straightened, hefted the carrier, and took off sideways across the clearing above them, cutting a horizontal path into the snow, headed for the forest that flanked the clearing on three sides.

"You! Shithead!" Gina screamed. "Hey, son of a bitch! Drop that carrier!"

A hot wave of rage flooded through Sam. Her body trembled with the frustration of knowing that neither she nor Gina could reach the wolverine snatcher in time to save Feisty.

The ground itself seemed to shimmer in commiseration beneath her snowshoes, and she noticed that the fringe of evergreens around the clearing were swaying, too. For a second, she had the insane thought that maybe divine retribution actually existed, Mother Earth quaking in outrage at the poacher taking one of her precious wild creatures.

But when a loud crack boomed somewhere near the top of the slope, Sam knew that something much more ominous was happening.

"Avalanche!" she screamed, turning. "Run!"

5

Sam did her best to race back to the woods. Her thoughts careened down the slope with her, colliding with one another in a useless jumble. Experience and training had informed her that the steep clearing was an avalanche chute, and instinct told her the only chance of survival was to reach the clump of trees that had survived for decades.

She was close to the first trees when the slide caught up with her. At first a spray of white enveloped her, blurring her vision into a fog. Then a tsunami of snow slammed into her back and shoulders, ripping her off her feet, tumbling her into a forward roll as the avalanche rushed over her.

OhGodohGodohGod. The air was thick and icy and she couldn't breathe, snow rushing into her mouth and nose, her pole straps tightening around her wrists like handcuffs, pulling her arms down when she needed to swim up. That was the only advice she'd ever heard about avalanches: Swim while the snow is still moving like liquid, and if you're lucky, you might end up on top.

The strap around her right wrist broke, and she had just begun to flail with that arm when the left side of her body collided with something immovable, slamming the air from her lungs. Stars sparked through a sudden darkness in front of her eyes, blacking out the wall of white surging around her.

Cracking, snapping, and loud crashes deafened her in a ferocious cacophony of surround sound.

The snow shoved against her back and head. Had she made the wrong choice? Would she be smashed between sliding trees and die a horrible death that way?

How could anyone swim when jammed against an immovable obstacle? Frantically clawing the snow away from her mouth to create a pocket of air, she focused on not passing out. She barely managed to fling her free hand upward before the cascading snow settled around her like a load of wet cement.

Her heart was thudding in her throat, her breath coming loud and panicky. She willed herself to inhale and exhale more slowly, hardly believing she was alive. She wasn't sure she was lucky in that. Her left cheek, and indeed, her whole body, was jammed against a tree trunk that she prayed was still vertical. Throwing back her head as far as she could, she wriggled, moving as much as possible, waving her arm over her head, trying to raise her feet, and thrashing against the weight of the surrounding blanket of snow that would only become heavier as gravity continued to solidify it.

Only an inch or two separated her face from the tree trunk. Instead of the icy taste of snow, her tongue now identified the rusty tang of blood. Her upper lip felt wet, and she was pretty sure her nose was broken. With one hand imprisoned above her head and the other trapped below her waist, there was no way to touch it. She was grateful that she could still breathe. But she knew that might only be a momentary relief.

The world was dark and smothering, and for a second, she felt a black rush of panic, the terror of not knowing up from down. But then her brain waves reset; the blood running down her lip and chin proved she had landed in a more-or-less upright position.

"Help!" she yelled. The shout seemed faint to her, even

though it was coming from her own mouth. And who was she
yelling to?

Shit. Double shit. Gina!

The wolverine. The trapper. They'd all been on the same
slope. Oh, holy crap, was everyone buried?

6

"It's starting to snow," Blake observed to Claude as they neared the top of the Chair 4 lift. "The freestyle competition at the Heather Meadows Lodge is over. Sam and Chase and Nicole have probably left for the day." The three of them had driven up to the resort together, and he and Claude had come in Claude's car. "Think we'd better drive down the mountain before the weather really sets in?"

"Last run," Claude agreed, wrapping his hands firmly around his ski poles as their chair approached the unloading zone.

Blake caught an edge and nearly did a faceplant as he and Claude pushed away from the chair lift.

"Klutz!" Claude joked. "Race you to Raven Hut." And then he was away, zigzagging down the slope before Blake could jerk his hand out of the snow and stand upright, tugging his ski pole back into position.

Blake watched his lover navigate the slope. Claude's ski jacket strained at the zipper across his stomach now, as did Blake's. Most people had gained weight during the boring shelter-in-place, no-social-life days of the pandemic. He and Claude were both still novices at skiing, having met years ago during beginner lessons here. Then, they'd skied the easiest route down, labeled "Big Creek" on the trail map. Today, it was a good thing that they didn't have enough experience to know what was great snow. While others had been complaining about the slushy snow underfoot today, the conditions seemed fine to them. It was just so nice to practice, to be outdoors having fun with others, after all the months of quarantine.

Even more fantastic was spending time with Claude again, now that the authorities had finally reopened the border between the US and Canada to nonessential travel. So many couples had been separated, allowed only to shout or wave to each other from across a ditch in Peace Arch Park or talk for a few hours inside the international park. Zoom meetings and phone calls were poor substitutes for laughing together. Touching a computer screen could never replace the warmth of human skin.

Blake had kept his greenhouse job throughout the quarantine and had even worked a lot of overtime because of the newfound craze for gardening, but potted plants were not conversationalists. His cooking classes had all been cancelled. He hadn't been able to see his friends or his daughter Hannah, except via computer or phone videos. If he hadn't been sharing a house with Sam and her cat Simon, he would have gone completely berserk.

Even though they'd been apart for most of the last two years, he and Claude had comfortably eased back into their relationship, like sliding into a pair of well-worn slippers. Many gay men would have avoided a long-term association with a man like Blake, who carried the baggage of a previous marriage and a daughter, and who made little more than minimum wage. He'd screwed up so many things over the years, first assuming he could be a hetero husband, then wounding Diane and alienating her whole family and most of their friends by finally coming out.

But he didn't regret being a father; he'd never regret

Hannah. Up to the time he'd met Claude, his daughter had been the brightest light of his life. Was it time to introduce her to Claude? Would she be jealous of the time he spent with his lover?

He wasn't too worried about Claude's reaction if he proposed that the three of them spend time together. Although he didn't have children of his own, Claude obviously thought family was important. He'd shown Blake photos of his sister and niece and nephew so many times Blake was sure he'd recognize that family anywhere.

Claude had the advantage of being single and well paid, and his job as a traveling sales rep for a wood products company provided a good excuse to cross the border reasonably often. Now that the border was open again to tourists, maybe Claude could show him some of the sights of British Columbia for a change, instead of the two of them always hanging around Bellingham. Blake hoped their relationship would evolve into something permanent, although he wasn't sure how they'd get around the problem of being from two different countries. Maybe he could move to Canada. Maybe Claude could move to the US. They'd have to check into all that.

Marriage? Well, he'd done that once before, to the wrong person, and he wasn't at all sure that he wanted to take that step again. Still, it would be good to evolve into a more stable, settled life. He'd soon be middle-aged, and as much as he loved Sam, he didn't want to live in someone else's house forever.

Claude was already well down the trail, so Blake pushed off to catch up. In the distance, Claude curved right on the trail called Holiday, which passed beneath Chair 6, the Experts Only lift. Blake followed. Claude had acted a bit insulted to be excluded from that lift, but Blake had no desire to see the steep terrain that awaited the expert skiers at the top of Pan Dome. Holiday was plenty challenging for him. As he passed below the lift, he noticed that most chairs were empty, which probably meant that the majority of experts considered the current snow conditions unsatisfactory.

He carefully zigzagged through the cut and carved to a stop at the edge of the trees to survey the trail leading down to the ski lodge. On the slope below, Claude stopped and turned, gazing up in Blake's direction. Claude's mouth opened in a shout, but Blake couldn't hear the words over a loud cracking sound that ripped through the air and seemed to reverberate through the snow beneath his skis.

Shouts erupted from the ski lift behind him, followed quickly by screams. A massive slab of snow plummeted down the steep valley in front of him. Alarmed, he shuffled sideways, closer to the cover of trees. Suddenly, every slope in sight was in motion, dumping its snow load into the horrific flash flood of snow hurtling down the canyon. Blake stared, his mouth open in disbelief and then in horror as a tsunami wave of white powder rose into the air, obliterating the sight of his lover and everything else below, swallowing every skier on the slope.

7

FBI Agent Chase Perez was relieved to take a break from the ski slopes to grab an IPA in the lodge. He was surprised the snack bar was still open, because few skiers remained on the runs and the snow conditions were crap today. But after the long shutdown, the lodge employees and vendors were probably eager to make any money they could, and the posted lodge hours were even longer today than usual.

According to his watch, the freestyle contest would likely be over, or nearly so. The crowd on the slopes and in the lodges was clearing out. Whenever Summer finished her assignment, they could pack up and head back down the mountain in Nicole's car.

A raucous group of teens had occupied the two best tables near the windowed front of the Raven Hut lodge, shooting spitwads at one another and clomp-chasing each other in their ski boots. He snagged a quieter table in the back room, where he had a view of two chairlifts and a could see down the hallway to the lodge front entrance. Nicole was still at the coffee counter, advising the clerk that the lodge really needed to invest in an espresso machine.

A massive double-sided fireplace, an impressive piece of rustic stonework, chopped the lodge into two rooms, front and back. The fire seemed a bit overkill for this day, but the coals were burning down. The staff would probably extinguish it soon as Raven Hut closed for the day. The locals had a quaint habit of sticking forks and spoons into gaps between the stones and hanging their hats and gloves from them to dry, giving the fireplace a whimsical air. He wondered if the lodge staff recovered the tableware at the end of every day or simply left everything there for the next.

Nicole shrugged off her mint-green ski jacket, and then slid into the chair across from his. She took a sip from the heavy ceramic mug in front of her. "Passible," she pronounced.

She hadn't changed a bit. Of course, she had proved to be a much better skier than he. Chase felt a stab of familiar annoyance, remembered from their partnership in previous years, when, as the more experienced agent, Nicole routinely performed most activities more efficiently than he did. Although they both now lived in Washington State, she and her sculptor husband made the trek to the slopes at Snoqualmie Pass or Crystal Mountain much more often than Chase did to Mt. Baker. Most of his work took place on Native American reservations, many of which were along the coast. He was more familiar with the foggy wild beaches of the state than with its groomed ski slopes.

They worked in different areas of the FBI now, so they each had interesting stories to tell. His often involved investigating nefarious behind-the-scenes transactions at the reservation casinos or the sad cases of women who had mysteriously vanished from their reservations, interspersed with exposing illegal deals in poached marine life or busting a drug-trafficking gang. Nicole's stories were mostly about internet fraud of one kind or another. These days, he had by far the more fascinating job, and his Lakota blood was satisfied by finally spending more time with other tribal members.

Chase raised his beer glass to clink against her coffee mug. "Nice to spend time with you again, former partner."

"Same here. How's the dump coming along?"

He raised an eyebrow. "The remodel of my *cabin* is proceeding nicely. Summer helped me add a deck, and I have double-pane windows now."

"Ah, progress." She licked a speck of foam from her upper lip. "Have the racoons moved out of the attic?"

He smiled. "I believe we've finally reached détente. The masked marauders don't come into the house, and I don't shoot them." As if Summer would ever let him do that. She didn't even kill spiders. He sighed and changed the subject. "What's Oscar working on these days? Or is he just a house husband after the pandemic?"

Nicole's lips curved in her trademark Mona Lisa smile. "Oscar has a longer list of commissions than ever. While the superrich were in quarantine with the rest of us peons, they had plenty of time to redesign their gardens and dream about the perfect marble orca or granite grizzly or bronze flamingo to show off there."

"Flamingo?" That seemed out of place for Seattle.

"A trio of them, actually." She took another sip of her latte. "They're six feet tall, weigh nearly a ton, and they're on a ship right now, destined for a new resort in the Bahamas. The company is flying us down there to install them in two weeks."

"Nice." Chase took note of Nicole's "us" with mixed emotions. His former partner's marriage had seemed on the rocks a few years back. But Nicole and Oscar had worked things out and had settled back into their cushy life in Seattle, where they'd moved to accommodate Nicole's new position. Chase was at times amazed that Nicole chose to continue her career in the FBI when she could easily retire to a life of luxury. Then again, he couldn't imagine Nicole Boudreaux as a kept woman. Her hyperactive brain would never allow that.

His former partner and Summer were both alike in that

way; sharp-witted, determined, eager to tackle challenges. He wondered when, or if, Summer would ever start thinking of them as a permanent couple. Would they ever share a comfortable life together? Even if they pooled resources, they could certainly never equal Nicole's and Oscar's lavish lifestyle. Not to mention that Summer would choose adventure over comfort until she was an ancient woman leaning on a walker. If she lived to be ancient.

He was grateful that she was covering the aerial competition at the higher Heather Meadows Lodge today instead of traipsing around in the snowy wilderness searching for grizzlies or something equally insane. Maybe after they dropped Nicole off at her hotel, Summer would come back to his cabin with him and they could cook dinner together. And after that, surely she'd stay the night and leave her own house to Claude and Blake for a while. He took another sip of his beer, contemplating the possibilities with his lover in his bed. Their intimate times had been few and far between in the last two years.

Pulling his phone from his pocket, he thumbed it to Summer's number, pressed the call button and raised it to his year. Something between a chime and a beep sounded in his ear. "Summer?"

The building shuddered, sloshing his beer over the rim. Simultaneously, Nicole's coffee slopped over the rim of her cup. They both scooted their chairs back from the table, and Nicole wiped at the coffee stain on her sweater. "What the hell?"

Around the room, adults rose to their feet, grabbing their children, murmuring questions. The low hum of noise grew in volume. The teens standing in front of the window, staring up the ski slope, suddenly erupted in a barrage of swear words. "Shit!" "Fuck!"

These exclamations were quickly followed by "Run!" as the

teens thundered away from the glass.

The entire crowd turned away from the windows at the front of the lodge, fleeing like a herd of antelope under attack from a pride of lions. Few made it through the exit doors before the wall of snow slammed into the lodge.

8

No one knew where she and Gina were. Nobody was going to come to their rescue. Nobody! Adrenaline flooded through Sam's veins as she pictured the world above, beautiful and serene and silent again, no sign of those dying under the shifted snow. Was Gina suffocating right now? The poacher? Feisty?

Focus. Slow down your heartbeat and breathing. Her heart didn't want to respond to those commands, so she held her breath for a few seconds to force her body to listen. The cocoon of snow already felt frozen against her back and legs. Clenching her jaw, she moved her right hand above her, waving it as best she could. A shower of snow sifted down onto the top of her head. That inspired a turbulent mix of panic and hope. Tilting her head back the inch that her tomb allowed, she strained her gaze upward.

Was that a patch of light above, somewhere near her wrist? Not sunlight, but at least a *lighter* patch of snow. Was her hand sticking out above the snow?

All she could feel with the fingers of that hand was cold— snow, air, she couldn't tell. And trapped as it was above her heart, soon it would be completely numb. She twisted the hand around, waved it, and felt it bang against something solid on the right side. She willed her fingers to explore. A sharp projection of some kind. Maybe the stub of a snapped-off branch? She hoped so. It had to be.

Flattening herself against the tree trunk, she stretched and sucked in a breath. Clutching the projection as tightly as she could, she pulled. Did she move up a few inches? The painful scrape of tree bark against her cheek seemed to promise that she had. She thought she had succeeded in even moving her left hand up a bit, although she could feel the leather ski pole strap strangling her wrist, impeding her efforts. Her left foot seemed stuck, too. Was the damn snowshoe still strapped to her hiking boot? Her right foot could slide a little.

She couldn't feel the constraint of straps around her shoulders or hips. Her pack must have been ripped off by the cascading snow. Her back and buttocks and shoulders, pressed against the enveloping snow, felt wet, making the frozen wall behind her slick. Her body heat was melting the blanket of snow. For now. How long would it take to turn back into ice?

She swallowed hard, trying to quell the panic rocketing through her brain. She was a toddler who'd fallen down a well. Or an unborn infant stuck in her mother's cervix, waiting for the next contraction to free her. Or crush her.

Sucking in a deep gulp of air, she expanded her chest as much as possible, and using every muscle in her body, she pushed against her frozen surroundings, trying to pack the snow as far away and as densely as she could. If she succeeded in making some sort of birth canal for herself, she didn't want loose snow to shift and fill the space, entombing her forever.

She couldn't die like this, in a coffin of snow. This would fulfill her father's worst nightmare, that she would die in some horrific event in the wilderness. Reverend Mark Westin had mellowed over the years, gradually coming to accept her gay housemate and her erratic career choices, but he still didn't understand why any sane woman would choose the life his daughter led, when she could have chosen marriage and children and a stable home life like most of his parishioners did.

Right now, Sam had to admit that maybe her father had a point. "Sorry, Dad. I'm going to do my best to get out of here. Pray for me." She didn't believe in prayer, but her father did, and maybe he had an open line to God that she had never discovered.

"Summer?"

Sam's heart thudded in her chest. A faint, tinny sound, muffled by snow. A voice?

Shit, was that her cell phone in her jacket pocket? There was no way to reach it. That one word was all she heard, just her given name. Only two people in the world called her by her given name: her father, and Starchaser Perez.

"Dad?" Her voice now seemed loud in the tight space. She held her breath for a moment, listening. "Chase?"

The cracking sounds around her had stilled. Nothing more. Had she only imagined hearing her name? Had she somehow summoned her father by imagining how he'd feel about her death? The longer she listened, the more the quiet seemed oppressive. Ominous. Total absence of sound.

She was listening to the silence of a tomb.

9

Time seemed to move in slow motion as the snow shifted beneath Blake's skis. He tensed for the collapse and his inevitable fall into the snow sliding down the canyon, but the slope he stood on merely sank a few inches and then stopped like an elevator lurch, sending a vibration through the landscape. He crouched, paralyzed, afraid to move.

The cloud of snow filled the air like a fog of icy flour. Shrieks from the ski lift echoed behind him, but for a few long moments, he could see nothing beyond his own black-gloved hands clenched around his ski poles. Then the snow finally sifted from the air around him and settled to the ground. The cloud of white fog below emitted screams and horrendous cracking sounds, as if an unseen battle with the devil was taking place within it.

When the air finally cleared, Blake's jaw dropped. The scene at the bottom of the slope didn't seem real. He didn't want it to be real. The avalanche had buried the bottom of the chairlift. He could see only a bit of the lodge, or what used to be the Raven Hut Lodge. From his position, it appeared to be only a crushed shell surrounded by snow. The tsunami of snow had washed over and around the lodge and snapped most of the trees that stood between the lodge and the road below.

Blake's heart pounded in his throat. He'd just witnessed a mass burial. How many skiers had been on the slope? How many were in the lodge? The word that leaped to his tongue was one of Claude's Quebecois epithets, and he murmured it aloud. *"Tabarnak!"*

Such a weird swear word, something to do with the Catholic church, but Claude had told him it roughly translated as "fuck."

Some figures were struggling to free arms or legs from the snow. A handful of individuals were running or skiing or limping toward the collapsed building. Skiers who had managed to get off the chairlifts were breaking free from their catatonic states and careening down the slope, well off to the side of the rough avalanche field.

Dozens of people were shouting or screaming names of friends or family. Cacophony. People trapped on the lift screamed from their seats. As Blake watched, two of them kicked off their skis and dropped to the snow below.

Claude! Where was Claude? Blake raked his gaze over the spot where he'd last seen his lover standing on his skis, staring up at him. Nothing but chunks of ice and snow now. No sign of a human there. He searched farther down the slope, toward the lodge, spied a woman half-buried, trying to dig her legs out of the snow, and farther on, a man pulling a child out.

He saw no sign of Claude. *Merde*, as Claude would say. *Shit.*

Sam had been near the Heather Meadows Lodge covering the competition, so unless that area had also been buried, she'd probably be safe. But Chase and Nicole? He hadn't seen them on the lifts or slopes. Had they already gone home, or had they been in the Raven Hut lodge?

Clenching his teeth, Blake angled his skis into a snowplow and slowly slid down the littered slope, his skis chattering over ice chunks and small rocks.

Claude had been wearing a blue ski jacket and a striped blue knit hat, which he insisted on calling a "tuque." The first skier Blake encountered was a woman in a gold jumpsuit, lying sideways in the snow, one ski on her foot. He stopped beside her still form, dug the snow away from her face, and was rewarded when her eyes opened.

"Are you okay?" he asked.

"I . . . uh . . ." Seeming stunned, she struggled to push herself up out of the snow, and he helped by pawing the icy crystals away with his gloved hands and then offering her his arm for leverage so she could sit up. All around him, he heard cries of anguish or pain. These were the victims who could breathe. How many were dying right now under the snow?

"My boyfriend . . ." the woman sputtered, glancing around.

She would survive. He stood up. "I have to go."

Dazed, Blake moved off, searching for a blue ski jacket and a striped tuque.

10

Inside the ski lodge, after the surge of snow and furniture and the hail of falling beams and rocks finally stopped, Chase found himself sandwiched between two chairs. Nicole was face down on the floor a short distance away, her torso under an overturned table. They were imprisoned by hard-packed snow in a nest of debris and furniture broken by the impact. Somewhere close by, a child was screaming.

Shards of glass glinted in shafts of light that shone through the wreckage, and a jagged piece of thick glass was embedded in the crown of Nicole's head. Blood stained her auburn hair a darker red.

"Nicole!" Chase struggled to pull his right leg from between the seat and back of a chair. The leg of another chair pressed against his neck. He'd bitten his tongue, and blood streamed down his chin. His lower back hurt like hell where he'd been hit by a falling beam. His abdomen echoed the pain from colliding with a flying table. A large rock lay by his head, and he pictured the two-sided fireplace in the lodge, a beautiful structure built of native stone. And the fire had been lit. He inhaled, gasping as pain ricocheted through his lungs, but didn't smell any smoke. With luck, the snow had snuffed out the flames.

Luck seemed a completely nonsensical concept right now. He tried to wipe the nightmare fears of fuel and broken electrical wires from his frantic thoughts.

Although he could see his former partner, he couldn't reach her. "Nicole?"

It was an eternity before her head moved. Groaning, she twisted her head in his direction.

"You *are* alive!" He blew out a sigh of relief, but winced from severe pain in his lower ribs. They were probably broken.

"Barely." Pulling a hand from under the table, she moved it toward the shard of glass.

"Don't!" he yelped. "There's a big piece of glass in your scalp." He didn't voice his fear that it might extend through her skull and into her brain.

"Wonderful." Her hand flopped back to the ground. "So we both look like Frankenstein's monster."

That told him about his appearance. "Are you injured anywhere else?"

"Hard to say. My left ankle is shrieking almost as loudly as my head." She closed her eyes for a moment, braced her forearms on the debris beneath her, tried to push at the table top across her back, panting with the effort, then finally gave up. "I'm pancaked here. You?"

He pushed at the chair leg that rested against his neck. It shifted a few inches, and he was able to move his head out from beneath it. Pain shot through his body like a lightning bolt. Yes, broken ribs for sure. A few inches above his head rested a section of wall, or maybe part of the roof, with a heavy beam still attached. "I'm okay," he finished. "Maybe. Sort of."

"Lucky you." Nicole sighed and rested her cheek on the floor. Through the debris piled above them, a fine dust of snow sifted down onto her hair. "I have an ominous feeling that it's going to get cold in here real soon, and I left my ski jacket on my chair."

"I did, too," Chase said.

"I don't suppose those chairs followed us, along with the
rest of this furniture."

Chase lifted his head a couple of inches off the floor to scan
the immediate area. "No coats in sight," he reported.

The child's shrieks had softened to sobbing now, but he
heard at least two other voices. Somewhere outside, a woman
was calling for Emma, and a man yelled "Jeremy!" Moans came
from different locations inside the building. Then the structure
overhead shifted with a loud screech, followed by a crash.
Several voices screamed in terror or in pain.

11

A trickle of icy water descended Sam's neck and slithered down her backbone. Her parka hood was probably filled with snow. Her body heat was leaching away by the second. She had to move now if she was ever going to move again. She shoved backward against the snow again. After she'd strained outward for a minute, Sam reversed her motion and did her utmost to wrap herself around the tree trunk. She pointed her left toe down, or at least envisioned pointing it downward so the damn snowshoe, if there was one attached, might hang more vertical from her boot when she pulled up her foot. She also tried to straighten her left hand so the pole strap might slip off. Pushing her chin and chest and the thigh of one leg against the rough bark of the tree, she pulled hard on whatever she held onto above, and wrenched herself up a few more inches.

Every muscle in her body screamed with the effort. Slushy snow slid down her upright arm into her face, obscuring her vision, slithering into her nose and mouth. She exhaled through her nose, snorting, and was rewarded with another trickle down her lip—snowmelt or blood, she couldn't tell. Using her tongue, she pushed a wad of slush from her mouth, whimpering.

At least she had air. For now. Maybe not for much longer. Her own labored breathing and moans were the only sounds her ears could pick up. Snow pressed against her right shoulder and

her backside, crowding her. She pulled again. Something—a
tendon or muscle, *please not a vertebra*—popped in her back.
The tree bark scoured more skin from her face. But she was
alive, and she was climbing. Well, dragging herself up inches at
a time with only one usable arm, like a zombie arising from a
grave.

No, like a one-armed chimpanzee—she liked that vision
better. An amazingly strong chimp. A champion weightlifter
chimp. She willed that image into her imagination—an ape so
muscular and skillful that it could haul itself upward with one
arm and swing through the trees like Tarzan. An orangutan.
Maybe a gorilla; they were even stronger. Blake had shown her
an article about Neema, a gorilla in Evansville that had learned
sign language. She pictured herself as Neema, who could no
doubt lift her entire body weight with one arm. Wouldn't it be
amazing to actually communicate with an ape? If she survived,
she hoped she'd get a chance to see that gorilla in the future.

Chimp, orangutan, gorilla, pull! Blink and snort away the
sinking snow. Embrace the tree. She tried to wrap her right leg
and foot around it, stay positioned so that she didn't slip back
down. Pushing her right shoulder as hard as she could against
the snow, she struggled to create space to bend her elbow.
Another icy trickle snaked down her back between her skin and
her clothes.

Pull. Again. Push against the snow with her back, against
the tree with her right foot, her chin, her cheek. She could no
longer feel her toes. Her teeth were beginning to chatter.
Hypothermia would soon render her muscles useless. How
many more minutes did she have?

Pull! She managed to drag her left arm a few inches upward
with every effort, although the strap still cut painfully into her
wrist. Her left foot was harder to slide than the right, so
aggravating, the damn snowshoe still dragging on its straps,

threatening to break her ankle. If only the binding would break instead.

But finally, her face was out. Air! As she leaned her head back against the snow, her brain abruptly replayed a déjà vu moment of near-drowning in the Galápagos, when after finally surfacing, she'd been so thrilled to suck in air again from earth's atmosphere instead of from a scuba tank. But here, instead of relishing the sudden brightness of warm daylight and the return to her normal environment, the world was frigid, her whole body was trembling, heavy snowflakes were plopping onto her wet face, and she was not yet saved.

But she could finally push her right elbow down on top of the snow, and she slowly inched her shoulders and other arm out. Yep, the damn pole was still attached to her wrist. The basket was broken half off and the shaft was bent. Her wrist was ringed with a red welt, and her left arm and shoulder hurt like hell from being stretched. Laying the ski pole horizontally on top of the snow, she pushed down on the shaft with both arms, gasping in pain, and slowly extracted her legs. She was grateful to see both her feet still wore boots. And one damn snowshoe. With numb fingers, she unbuckled the straps and kicked it away.

Thank God she'd run for the trees. The avalanche had launched her the last few yards into the grove of firs. Many of the surrounding trees were bent, and a few at the leading edge had snapped as the snow piled up against the upper sides of their trunks. Although she'd lost her hat and her gloves, she counted herself lucky to still be wearing her ski jacket and pants as well as her boots. She'd read stories of avalanche victims stripped naked by cartwheeling through speeding snow.

I'm alive, Dad. Survived another adventure. At least so far.

Sam took a shuddering breath through her teeth, clamping her chattering jaws together as she analyzed her injuries.

Everything hurt, especially her left ankle, her left shoulder, and the side of her face that had scraped against the tree. Her nose was numb, probably a blessing.

But she couldn't rest. Her clothes were wet, and if she didn't keep her body in motion, she'd soon be reduced to a shivering statue. It would be mortifying to crawl out of an avalanche only to freeze to death on top of her former coffin.

She wasn't sure she could stand up. Stabbing pains shot through her lower back and legs as she rolled to her hands and knees, but she finally pushed herself to her feet. Wiping blood off her face, Sam glanced up the slope. Gina had been above her. Red parka.

The upper edge of the snow chute had been scoured of snow and was now a dark stripe of dirt and rock, but the rest of the clearing was a sheet of solid white. The log trap had been ripped apart. Sam prayed that somehow Feisty had escaped. Then she had to remind herself that was impossible; she'd seen the poacher stuff the wolverine into the carrier.

Sam cupped her hands around her mouth. "Gina! Gina!"

She panted in pain, her lungs or diaphragm or something inside her chest protesting the effort of yelling. Staggering toward the upper edge of the trees, she tripped over broken limbs thrust up from the icy surface. The snow in the clearing was now so solidly packed that she could stand on it without snowshoes, her boot soles only sinking an inch or so into the white cement.

At least the sky was barely spitting now; it wasn't snowing hard. Yet. Clouds raced one another across the sky in a strobe effect. Sunshine. Darkness. Sun. Dark.

"Gina!" she shouted again. And then she remembered the bearded man. "Trapper! Poacher! Anyone?"

She held her breath, listening. It was so quiet. Too quiet.

After exhaling on her frozen hands for a minute to warm

them up, she pulled her cell phone out of her pocket. The glass cover was cracked, and although she tapped it several times, the screen refused to light up. She couldn't have heard Chase's voice, could she? He might have a satellite phone, but her cell had poor coverage in the mountains. And now her phone was dead, anyway. She wondered if her videos of the freestyle ski competition had survived. And then she wondered how her thoughts could even go to her job now.

Was she the sole survivor? Stepping out farther into the clearing, she scanned the avalanche chute again, raking her gaze back and forth over the snow above. A few small clumps detached themselves from the cornice above and rolled down the slope, gathering more snow as they tumbled, and for a moment, she feared another avalanche was coming, but the clumps remained golf-ball size as they traveled. She turned to scan the area below her.

A low moan rippled from the edge of the trees fifty feet below her. Or had that been her imagination? Tree branches rubbing together? She stopped breathing again to listen.

Squinting, one hand held over her brow, Sam scanned the dappled pattern of tree trunks and snow. She was finally rewarded by a flash of red among the evergreens.

"Gina!"

12

Blake awkwardly zigzagged over the chunky snow above the collapsed lodge, searching for any hint of blue. Stripes. Or a hand or foot. Anything sticking out of the snow. Anything. He pulled one man out of snow that now seemed as heavy as concrete. The zipper on the man's ski pants had broken and his pants and undershorts had been pulled halfway down his legs. He'd also lost a ski boot.

"Sorry, man," Blake told the stranger, helping him pull his pants up.

"Are you kidding?" The stranger stuffed his testicles into his shorts. "I'm just happy that I still have my junk, even if it's frozen right now."

"I hear you. Have you seen a man in a striped hat?"

"I didn't see anything after that snow wave hit." The stranger surveyed the area, then shouted, "Hey, Allen! I'm alive!" He waved at his friend, who stood a short distance away. Then, turning to Blake, he smacked him lightly on the arm. "Thanks, man. Good luck finding your friend."

Blake moved on, searching. After kicking out of his skis and kneeling to dig out a blue glove half-buried in the snow, he saw it—a piece of blue-striped knit, just a tiny fold sticking out of the snow.

"Claude!" He crawled to the scrap of fabric, scraped at it

with his gloved hands. Uncovered a bit more. Yes, it was Claude's tuque. He yanked, and the hat came away, revealing blond hair beneath. "Claude!"

Frantically clawing at the icy ground with his fingers, Blake shouted, "Help me, somebody help me!"

The knees of black ski pants slammed into place a couple of feet away, and a ski patrol guy with Asian features began to dig alongside Claude's head with a snow scoop like the one Sam carried in her pack. Blake was ridiculously, disastrously, unprepared with only his gloved hands, but he pawed at the snow as best he could, scraping frantically to uncover his lover's head.

As Claude's nose and mouth were revealed, another volunteer joined them, a woman who scooped away snow from Claude's chest, and then another red-jacketed woman, and between the four of them, they finally uncovered enough of Claude to begin CPR. The two women continued to dig the rest of his body out.

The Asian ski patrol guy bounced his stacked hands on Claude's chest, and nodded every so often to Blake, who did his best to puff air into Claude's mouth. His lips were lukewarm, not ice cold; was that encouraging? Finally, the team managed to extract Claude's limp body from the snow and lay him out on the chunky surface. But Claude wasn't breathing.

Claude wasn't moving. The ski patrol woman pushed herself to her feet and jogged away from the body. Oh *merde*, *tabarnak*, they were too late. Blake raised a gloved hand to his mouth and bit down on it to keep from screaming. Returning, the ski patrol gal slammed a defibrillator into the snow beside Claude.

Her colleague ripped open Claude's jacket, yanked up his sweater and applied pads to his chest. "Back off! Get back!" The team pushed themselves away from Claude. "Shocking."

Claude's body stiffened for a moment, then went limp again.

Blake clenched his jaw, tried to staunch the flow of tears down his cheeks.

The Asian man shocked the body again and again—a horrific thing to witness. Blake was on the verge of asking them to just leave his lover in peace, when suddenly Claude gasped. The four onlookers cheered in unison, and Blake positioned himself, leaning over Claude, to be the first person Claude would see when he opened his eyes.

That didn't happen. Claude remained limp, unconscious. But his chest continued to rise and fall.

"Hey, man." Red Jacket touched Blake's shoulder. "He's alive. There's hope."

The rescuers swaddled Claude in two metallic emergency blankets and laid him on a ski patrol sled, then focused on Blake. "Stay with him, okay? Sometimes we gotta do the jump-start again."

Blake wanted to hold Claude's hand, but it was cocooned inside the emergency blankets. He settled for touching his fingertips to Claude's cheek. He murmured, "I'm here."

"We gotta recharge the pack, Matt," the female red coat told the other. "The juice is still on at the other lodge."

"Will he regain consciousness?" Blake couldn't bring himself to ask about brain damage from lack of oxygen. But hadn't he read that ultracold water helped save drowning victims? Maybe that worked for avalanche victims, too?

The ski patrol guy—now Blake noticed that the name tape on his red jacket was Zhao—shrugged and repeated, "He's alive. There's hope. Holler if you need us."

13

Although the pain of moving made him nearly black out, Chase twisted his body and pushed with his hands to drag himself closer to Nicole. Waves of shivering radiated through his torso.

After studying the debris piled around them, he located a broken chair leg within reach and managed to wiggle it free of its nest of snow and broken wallboard. It was splintered at one end where it had ripped apart. He estimated its length at around eight inches.

"Can you push up against that table on your back?" Chase held the piece of wood in her sight. "Maybe I can wedge this underneath to give you some breathing room."

Nicole swore as she tried to pull her arms and legs beneath her torso and lift the table top, but managed only an inch before she collapsed against the floor again.

"That's not going to work," Chase said, his tone grim. "I'll try to find something else."

"No." Nicole's breathing was harsh as she panted. "Give me a m-m-minute." Then, inhaling sharply, she commanded through clenched teeth, "Now."

The table rose a few more inches, and Chase managed to shove the leg under the corner of the table and then hammer it into an upright position with his fist. The wood collapsed on the splintered end, losing an inch, but managed to take some of the weight from his partner's back.

Chase leaned back, gasping, his head forced upward by a horizontal section of pipe in back of them. He and Nicole both gulped air for a few minutes, like a pair of draft horses pulling a heavy wagon. Sweat rolled down his face, and he raised a hand to wipe it out of his eye. His back and ribs were screeching, the noise of the pain threatening to drown out all other sounds.

"I think mm-maybe I can rr-roll over," Nicole told him.

"Don't hurt yourself worse."

She curled an arm beneath her torso, then her shoulder, then twisted her hips, bumping against the table. A shower of snow rained down on them. "This is *not* my idea of a g-g-good t-time." She bit off each word, her teeth chattering audibly now between *uhn-uhn-uhn* grunts of pain. Finally, she managed to turn her back to the ground and lay her head against the floor, whimpering.

"Better?" Chase asked.

"Don't know yet." She licked her lips, then slowly inhaled and exhaled. "My left ankle, or maybe my lower leg, is definitely broken. At least I hope that's all that's wrong with it. Do you have a plan to get out of this?"

Plan? The sound that issued from his mouth was halfway between a laugh and a huff of despair. "My plan is to wait for help. This avalanche can't have gone unnoticed."

"Ya think?" Through cold lips, Nicole's words sounded more like "Ya ting?"

What was going on outside? Was Summer safe? Chase's brain flashed a horrific vision of her buried in snow, but maybe that was only because his own body was so cold. Both he and Nicole would soon be hypothermic. Preserving bodily warmth was crucial. Groaning, Chase inched his upper body closer, pushed his arm beneath his partner's neck, and wrapped it around her shoulders, carefully avoiding the shard of glass sticking up from her scalp.

"Pain?" Nicole asked.

"Worse than being shot." At least as far as he could remember. The bullet he'd taken in the Arizona desert had burned like he was being branded. The current pain in his back and side felt more like something had torn inside, or a maybe like a bruise so deep that it might never heal. Broken ribs seemed probable. He hoped a splintered rib had not punctured a lung, but so far, he seemed to be able to breathe okay. "You?"

"I think I might be developing a migraine."

"I'll get you an aspirin in a minute."

"What do you think the Bureau will . . . say . . . when they hear about this?" Nicole's jaw moved against his armpit. "At least it could have been a terrorist bomb."

He snorted, then immediately regretted it as the sharp exhalation rippled down his lungs to his aching belly. "They'll disa- . . . disavow . . ." Such a hard word to enunciate, but no synonym came to mind. ". . . any knowledge of our . . . existence."

"Sounds about right."

"You're gonna get so much shit, Nik."

"Why?"

His lips were growing numb, barely able to form sounds into words. "Rumors. Affair."

"Us? We're not even partners any more. Oscar won't . . . Summer?"

Nicole's words seemed to be fading. And so was the little light filtering into this pile of debris. "So damn cold," he muttered. "Getting dark." The pain in his back seemed to be snaking around, filling his abdomen now. Clenching his teeth, he closed his eyes, wondering how long he'd feel this increasing agony. If he'd had his pistol, he would be contemplating shooting himself about now.

"Chase? Stay with me." Nicole pulled at his arm. "Chase?" Nicole sounded more distant with each passing second.

"Summer." He sighed her name in his head, wasn't sure it had come out of his mouth. *Please let her be okay.*

"Chase!"

Nicole's shoulder moved against his armpit as she snuggled closer to him.

14

The snow beneath her boots had set up so hard that Sam had to kick steps into the steep slope to descend. The bent pole with the half-basket was at least semi-useful, allowing her to punch its point into the icy snow to steady herself, using her right arm. The maneuver seemed to take forever, but she was terrified that if she started sliding, she wouldn't stop until she reached the valley below after ping-ponging off every tree branch and rock along the way.

Gina had ended up with her back against a tree trunk. She was buried up to her chest, and was frantically trying to claw the snow away with one free hand as she gasped for air.

Sam threw herself down in front of her friend and clawed frantically at the snow that was compressing Gina's abdomen and chest. "Hang in there, Gina."

"*Unhh*," the other woman whimpered. Then she abruptly hissed, startling Sam into looking up at her. Her face was blue-purple, and she was panting, her eyes darting to one side and back. Gina darted her eyes sideways again.

Sam followed the motion, and saw that, miraculously, her pack rested half-buried in the snow only a few yards away from her friend. On hands and knees, Sam scrambled to it, snatched it up, and with trembling fingers, finally managed to unzip it. It seemed a miracle that her snow scoop was still inside.

"Thank God!" The scoop was a rigid plastic sheet with handholds on each side. It doubled as a scraping device and also as a convenient seat when she wanted to sit on top of the snow.

She crawled back to Gina, and grabbing the device with both hands, knelt in front of her friend, who hadn't yet said a word. Sam understood that the pressure of the snow against her lower limbs and diaphragm was making it nearly impossible for Gina to inhale. The deep purple color of her face was due to blood being forced upward. If Sam didn't manage to free her soon, Gina would stroke out or die from lack of air.

"This will work, Gina." She panted the words, digging the edge of the snow shovel into the drift in front of her friend's chest and dragging it backward. The snow was as heavy as wet clay, and Sam's ribs and arms ached with the effort. A sharp pain zinged through her gut to her back with each pull, but Gina's chest seemed to move a little easier with every scrape. The dark color slowly drained from her face.

"Shit," was the first word out of Gina's mouth, followed by "God almighty," and then "Fuck, never want to do that again."

"Ditto," Sam panted, scraping with all her might.

Soon Gina's other arm was free, and she could help a little, clawing snow away with her fingers. Sam experienced a pang of jealousy that her friend had somehow retained her gloves, when she had lost both of hers. Then, Sam's snow scoop raked across cloth instead of snow.

"Ow!" Gina growled.

"Halleluiah!" Sam chortled. "Legs!"

Why was it that the only expressions that came to her at times like this were from her churchy upbringing? Her father might still be a preacher, but these days, she wasn't even remotely religious.

To their mutual delight, they discovered that Gina had ended up with her legs extended in front of her instead of being buried in a standing position. Sam was able to free her friend's legs with only a little more effort.

"Do they work?" Sam stared at the black fabric of Gina's snow pants.

Gina waggled her feet. "I think so." She frowned at her boots. One had been pulled halfway off her foot. Both had drag marks across the toes. "Damn, those snowshoes were nearly new." She slid her hands across her shoulders. "And my pack's gone."

"Maybe we'll find them downslope," Sam told her. "I ended up with one snowshoe and one bent pole."

"More useful than none?" Gina questioned, raising her knees to massage her ankles. "Hurts some, but nothing like my head." Reaching back where her head rested against a tree, she felt her scalp. Her fingers were bloody when she pulled her hand back. "And my ribs may never be the same."

Inhaling slowly, she brushed the hand across the front of her parka, leaving a darker stripe of blood on the scarlet fabric. "But it doesn't feel like anything is really broken." She inhaled, coughed, and winced. "At least not too much."

"I'm so glad you're alive." Sam smiled stiffly, trying not to betray her anxiety that her friend might have broken ribs and internal damage. "But you look like shit."

"You should see your own face," Gina retorted.

Sam started to reach for her swollen nose, then thought better of it and let her hand drop, settling for brushing across her chin, where she had to have streaks of blood.

"Zombie Apocalypse: The Undead Return," Gina commented, still wincing and gasping.

"I'll suggest that to my agent." Sam shakily stood up and held out both hands to pull her friend to her feet.

They both stood for a moment, breathing heavily.

"So the women survive," Gina finally said, scanning the

snow above them. "X chromosomes rule."

"Any idea where the guy ended up?" Sam asked. She was afraid to mention the wolverine. She was having a hard time summoning sympathy for the trapper. If it hadn't been for him, none of them would be here now. He wouldn't be suffocating under the snow, and Feisty wouldn't be entombed in a dog carrier. "I have a probe in my pack."

Gina groaned. "Guess we've got to try." Clamping her right arm against her chest, she began a slow trudge upward toward the log trap, kicking steps into the icy slope.

When they reached the altitude of the trap, they moved horizontally to approximately where the trapper had been when the avalanche had let loose. There was no sign of any creature there, alive or dead.

Gina focused on the area below them. "The avalanche would have shoved him downslope."

Extracting her probe from her pack, Sam extended the jointed pole and made a first jab into the hard-packed snow, leaning on the pole to sink it as far as possible. Then she yanked it out, took a couple of steps, and thrust it into the slope again. The clearing was relatively small, but this was probably a useless exercise. The methods she'd been taught to search for avalanche victims involved dozens of volunteers, advancing in lines less than a foot at a time, each jabbing a pole into the snow. With only one pole, the odds of contacting anything below the surface were slim. Sam tried not to think about a person or an animal suffocating right now in the cold and dark.

After five tries, Gina took her place as they zigzagged across the steep chute. They both knew it was a long shot that the pole would connect with anything. The snow could now be so deep that the pole wouldn't reach, or they could easily stab the slender probe on either side of a body and totally miss an arm or a leg or a torso twisted sideways.

But on Gina's fifth try, the probe abruptly stopped about two feet in. She pulled it out, moved it six inches to the side, then jabbed again. It sank its full length. Pulling it out, she tried six inches below the first hole. Again, it stopped about two feet down.

Sam picked up her snow scoop, sank onto her knees in the snow, and went to work. She didn't know whether she wanted to find the trapper or not. No way could he be alive; her watch had been ripped off but she knew it had been at least an hour since the avalanche. Probably more like two. With luck, the pole had struck the carrier, with Feisty inside.

Wolverines were supposed to be incredibly tough. If the carrier hadn't been crushed, it might have given Feisty enough air. She might still be alive.

As she scraped at the snow beneath her, Sam became painfully aware that the snow from above was falling faster. The daylight was waning. They were miles from the lodge. "Did you feel trembling before the avalanche hit?" she asked Gina.

"Yep," the other woman answered. "Earthquake, I'm pretty sure. Koma Kulshan reminding us of our humble place on the planet."

Sam bit her lip. She hadn't really wanted Gina to agree. Mount Baker, or Koma Kulshan, as the native tribes had named it, was still classified as an active volcano, part of the Pacific Ring of Fire or Circum-Pacific Belt, a horseshoe-shaped belt of seismically active volcanoes and tectonic plates that fringed the Pacific Ocean. Most of the time, the mountain was a stately focal point among the jagged peaks of the North Cascades, but now and then the volcano rumbled or vented steam or sent a lahar flowing down a valley to demonstrate it was still alive.

An avalanche could be a narrowly focused local event, but a quake could set off multiple slides all over the area. The volcano, if it had been the epicenter, was a couple of miles away from their current location. Had the quake reached the lodge or the ski slopes? Chase, Blake, and Claude were down there. Nicole, too.

Were there more earthquakes to come? Would there be aftershocks?

She reached for her cell phone, found it in her jacket pocket, along with a handful of snow. Still dead. Wasn't that the definition of insanity, going through the same motions but expecting a different outcome? Cursing, she zipped the useless device back into her pocket and began to dig again at the snow.

15

Soon the snow scoop raked across purple fabric, and it took a few more scrapes to recognize they'd uncovered a shoulder. Sam blinked in surprise; she would have sworn the poacher was wearing a black jacket. Moving up the neck, they dug out the head, which was buried a few more inches down.

The trapper had ended face up. A nose and chin emerged first. They both stared. A mask of ice covered the blue-white skin of his face, converting human details into the plastic features of a department-store manikin. Unfortunately, Sam knew this meant the snow had melted around his face and then froze again. Which meant the wolverine poacher had been breathing when he'd been buried.

There was no hope for this person now. What a god-awful way to die.

Gina brushed her hand over the hairline, pushing back the remaining snow around the face. Long blonde hair. A sparkly pink earring gleamed from an ear. "What the—"

"Hell," Sam finished for her. "I would have sworn I saw a man. Or a boy. He had a beard. And a black jacket."

"I did, too. And he did. She"—Gina nodded toward the corpse—"must have been waiting for him in the trees."

The girl's parka had been ripped open and hung halfway off the shoulder they'd uncovered. Gina pulled off her right glove with her teeth, then plunged her hand down inside the purple coat, next to the girl's chest.

"What are you doing?" Sam asked. "She's gone. Her body is already freezing."

"Inside chest pocket," Gina grunted, reaching farther into the parka. "That's where I keep my ID." After a moment of rooting around, she pulled her hand out and shook it free of snow, then slid her hand back into her glove. "Nothing."

Wiping snow from her brow, Sam regarded the girl. "Could be in a lower jacket pocket. Or in a pants pocket." She tugged at the neck of the jacket, but it didn't budge. The girl's lower body was buried lower under a heavy weight of snow.

"Or she left it in the car." Gina stared at the ice mask. "Christ, she's so young."

"Was," Sam turned away, still horrified by the frozen face. She inhaled deeply, rejoicing that her lungs could still suck in air.

Frosty air, thick with snow. Clouds had blotted out the sun now. She pushed herself to her feet, shaking snow from her hands.

Gina straightened. "We've got to get out of here."

"But, the poacher? The boy, man, whoever." Sam jabbed the probe off to the side of the corpse. "And Feisty." Her teeth were beginning to chatter again.

By silent mutual agreement, she and Gina circled the body, Sam pushing the pole into the snow. Nothing.

Gina finally made the decision. "Let's go. They could be anywhere. But they won't be alive. It's getting dark. And it's snowing harder." Shivering, she added, "And neither of us is in the best of shape."

All true. Sam's entire body was trembling again, too. But it still felt like giving up to leave. Hell, it *was* giving up. She recovered her remaining snowshoe, hoping her other might be found, and stuffed it into her pack. One of the straps on her backpack had been ripped apart, but she hung the pack over her right shoulder, grimacing as she stretched her arm through it.

They trudged slowly down the slope, alternately sliding on hard pack or stumbling as their feet sunk into soft, deep snow. There was no sign of more snowshoes or poles, their hats, Sam's gloves, or Gina's backpack.

Sam couldn't stop thinking of that ice-covered young face. Two ice-covered faces, actually; the male trapper had to be under the snow somewhere. Why were they trapping a wolverine?

An innocent wolverine they'd drugged and imprisoned in a cage and now buried in an icy sea of white cement. Adding to the ache in Sam's chest was the thought that somewhere, baby wolverines might be crying for a mother that would never come home.

She also could not quit worrying about what might lie ahead. Gina concurred that they'd felt an earthquake. How localized was the tremor? Would the ski resort be intact? Were Chase and Blake alive and unhurt? Nicole and Claude? She tried to envision them happily oblivious to the disaster she and Gina had barely survived.

They still had such a long way to walk. *One foot in front of the other*, she told herself. *One step at a time.* Behind her, Gina coughed, ending with a stifled moan. *We'll make it. Both of us will make it. And then we will deal with whatever we find.*

Sam's left foot and hand ached. Her back muscles chimed in with every stumble. Her hands felt frozen, and she jammed them into her pockets whenever she didn't require them for balance. Beneath her parka hood, her hair was still wet. Her nose and face were so raw the skin there felt as if it was being scoured by the falling snow, which was now coming down in a thick white curtain. Although she knew the ridge back up to the trailhead had to be ahead, the snow-covered mountain had blurred into the snow-filled sky.

Gina was having a hard time keeping up. Larger and heavier than Sam, she sank deeper into the snow with each step. She labored for every breath, grunting in pain each time she stumbled, holding her arms tightly to her ribs. Sam worried that her friend had broken multiple bones or torn internal organs. She held out her bent ski pole with the half basket. "Maybe it'll help?" Her fingers were so cold she could barely clutch the grip, anyway.

Gina grimaced as she curled her fingers around the handle. "Thanks. Do you know where we are?"

"More or less," Sam confirmed.

"Me too." Gina coughed wetly, and then wiped a hand across her mouth. "But I need to rest now. You should go on ahead. I know you've got to be worried about Chase and the others."

Sam hesitated. "We're still at least ninety minutes from the lodge."

"I'll make it," Gina said. "Slowly, but I'll make it."

Sam bit her lip. Her friend's face was haggard, her brow lined with pain. Where had that blood on Gina's lower lip come from? Was she hemorrhaging internally?

Gina sank to her knees, then collapsed onto her backside, sitting in the snow. "It will just be a short rest. Then I'll start again, I promise. If I don't show up in an hour or so," she said, "you can send help back for me. I'll stick to the trail, or at least as close by as I can determine."

Sam was itching to scale the ridge as quickly as possible, to have the ski resort in sight, to see that her friends had survived. "Are you sure?"

Gina nodded. "Go."

Sam dug in her pack, extracted her headlamp, and was

gratified to find that it still worked. "I'll send help immediately, the first ski patrol I see, I promise. Take this. Keep it on so they can find you. And I'll be back as soon as I can."

"I know you will. Go."

Ashamed of her eagerness to leave her friend, Sam hurried away into the snow, still stumbling, but stumbling faster now, and feeling warmer for the faster activity.

For a few moments, Gina was a dim red-and-black figure topped by a tiny bright light, and in another minute, Sam could no longer see her at all in the fog of white. Jogging whenever the snow was packed hard enough to stay on top, she strained to see the terrain ahead, trying to picture the area in summer, trying to guess where the Lake Ann trail crossed the creek. Traversing the valley floor, she soon came to the area where she thought the path should be, based on the scraggly small trees on either side of a hump of snow. Those indentations could be the footprints she and Gina had made on their way to the trap site.

In the falling snow and growing darkness, her eyes couldn't see anything more than a curtain of white ahead, but she knew the ridge should be less than half a mile farther. She'd know when the terrain started to climb again, back up to the trailhead above the ski resort.

She had taken two steps out onto the hump of snow when it collapsed beneath her boots. She didn't even have time to get the curse words out before she crashed through the snow.

16

Her feet hit, first left then right. Then her legs collapsed at the jolt of pain, and Sam fell to her knees, gashing one kneecap on a rock, finally coming to rest on all fours in six inches of freezing cold water.

"No," she moaned, shaking her head. "No!" This couldn't be happening.

Wasn't an earthquake and an avalanche enough for one day? She pushed herself to her feet, every muscle in her body quivering now.

The snow bridge she'd fallen through was less than four feet off the ground. When she stood up, she could rest her arms on top of the hole, but when she tried to climb out, a wedge of snow broke off under her elbows and fell onto her feet, which were soaking in the icy creek below.

If anyone had been with her, they probably could have pulled her out. But, as usual, she was on her own. Why was it that in real life, heroes never showed up in the nick of time, like they did in the movies?

"Shit! Crap!" she yelled in frustration, knowing nobody could hear.

Thin layers of snow over tunnels of running water were one more reason why it was so dangerous to explore the backcountry in the mountains in April.

In a snowstorm.

In the dark.

After being buried, digging out an injured friend, and watching two people and an innocent wolverine die.

Furious, she tore at the snow with her bare hands, praying she could claw enough of it away to worm her way out before she succumbed to hypothermia from the freezing water.

Before Gina caught up with her and fell in, too. If Gina was moving at all. Should she have left her friend alone?

Sam slapped at the snow. If this wasn't proof that God didn't exist, she didn't know what was. Was this some sort of curse? What more could happen?

The snowshoe. She still had the lone surviving snowshoe strapped to her pack. Pulling it out, she used the jagged metal teeth on the bottom to chew away at the ridges of snow until she created more solid steps that would bear her weight.

Damn it.

17

Maya didn't understand why Eaze wanted to meet the dealer after dark, and at Whatcom Community College. Surely Eaze could just slip him a few bills in daylight as well as in darkness.

"JW and I have come to an agreement," Eaze told her, wiping his nose on the back of his hand. "I'll wait inside, and later we can go get an Oreo blizzard or something at Dairy Queen." Taking her chin in his hand, he pursed his lips in a kissing motion. "Sweets for my sweetheart." Letting go of her, he strode off toward the library entrance, almost jogging.

"Eaze!" Maya yelped, surprised that he was leaving her alone with this guy in the shadows next to the building. She watched as Eaze walked through the pool of brightness spilling from the streetlight and then into the semi-darkness near the library entry.

"Where the hell are you going?" she yelled. Eaze had said they were here to talk about the debt.

The dealer's hand landed heavily on her shoulder. "So, Maya."

She was still unnerved at the news that Eaze's dealer had turned out to be James Winnow, the clean-cut leader of the conservative group on the campus. They called themselves Winning Leaders of America, WLA. Most of the kids she hung out with called them Whining Losers of Antarctica. She'd never understood the "Antarctica" part, although she too wanted to see them exiled somewhere far from campus.

Had wanted. She wasn't part of that debate anymore.

She faced James. "Eaze explained that he's gonna pay it off over time, right? So we're good now, right?"

"C'mon." James's smile was more of a smirk. "Don't play dumb." His fingers curled around her shoulder, urging her to step backward around the corner of the building into the pitch blackness. "I promise you'll have a good time."

"What are you talking about?" Maya tried to pull away, but his fingers pinched her left shoulder. She felt her neck abruptly go numb. The sensation radiated down her left arm. "Stop it! You're hurting me." She pushed her right hand against his chest.

Grabbing that hand, he forced her fingers down against his bulging groin. "You can start here."

"The hell I will!" She tried to pull her hand away, but his fingers clamped even more tightly onto her wrist.

He abruptly bent that hand backward. His other hand leaped to the top of her head, grabbing a handful of hair as he shoved her down. "Get on your knees, like the good little bitch Eaze promised you'd be. Unless you want your throat slit instead."

Did James really have a knife? It seemed likely—a dealer would need some sort of protection. He outweighed her by at least a hundred pounds, and his wrestling prowess showed in his muscular frame. He was too damn strong, and the night was too damn dark. Had Eaze really promised James this? Unbelievable.

Why wasn't the lighting on campus better? Why weren't students and teachers strolling around? It was the damn quarantine restrictions; although most had been lifted, Bellinghamsters were still sticking to their own homes for the most part.

She knelt on the cold ground, feeling the dampness immediately soak through the knees of her skinny jeans. James let go of her wrist, and she rubbed it with her other hand. She heard the rasp of the zipper on his fly as he slid it down, snarling, "You bite me, you're dead."

"Oh, I'd never do that." Reaching for his erection, she curled her fingers around his penis.

James kept his grip on her hair, but threw his head back. "Oh yeah, baby," he murmured. "Let's go."

Maya grasped his penis firmly, then abruptly clamped her fingers into a fist, twisting as hard as she could and wrenching upward at the same time.

"Bitch!" he screamed, yanking on her hair. His other fist slammed into her temple.

She blinked away the stars that flashed in front of her eyes and twisted harder until he staggered back, letting go of her hair, swearing as he reached into his jacket pocket. Shit! Was he going for the knife? Maya leaped to her feet and kicked out, aiming for his groin. James screeched again as her boot connected with the softest part of his body.

He fell to his knees, whimpering. As she fled for the library entrance, she heard him hiss, "You're dead. So dead. And so's your fuckin' boyfriend."

18

Breathless, Sam finally crested the ridge at the top of the Lake Ann trail. It had taken her most of an hour to dig her way out of the damn hole she'd fallen into. Her pants, soaked by the frigid water, were now covered in a thin layer of frost. They were a mix of wool and synthetic blend, so the moisture next to her skin wasn't too bad. If she'd worn cotton jeans, she'd have been completely hypothermic before she managed to claw her way out of the collapsed snow.

Her feet were another story. Her boots were waterproof, but that only meant that they kept water in after it flooded over the tops. She could feel blisters forming as the wet wool socks chafed the skin of her heels. She wanted to stop and wring out her socks, but she was afraid to halt for fear she'd never get started again. Not to mention that her socks might freeze before she could get her feet back in her boots.

She'd expected Gina to catch up with her before she managed to crawl out of the hole. But when she stood up, the other woman had been nowhere in sight. Had Gina even started walking again? Sam feared she'd abandoned her friend to die alone. But now, the best bet was to get help to rescue Gina as soon as possible.

Taking a break for a few minutes, she surveyed the valley below. Had she stood here only a few hours ago? It felt like she'd been out in the frigid weather and dark for days.

Through the blowing snow she could barely make out a few lights at the upper ski area. The slopes would be vacant now, the freestyle contest long over. Her exhausted brain coughed up the errant thought that the editor at *Out There* would be anxiously awaiting her story and photos. Tough. She had a better story for him now.

The faint whine of a snowmobile engine reached her ears. "Hey!" she shouted. "Over here!"

"Hey!" she tried again. Like whoever was driving that machine would hear her faint cries in the blowing wind and sound-muffling snow. If only she had the headlamp. But she'd left that with Gina.

The tenor of the snowmobile engine slowed, like the driver was carefully navigating a dangerous area. "Hey!" she yelled, then abruptly remembered the plastic whistle built into the chest strap of her pack. She fumbled for it, her fingers numb with cold. Still on the strap, thank heavens. Putting the whistle to her lips, she blew. Taking a deep breath that hurt her ribs, she blew again. And again.

The rumble grew faster. Was the engine noise also getting louder? She blew the whistle until her ribs ached and she became light-headed.

Finally, two headlights appeared out of the gloom, glowing ever brighter, then abruptly stopped. "Hello?"

"Here!" Sam yelled, and then used her whistle to guide him close. As the machine neared, the headlights blinded her and she had to focus her gaze on the dark forest for a moment before looking back.

"Am I glad to see you!" she told the man on the seat. Up close, she saw that he was young, with a fashionable three-day stubble of whiskers. He wore the red jacket of the ski patrol.

"You were in that earthquake?" Shoving the snowmobile

gear into neutral, he stood up from the seat to eye her. "I'm Kevin Zhao. How badly are you injured?"

"I can walk," she told him, although she wasn't sure how long that would remain true. Her throat was raw from blood and snot and breathing ice crystals, and her voice was hoarse. "You need to go get my friend, Gina Canfield. She's in bad shape. We had to dig out of an avalanche. I think she has broken ribs." Sam gestured vaguely in the direction of the area south and below them. "She's down in the valley."

He glanced in the direction she indicated, but all that could be seen was white fog pierced by the dark ghostly spikes of nearby trees.

"Down close to where the Swift Creek trail meets the Lake Ann trail," Sam clarified, beginning to cough. "She has a headlamp. But the snow bridge over the creek has collapsed, so . . . " She couldn't think of what should come after the "so."

Twisting, Zhao pulled up the seat behind him and extracted an energy drink from the compartment below, then extended the bottle to her. "Get on," he ordered, slamming the compartment closed and sliding forward on the seat.

"But Gina—" Sam coughed as she struggled to twist off the bottle cap.

Taking the bottle from her, he deftly removed the cap, putting it in his pocket. "Drink some of this down; you look like you're going into shock."

"You should see the other guy," she said between gulps. The drink tasted simultaneously salty and sugary. When she was halfway through, he grabbed the bottle back from her, screwed on the cap, and stuffed it into the pocket of his jacket.

"Thanks. But Gina—" she tried again.

"Get on. I'll deliver you and then I'll get Tyler and we'll go get her."

Wincing, she lifted her leg and straddled the seat behind him.

"We're getting out the heavy gear from the maintenance shed, but there's not much we can do at the lodge right now."

What was he trying to tell her? Heavy gear? Which lodge?

He gripped the handles of the snowmobile. "Can you hold on to me?"

Her shoulder and neck protested when she leaned forward, but she managed to wrap her arms around him. "What's happening at the Heather Meadows Lodge?" she asked into the back of his neck. "Did everyone get away after the contest?"

"Far as I know, Heather Meadows is mostly okay. The earthquake shook things out of plumb, so they'll have to pry the equipment bay doors open or saw their way through, but that's kind of minor compared to everything else." He revved the engine and they slid forward. "Everyone's at Raven Hut."

Sam's heart skipped a few beats. Chase and Nicole, Blake and Claude had been skiing above Raven Hut.

"What happened at Raven Hut?" she asked, nearly shouting to be heard over the engine noise.

He turned his head to tell her, "Major breaks on the slopes above. Everything just came loose down the canyons. The hut's crushed."

She buried her face in the red parka on his back, praying that all her friends were long gone from the lodge before the avalanche hit.

"The road and half the parking lot's buried, too," he added.

Please let everyone be okay. As petite as she was, Sam couldn't see over her rescuer's shoulder. The wild downhill ride from the ridge, her first on a snowmobile, might have been thrilling if the zigzags and bumps hadn't hurt so much.

19

Maya found Eaze sitting on a bench just inside the double entrance doors of the library, reading the college magazine in the dim light of the overhead fluorescents. He frowned slightly at her, straightening his back as he slid the magazine from his lap to rest beside him. "Wow. JW must be a lightweight. That didn't take long."

"How could you?" Pulling her Android from her pocket, she flipped to its call screen. "How could you leave me with that creep?"

Eaze leaped to his feet, grabbing her bruised wrist. She nearly dropped her cell phone. "What are you doing?"

"Calling the cops," she said. "That dickwad just tried to rape me. He told me you promised him I'd do him."

"Maya." Eaze kept his fingers curled around her wrist. Raising his other hand, he stroked her cheek with the back of his fingers. "What's the big deal? It's not like you're a virgin. Three times, babe, that's all. Only twice more after tonight, and James was going to shave five hundred off the debt."

Maya stared at him for a long moment, her mouth open. Then she shook him off. "You're both scumbags."

"You turn him in, you turn me in." His dark eyes implored her. "Aww, baby, be reasonable." He held out his arms again, but she stepped back away from his reach.

He crossed his arms against his chest. His face hardened. "You got no proof. It's your word against his." His eyes glittered. "And mine."

"Un-fucking-believable." Turning on her heel, Maya strode toward the door. "I don't want to see you ever again."

Before the door closed behind her, she heard Eaze whine, "Where am I supposed to sleep tonight?"

"Try a garbage dumpster."

She paused in the shadow between the library entrance and the streetlight, holding her breath, her gaze searching the darkness as she listened for any sound of footsteps. A police cruiser drove by. She trotted toward the lighted bus shelter on Cordata Parkway, hoping a Whatcom Transportation Authority bus would arrive soon. WTA didn't run many buses late at night, and she knew some runs had been cancelled during the quarantine months. If a bus came, it would still be a long walk from the end of the line back to her tent in Sam's backyard.

If a bus didn't come, who could she call? Sam was probably going to spend the night with Chase. She'd try Blake if the bus didn't come in half an hour; he was usually a soft touch. But then she remembered that he'd gone skiing with Claude today, so if he came back, he might be late. And if Claude was staying over, Blake might not answer at all. *Shit.*

Maybe Troy Johnson? Her former boss once said he thought of her like a daughter. But then, just a month or two ago, he'd told her he wouldn't hire her again this year, and after that he didn't even answer the last two voicemails she'd left. *Shit, shit, shit!*

She chewed a fingernail. Was Nick Lewis still in juvie? He'd be old enough to drive now. She'd promised to visit him when he was sentenced, but she hadn't, not for the last two years. If Nick was out, he'd probably be in foster care now because his father was still in prison for double murder. Which probably meant Nick wouldn't have a car. Her shitty foster parents sure never bought her one. And Aidan Callahan was definitely still behind bars. Some friend he'd turned out to be. Some mentor.

And now she'd discovered her one friend, Ethan Zeran, was just as much of a jackass as Aidan had been. All kind and sympathetic one minute, ready to throw anyone under the bus when that was more convenient.

How could everyone she knew be a scumbag or a convict? Or else they were just plain dead, like her mother and father, like Jade and Alice, Kim and Kyla. Brianna. What a shitty world.

Maybe her counselor at the community college. What was her name? Connie Something? Carol? Cammie? She hadn't heard from the woman since she'd dropped out. But practically everyone had dropped out because of COVID, hadn't they? Nobody could be expected to live on Zoom or Google Meetings or whatever the fuck the college called whatever shit programs they were using online. And without her apartment, she didn't have anywhere to study, even if she'd stayed enrolled.

An old blue Subaru screeched past. That was the car she and Eaze had come in, the Outback Eaze said he'd borrowed from a friend. Maya recognized the duct tape on the side mirror even before she spotted James's malevolent smile in the driver's seat. Was that his car? Was that Eaze beside him?

A hand emerged from the driver's and the passenger's windows, each with the middle finger extended. Stereo fuck-you signs. As they passed, Eaze's snarl wafted back to her. "Bitch!"

The hair on the nape of Maya's neck prickled. It was only a fifteen-minute drive from the college to Sam's house. Had Eaze told James where she lived? The scumbags could easily beat her there.

Maybe Eaze was only going to retrieve his sleeping bag from her tent. The raised finger seemed to promise more than just an errand. She chewed on her lower lip, trying to envision what other things he'd left there. Was the gun in her tent, or did Eaze have it on him? *Fuck!*

Please don't let anything happen to Sam or Blake. Or Simon. Maya wasn't sure who that little prayer was supposed to go to. Nobody had answered any of her prayers for the last twenty years. She pulled out her phone and texted a warning to Sam and Blake: Watch 4 trouble. Vague, but she didn't know what else to say. *Eaze might be gunning for you?*

Lights shone in the distance. Was that the bus? The route sign on its destination board told her that it would take her to Western Washington campus. And she knew it continued on from there toward Sam's house. She redirected her thought prayer in that direction. *Please get me back to Sam's house as fast as you can.*

20

Kevin Zhao slid the snowmobile to a stop a short distance away from a cluster of people, but he didn't kill the engine. Over his shoulder, he murmured, "Okay to leave you here?"

"Yeah." Realizing he was in a hurry, she painfully peeled her body from his back, reluctant to give up his warmth and comforting bulk. It hurt to stand upright again. Her parka was damp. The wind was blowing the snow sideways here.

"I'll find Tyler and a sled, and we'll get your friend."

"Thanks, Kevin. Her name's Gina Canfield."

"Gina." He nodded, then gunned the machine off into the darkness.

Soon after he left, she realized that she should have told him there had been three more victims. That man or boy, the girl. And a wolverine. But it was already too late to rescue them.

A generator rumbled somewhere in the shadows, probably powering the two giant spotlights that painted stripes of bright light across the scene. Sam faced what should have been the Raven Hut lodge, but the heap of snow-covered wreckage in front of her did not seem even remotely familiar. A few in the small crowd glanced at her briefly. Most were focused on the debris in front of them. Some held out their cell phones, sweeping them around, but the flashlight mode of the phones did little to illuminate more than minute areas of the collapsed building. No lights were visible inside the structure. Behind them, the overhead lamps in the avalanche path had been swept away, but the edges of the area were still illuminated by lamps on tall poles. In the distance, Sam heard the hum of generators.

One woman in a pink ski coat seemed hysterical, futilely yanking on shattered pieces of broken lumber that poked up out of the mountain of snow. "My baby," she sobbed. "Emma! Somebody help her!"

Sam had never wanted children, and now, as she watched, she couldn't imagine what it was like to be this anguished mother right now. That her own father had never been present during the many occasions she'd been in danger was probably a blessing for them both.

A short distance away, a man was shouting into his phone. "Why the fuck not?" He stared up toward the sky as he asked, "Well, when *can* they fly, then?"

Asking for a helicopter? No aircraft could fly in this weather, at least not low enough to be of any use. A stubby antenna poked up by the man's ear. Sat phone, then. She was surprised it could locate a satellite in this blizzard.

Why was no rescue coming up the highway? She squinted in that direction, trying to make out the scene through the blowing snow and darkness. There should have been a parking lot and a road below Raven Hut, but she couldn't make out anything there but a massive field of snow. Were cars buried beneath that snow?

How far had the avalanche traveled? The highway to the ski resort snaked up the steep mountain. Had the earthquake caused multiple avalanches along the road? How much of the highway was blocked?

She limped around the collapsed structure, biting her lip as she heard Chase's voice echo in her head. "*Summer?*" Had she actually heard him call her?

The rear of the building was not totally flattened, as far as she could tell. The massive load of snow made it difficult to see how damaged the front was, but it was obvious that the two-story window wall at the front of the lodge had been obliterated. She didn't want to think about all that glass shattering on impact, or about how far surging snow could carry lethal shards.

"Chase?" she murmured. Please, God, if you exist, let him have gone home before this happened. Nicole, too.

She had no idea if Blake and Claude were safe, either. Sam circled the observers, studying each person gathered around the ruined hut, searching for familiar shapes and faces. When the mound of collapsed building debris abruptly emitted a faint wail, everybody gasped.

The woman in pink screamed, "Emma?"

Someone, at least one person, was alive in there. Two men in ski patrol jackets were down on their knees, shining a flashlight into a hole in the collapsed building.

"I can't tell how far it goes," one said.

"Maybe I could . . ." the smaller man said, leaning forward and thrusting his head and shoulder inside.

"No way, dude." His friend shook his head. The smaller man pulled his head back out. "It wouldn't be safe, anyway. The whole thing could shift again. They'll just have to wait."

"Until?" The smaller man stood up, brushing snow from his jacket. "Who knows how bad the situation is in there? Who knows how many people are trapped? How badly they're injured?"

The distraught mother was beside them now. "Have you found a way in? Emma's in there. I can hear my baby!" Falling on her knees in the snow, she tried to wriggle her shoulders through the opening. She was bulkier than the ski patrol guy who had just tried, and it was clear that even if she managed to wedge her head and shoulders through the gap, there was no way her hips would fit.

"Emma!" she screamed into the tunnel, then backed out, crying. Still on her knees, she tugged at the boards that crisscrossed above the dark hole. "Jerry!" "Amber!"

"Ma'am." The two men tugged the woman back to her feet.

Sam studied the opening. She was the smallest person in the crowd. She might fit. But for how far? The hut had been blasted down by the avalanche. Broken glass would be everywhere. Could there be gas, or live electrical wires? And like the ski patrol guy said, the whole structure could shift again at any time. She didn't want to do it.

Then the wail came again. And then a man's voice, muffled, barely audible. "Help!"

Chase? She couldn't tell.

"Jerry?" the hysterical woman shouted. "Jerry, is that you?"

A higher voice next, a woman or maybe a child. "Is anyone out there?"

A man in the crowd thumped on the nearest piece of the collapsed building in response until someone shouted, "Stop! You'll bring it all down."

The smaller ski patrol guy yelled, "Everyone, shut up! Silence!"

When the crowd had hushed, he bent over and bellowed into the tunnel, "We hear you. We'll get help to you as soon as possible. How many are in there?"

"At least three alive," the male voice answered, sounding distant.

It sounded like Chase. Didn't it? Maybe. Was that her imagination?

"Anyone injured?"

"Everyone," the male voice responded.

That was followed by another pitiful wail. Beside her, the mother sobbed.

After sucking in a big gulp of cold air, Sam said, "I'm going in."

21

The ski patrol pair studied her. "You're injured," the taller one said. The glow from his flashlight revealed the reflective name tape on his jacket front. Malley.

"Superficial." She brushed her fingers across her scraped forehead, and was immediately sorry when her skin burned at the touch. "Do you have first aid supplies?"

The shorter one turned away, saying, "I'll go get the bag."

"We can't let you—" Malley began.

"At least I can try."

"Sam?" A familiar figure materialized beside her.

"Blake!" They reached for each other simultaneously. Although the embrace hurt her shoulder and arm, her friend's hug still felt good. "I'm so glad you're okay, Blake. Where's Claude?"

Her housemate's eyes filled as he thrust his chin toward a dark shape beneath a blanket on a ski patrol sled several yards away. Sam clutched Blake's sleeve. "Oh, no, I'm so sorry . . ."

Blake shook his head. "Claude's not dead." He raised a hand to wipe away a tear from his cheek. "At least not yet. But we had to dig him out, and he's unconscious."

"Do you know about Chase? And Nicole?"

Blake surveyed the wrecked building. "I think maybe . . ."

Sam raised a fist to her mouth in horror.

"But I don't know for sure. They might have been in the parking lot."

The parking lot was not even visible. How many people were trapped in cars under that snow? How many people had been walking on the road that was now buried?

"Or maybe even down the road," Blake amended, trying to inject a note of hope. "All the way down, to the bottom of the mountain."

The shorter ski patrol guy was back. The name on his jacket was Sharpe. He thrust out a helmet with a headlight and a device projecting from the front that Sam recognized as a GoPro Camera. "And here's the first aid bag." He set a small red nylon bag down next to her. "Although how you're going to carry it, I don't know."

"Got a rope or a strap?" She jammed the helmet on her head. "I'll tie it to my ankle and tow it behind."

Sharpe unzipped the bag and extracted a yellow nylon strap. "There will probably be broken glass." He dug around in his jacket pockets, pulling out a pair of leather gloves. "These belong to Ashley. She's not on duty today." He handed them to Sam.

"Lucky girl," Malley commented.

Sam pulled on the gloves. They were a bit loose, but they'd probably stay on.

"Sam, you can't go in there!" Blake protested.

She pointed toward the small opening and then gestured at the people standing around them. "See anyone else who could?"

Blake surveyed the crowd. "We need a rescue dog."

"See a dog?" she asked.

All three men stared at her.

"So I'm going." She knelt in the snow to tie the strap to her right ankle, clenching her teeth against the pain that bending caused her. Switching on the headlamp, she then crawled toward the opening. With her palms and knees against the icy surface, she began to shiver. Oh well, she couldn't possibly be any colder inside this tunnel than she was outside.

The narrow beam of the headlamp revealed a tangle of massive timbers and wallboard, broken tables, chairs, and, surprisingly, rocks. She hadn't even gotten her feet inside before she had to flatten her chest to the ground and use her elbows and toes to inch along under an X of crisscrossed boards. Her shoulder and ribs shrieked with pain as she stretched out like a worm.

Probably be broken glass? The debris beneath her—it was no longer a floor—was littered with shards that glittered in the headlamp beam. They shredded her parka as she slithered over them. She was grateful for the leather gloves.

"Anyone in here?" she yelled. Several muffled voices drafted toward her from different directions. At least one man's—Chase?—and a woman's voice, but she couldn't make out their words behind the wailing that seemed to grow louder with every inch she moved. Then the debris overhead groaned, and for a torturous moment something up high above her ticked, like an old-fashioned clock. Or the timer on a bomb in a horror flick. Was the building shifting?

Her breath caught in her throat. A sliding screech squealed above. A shower of snow sifted down onto her head. Then she heard nothing except the wailing. That seemed the closest sound. She'd try to move in that direction.

Every foot or so, she had to crawl over rocks or across a two-by-four, yanking the first aid kit behind her with her foot. The constant pattern of two-by-fours beneath her made no sense until she realized she was crawling on top of a collapsed wall. Her headlamp snagged on a wire, and when she raised her chin to disentangle it, the light illuminated a spiderweb of wires that she'd have to find her way through. *Please let the power be off,* she prayed as she snaked over and under the tangle, pushing the wires aside when she could.

The wailing grew louder. "I'm coming," she said aloud. The first aid kit, anchored to her ankle, got caught up in the wire web, and she had to contort her frame to pull the bag through. A sharp pain shot through her shoulder, but she managed to clasp her hand around the strap and yank the nylon bag out of the tangle. Ahead, she saw a sneaker suspended in the air among a pile of rocks and broken beams. Sam had never been in the Raven Hut Lodge, but she'd seen photos of the stone fireplace. That explained the rocks. Farther on, a blue plastic structure, half-embedded in snow, had been shoved partway under a broken chair. Her helmet smacked into a table leg, and she was forced to press her face practically to the ground to slither beneath it.

Reaching up, she took hold of the sneaker. Purple, small. Her memory tortured her with a flashback of the dead girl in the purple parka, ice covering her young face. Purple seemed to be an unlucky color today.

Oh, sweet Jesus, it was not just a sneaker; there was a foot inside. Which she assumed was attached to a leg and eventually a whole human being, but she couldn't see anything more than the bottom part of the shoe wedged into the rock pile. "Hey," she said, shaking the sneaker. "Can you move? Are you okay?"

No movement. If there was a verbal response, she couldn't hear it above the shrieking ahead. Was she holding onto a corpse's foot? Of course there would be bodies, she told herself—what did she expect inside a collapsed building? Pulling her hand back, Sam closed her eyes for a second, hoping for tranquility, and then moved on.

There! Another foot, this one tiny, alive, wearing miniscule white leather booties, kicking at the snow. She thought she heard muffled cheers outside, and remembered that the camera on her helmet was recording. Whoever owned it—probably one of the ski patrol guys—must be watching on some electronic device. Did it have a microphone, too? "Yes, it's a baby," she said, brushing the snow away, thankful that the infant had been strapped into a sturdy carrier that had come to rest on its back. That carrier had saved the little girl's life.

The child seemed unhurt except for a bleeding scratch along one cheek. She was no doubt cold and scared to death, and she wouldn't stop crying. This close, it sounded more like screaming. "Are you Emma?" Sam crooned, trying to make her voice soothing. "I hope so. Your mama misses you."

The baby wasn't buying it. Her shrieking seemed to grow in volume. Now what? Sam hadn't thought any farther than seeing what—or who—was in here. There was no space to turn around, she could barely bend her knee to drag up the first aid kit. Should she try to reverse course and take the baby out, or continue on her search? There could be other victims who needed her more.

The little girl grabbed a handful of Sam's long blonde hair and refused to let go.

"Okay, okay." Sam struggled to unleash the nylon bag from her ankle and buckle it onto the baby carrier. Then she began to shove herself backward, dragging the baby carrier with her hands. Close up, the child's shrieks were deafening. When Sam reached the tangle of wires, she found just enough space to fold herself like an inchworm and turn so she could push the carrier in front of her.

How could she be sweating and freezing at the same time? Her hair was full of glass shards and snow. Every muscle in her body ached. At one point she had to tip the baby carrier on its side to slide it under the debris. That made the baby scream even louder.

Then she finally saw the opening ahead, and a pair of hands

reached in and pulled the carrier from her. Sam collapsed against the ground and laid her head on her outstretched arm for a minute, panting.

Blake's face appeared in the opening. "Sam? Are you okay?"

She stretched both arms toward him. "Can you pull me out?"

Grasping her wrists, he pulled her outside. It hurt like hell, but then everything had been hurting like hell for hours. She sat up, stretching her back, tilting her head back to relax her neck muscles. Her face met an icy blast. The snow was falling harder now.

A few feet away, the mother clutched the baby, murmuring to her, and mouthing "Thank you" to Sam.

Sam briefly blinded Blake with the headlamp before she remembered to switch the thing off. "Any word on rescue?"

He unscrewed the top of a thermos and handed it to her. "The road's closed by the avalanche, and the choppers can't fly in this."

She grimaced at the taste of sweetened coffee. But at least it was lukewarm. "I meant any good news. So it will be hours."

"They're going to try to get snowmobiles up the highway from the closure. And the ski patrol went up to Heather Meadows to get a snowcat out of a maintenance shed, but the doors are jammed, so they're breaking their way in. Apparently, they can plow with that, or drive on top of the snow or something."

"Yippee," she whined. "What we really need is an excavator or a crane or a machine that can lift things."

The mother approached. "Did you see any sign of my husband, Jerry? Black parka, bald head. Or my babysitter, Amber? Sixteen, long dark hair?"

"Was Amber wearing purple sneakers?" Sam chewed her lip

as she waited for a reply.

Doubt overtook the woman's face. "I think so, maybe."

"Then maybe I saw her foot. She was sandwiched in a lot of debris."

The woman clutched baby Emma to her chest. "Good lord."

"There's still hope." Sam prayed she wasn't lying to the woman.

She scanned the area for a moment, studying all the people she could see. No sign of Gina. Sam's heart dropped. Had Kevin Zhao and his friend been unable to find her friend? Had she survived? Had she sent the two snowmobile rescuers to their deaths down in that snowy valley as well? Guilt gnawed at her insides.

22

A few bystanders in the crowd tugged at debris around the edges of the collapsed building, lifting small pieces away. A little farther down the slope, several skiers shoved avalanche poles into the snow in back of the collapsed building, hoping to locate the missing. They would only find corpses, Sam knew. Nobody could have survived this long under the snow. The only possibility of survival under the snow was if some victims had been inside a car when the avalanche hit, and by now, the air would be running out if it hadn't long ago.

This was supposed to be a celebratory outing for everyone who came up here. She and all her friends had looked forward to sharing sun and snow and happy people. And then she'd hoped to rescue a wolverine, finally see a skunk bear in the flesh instead of through a camera lens. Instead, she—and all these other people—had crash-landed in a snowy hell. As if she needed reminding, her brain flashed the unwelcome memory of the female poacher's ice-masked face across her mental screen.

Focus on where there's still possibility of life, she told herself. She shook the snow and shards of glass out of her hair and studied the frantic scene around her. She would enjoy the contrast of snow and the dark night if she weren't so exhausted. Even her bones felt tired. But Chase . . .

She faced the opening in the collapsed lodge again, putting

her gloved hands down onto the snow. "I heard several other voices inside. I'm going back."

"Sam . . ." Blake started to protest, but then stopped.

There really wasn't anything to say, was there? There was no indication that more capable rescuers would show up soon. She couldn't leave people to die in there if there was a chance of saving a single one. Deciding to leave the first aid kit behind so she could be more agile, she zipped several tightly wrapped metallic thermal blankets inside her pockets. She couldn't do much of anything in the way of first aid, but maybe she could save someone from freezing to death. If there was anyone to save.

She belly-flopped her way in and scrabbled to the wire web again. After she was through, she elbowed her way to the left, through a star-shaped opening surrounded by the sharp teeth of splintered boards. She'd managed to get her top half through the hole when her shoulder nudged a dangling piece of paneling, shifting it.

Abruptly, the structure above her groaned as if alive. Debris tumbled down like a rockslide. Something hard smacked her in the back of the head, and then a wave of snow washed over her face and shoulders. *OhGodohGodohGod*, she was buried again! Her scream was muffled by the snow. She twisted her head, bashing her aching nose into whatever was beneath her. Frantically waving her outstretched hand in front of her face, she shoved the icy clumps away.

Muffled calls from outside reached her ears. Or was that just her imagination? Her shoulder was pinned by whatever had fallen on her. The board at the bottom of the sharp opening she had crawled halfway through was pressing into her ribs and abdomen. She was being cut in half. A weight rested solidly on her back and shoulders. Holy hell—was she going to die in here?

"Summer?"

She clamped her lips together and stopped to listen. Had she really heard Chase's voice? She moaned and coughed, spit out a wad of snow and dust, tried to push herself off the floor. Maybe an inch, that's all she gained. The constriction at her waist hurt like hell. She could barely breathe. The weight on her back was crushing. An agonizing vision of the wolverine trapped and buried and smothering in a smashed dog carrier filled her head.

She bent her legs and feet as much as she could, tightening her thighs against the other side of the opening, at the same time shoving backward with her outstretched hands. The helmet strap under her chin threatened to choke her. With fumbling fingers barely wedged beneath her neck, she managed to unsnap the strap and then pushed backward again.

Whatever was crushing her shoulder slid up onto her neck and then, after ripping away what felt like half her scalp against the debris resting on her back, she succeeded in pulling her head and shoulders out of the opening. Coughing, she wriggled backward like a prairie dog that had just spotted a rattler lurking ahead in its tunnel. Her helmet and GoPro stayed behind, wedged beneath the rubble.

"Fuck!" She wasn't prone to cussing, but now seemed like the perfect moment for it. Resting her head against her forearms, she closed her dust-caked eyes and allowed herself a pause to reflect on her situation. "Fuck, fuck, fuck!"

A faint voice responded. "Help! Help us!"

Ahead and more to the left, she thought. Sounded female. Nicole? *Us*, she'd said. So at least two. Was Chase with her? The structure screeched again. Whining, cracking, gasps—were any of those human sounds, or just the unstable wreck of the building shifting into a new position?

Why had she imagined she could rescue anyone? She was more likely to die in the cold and dark here with the other victims.

Suck it up, Westin.

The opening she had tried to crawl through was now blocked with fallen debris, glowing eerily in the beam from the headlamp on the helmet. Only patches of very dim light filtered through the wreckage above. Everything else was pitch black. She needed that headlamp. Snaking an arm through the tangle of broken wood and sheetrock, she grabbed an edge of the helmet. She pulled. Nothing moved. The helmet was tightly wedged between fallen boards. Sliding her fingers over the helmet, she found the strap that held the lamp in place. She managed to slide the strap off one side, but it snagged on the other.

Damn. She yanked hard, wedging her shoulder against the wall of debris in front of her. Just when she thought the strap couldn't stretch any more, it snapped. She barely managed to keep hold of it, but finally succeeded in pulling the headlamp back.

Okay. She coughed again at a mouthful of sheetrock dust. She no longer had a helmet, but she had a headlamp. On a broken strap. Its beam revealed a possible opening farther to her right, back toward where she'd found baby Emma. She couldn't figure any way to tie the strap onto her head, so she resorted to pushing the strap down into her collar, letting the lamp hang out beside her neck as she inched her way forward. She was now a lighted inchworm. Or maybe a luminescent mole. A new species, born of necessity.

Was that a moan she heard? "Chase? Nicole? Anyone?"

Her words sounded as unintelligible as when she'd shouted underwater through a scuba mouthpiece. She'd been in bad circumstances before. She'd survived a near drowning in the Galápagos. *Don't go there.* That story was hardly inspiring. She'd lived, but her partner hadn't. She coughed again, tasting blood that she hoped was only from her broken nose.

Was that tapping? Faint human voices? Coming from inside or outside? She couldn't tell. Imagining herself as a lithe python now, she slithered over the end of a set of metal shelves and then between the shelves, elbowing her way through broken dishes that crunched beneath her.

Off to the right, she spotted the purple sneaker again, redirected her vision, studying where the baby had been. Beyond that small space was another web of wires, and beyond that, she could see a pale green gleam. Hadn't Nicole been wearing a mint-green ski jacket?

Something shifted overhead. Panic flared in Sam's gut. She inhaled, trying to sift the dusty cloud through her teeth, and then coughed on air that tasted of chemicals she didn't want to analyze. A powerful urge to retreat gripped her for a few seconds. But it would take her just as long to get back. And she would not have accomplished anything.

Calm down, Summer. It was her minister father's voice, soothing her as a little girl when she'd become hysterical about her mother dying. *Let's sing.* And then he'd launch into "Amazing Grace" or "How Great Thou Art" and the well-worn words would comfort her.

But it had been a long time since she'd sung a hymn. The song that came to her now was not the music of a hymn, but the holiday tune "Over the River and Through the Woods."

Over the debris and through the wires, she sang to herself in her head, *through Raven Hut Lodge we crawl. To find the living and not the dead, even without a helmet on head* . . . What rhymed with crawl? Trying not to bawl?

She reached the green. It *was* Nicole's jacket, or at least a jacket like Nicole's, wrapped around the back of a fallen chair and tangled in wires beneath a section of heating duct.

"Nicole?" she murmured into the blackness.

"Here!" The voice startled her. But it was a man's voice, not Nicole's.

Ahead, barely visible through the debris, a hand moved. She pulled the headlamp from her collar and focused the beam in that direction. A bloody face blinked at her from the shadows. "Jerry?" she asked, remembering baby Emma's father.

"Daniel." Not a man, but a boy. Sixteen, seventeen. He was shivering, pinned face down on a broken table, held in place by what appeared to be a section of wall. Sam couldn't see what topped the wood and drywall structure. Everything above was solid black.

"Can you breathe?" she asked.

"So far." A whine escaped as he exhaled heavily. "Barely. I think my shoulder's dislocated, and I can't feel my legs."

Sam rolled over onto her back and pushed at the wall section on top of him. She couldn't budge it, and she was afraid to try harder, lest she dislodge whatever was keeping him from being crushed. "We're going to get you out, . . ."

"Daniel," he reminded her. "There were two others, down by my feet. A man and a woman. They were talking, but I can't hear them anymore. I hope they're not dead."

Sam gulped. Chase and Nicole? "I'm going to see if I can reach them. Hang in there, Daniel."

"Like I have a choice," he mumbled, his voice grim.

She elbowed her way forward around a section of heating duct, moving in the direction of Daniel's feet.

We're going to get you out? How could she have promised the kid that? She wasn't even sure she could get herself out.

23

As the WTA bus cruised slowly toward Sam's neighborhood, Maya anxiously checked her cell phone. There was no response from Blake or Sam. It was dark; they couldn't still be on the mountain, could they? Probably eating out, having a good time. Typical. Nobody thought about her and her problems anymore. She tried calling Eaze. He responded with a text, an emoji hand with the middle finger raised.

When the bus finally slowed at her stop, she leaped off and ran the half mile to Sam's cabin, panting by the time she arrived, clutching at the stitch in her side. A year ago, she'd hiked for miles in the mountains, carrying a heavy backpack every day. What the hell had she done to get so out of shape?

She was relieved to see lights on inside the cabin. Maybe Sam or Blake or both were home, after all. But as she approached, she didn't see Sam's RAV4. Blake's old beater was there, but Claude's BMW was not. Crouched in the space behind Blake's Honda was James Winnow's car.

Light spilling from the cabin windows revealed her tent in the backyard, slumped like an injured animal, its spine pole caved in. Her sleeping bag lay stretched between two blueberry bushes, stuffing leaking out of the rips torn into its covering. She bit her lip. Now she didn't even own enough to call herself a bag lady.

She peered into James's car. On the passenger seat was her laptop. She quietly opened the door and removed the computer, tucking it into the space under the wooden steps that led to the back door. The window next to the steps, the one in the utility room, was broken. Twisting the door knob, she pushed her way inside.

The overhead light was on in the living room. As she watched from the doorway of the utility room, James aimed a kick at the television screen sitting on the console. It crashed to the floor. "Piece of shit," he growled.

Maya stepped back into the shadows and texted 9-1-1, typing break-in and Sam's address. She quickly put the phone on silent mode and shoved it into her jacket pocket.

In the living room, James was still raging, shouting a long string of obscenities. Turning to Eaze, who stood behind the kitchen counter, he asked, "Who doesn't have a single piece of crap worth stealing? I only found sixty-five dollars in the bedroom! How you gonna pay the rest?"

"I'll think of something." Eaze took a drag from the beer can in his hand, and tossed another in James's direction. "Chill."

Maya no longer recognized her boyfriend. Why was he doing this? He was a monster. What would he do to her next? What would James? She didn't want to be here. But she couldn't let this happen to Sam and Blake.

Her head aching with fury and her heart pounding with fear, she stepped out from the shadows. "I told you that Sam and Blake were not rich."

"Well, well, it's the bitch from hell." James's face twisted in rage. "Your fuckin' friends ain't even poor. They got nothin'!"

"They have everything any good person needs." Sam and Blake had friends and a home and a decent life. And they were respected and trusted. Maya strode toward the kitchen. Both men followed her movements like a hungry cougar tracking a deer.

Leaning against the kitchen counter, she jerked her chin at the beer in front of Eaze. "Got one of those for me?"

When Eaze turned to open the refrigerator door, she surreptitiously slipped a knife from the block behind her back.

Eaze shut the refrigerator. "Sorry, no more."

"That's okay," she told him. "No worries."

"*Now* you want to make nice?" James snarled, moving in her direction.

"No." Maya spat out the word. "Now I want you to leave."

"We could both do her." James's focus on her was as intense and impersonal as a snake's. "You hold her down. I'll go first."

A trill of fear rattled down Maya's spine. "I called the cops."

James grinned. "Yeah, right, like a slut's gonna do that." To Eaze, he said, "Get her now."

Eaze licked his lips. "Maya." He crushed his empty beer can in one hand, tossed it on the floor, and then took a step toward her.

She tried to back up, but her backside was already pressed against the counter. She gripped the knife handle behind her back. "Don't touch me, either of you. The cops will be here any second."

"Maya," Eaze murmured again. Which could have meant anything from "I'm sorry" to "Just do as I say." He pulled his gun from his jacket pocket.

She cringed. Coming from Eaze's lips at this moment, her name clearly didn't mean "I love you."

Simon chose that moment to rocket from Sam's bedroom through the living room, a black-and-white streak that startled them all. The cat danced by the front door, clearly desperate to get out. He yowled his request.

"I hate that fuckin' cat." Eaze aimed his pistol in the cat's direction.

Maya stabbed the knife into Eaze's shoulder just as the gun went off. Out of the corner of her eye, she saw Simon rise up in the air and then shoot off into the utility room. Blood spattered the door where he'd stood.

Through the ringing in her ears, she heard the faint sound of a siren.

James and Eaze heard it, too. They frowned at each other and then both ran toward the door, the knife still buried in Eaze's shoulder.

"Fuck you, girl!" James hurled his beer can in her direction. It smashed into the kitchen cabinet behind her.

Maya sank to the floor, her heart beating wildly. Cold evening air gusted in from the open front door. After she was sure she wasn't going to throw up, she pushed herself to her feet, walked over, and after peering out to be sure they were gone, she closed the door.

She stumbled over a heavy object, and it skidded across the floor toward the refrigerator. The pistol. Eaze must have dropped it when she'd stabbed him. She gingerly picked it up with her thumb and index finger, holding it at arm's length by the grip, then walked quickly to the utility room and stashed it inside the washing machine. She might need it if James and Eaze came back.

Simon was not in the utility room. An ominous splash of blood streaked the dryer lid next to the broken window.

Opening the back door, she called him. "Simon! Come here, kitty, kitty!"

There was no response. Was the cat dying under a bush somewhere in the dark? Sam would never forgive her. Shit, she'd never forgive herself. She didn't deserve to be forgiven.

Flickering blue and red lights strobed across the yard, and then the police were banging on the front door.

24

When she saw black and white ahead—the black of Chase's ski pants and the white of Nicole's turtleneck—Sam's anxiety clotted into a lump in her throat. She wasn't certain whether the tears streaming down her face were due to relief at finding them, horror that they were trapped in this disaster, or a mixture of both.

Nicole was wrapped half around Chase, her head on his shoulder, as they both laid on the ground, imprisoned by debris. Nicole's legs were hidden under a table that rested on them, and Chase's legs were tangled in broken chairs. Pieces of lumber and furniture and sheetrock pressed in from all sides, pinning them in place.

Snaking through the debris as carefully as possible, Sam used her elbows to drag herself close. "Chase! Nicole!"

Nicole opened her eyes and lifted her head an inch. "Summer," she stuttered, her teeth chattering. "So cold." Her head collapsed back onto Chase's shoulder. Blood, partially dried now, streaked the FBI agent's auburn hair and painted her face and sweater, dribbling from a large fragment of glass embedded in her scalp.

"Chase!" Sam stretched her arms over a chair seat to pull on the sleeve of his sweater. His eyes remained closed. Unlike Nicole, he didn't seem to be shivering, although neither one of them was wearing a jacket. The lack of shivering was a really bad sign. Sam pulled off her leather glove and laid a hand against his cheek. "Chase!"

His eyelids fluttered, and then his lips moved. "Summer," he sighed. Then his body went slack again.

"Chase, I'm here."

When there was no response, she felt like an idiot for saying that. Like she could rescue him just by being here. Like she could heal him with her presence. She couldn't see any wounds. Gingerly, she slid her hand beneath his head. Chase made a slight "*unh*" sound. To her cold fingers, his skin felt lukewarm. After slipping her hand back out, she examined it. No blood. Pulling the headlamp from beside her neck, she carefully thumbed up one of his eyelids and shone the light into his eye. The iris had nearly vanished into the top of his eye socket, but she thought his eyeball moved slightly. Whatever that meant.

"Chase!" Releasing his eyelid, she rubbed his cheek. "Where are you hurt?"

Nicole moaned again. "So cold."

"Nicole, what happened to Chase?"

"Slammed." Her speech was slurred.

Sam pulled a metallic rescue blanket from her pockets, popped its tiny plastic package, and spread it over Chase, tucking it in around the edges of his body as best she could. "Slammed" could mean almost anything. He might have broken vertebrae. He could be bleeding internally. Lungs, liver, kidneys, spleen, intestines. Chase might be dying.

Do something, her brain screamed. *No, wait. Analyze the situation.* She studied Chase's former partner. "And you, Nicole?"

"New . . . hair . . . style. Like it?"

The woman's lips were tinged with blue. Even hypothermic, Nicole remained a smartass. Sam had to admire her for that.

Reaching over Chase, she stretched another rescue blanket out over her, and though her hands were trembling, Nicole was able to tuck it under her chin and around her own torso.

Taking the last remaining packet from her pocket, Sam crawled toward the feet she saw nearby. "Daniel, I'm going to cover you as much as I can with an emergency blanket to keep your body heat in."

She could only reach up to his knees, but she tucked the metallic fabric around his feet and wedged it beneath the plywood and boards resting on top of the boy.

"Thanks, man."

His gratitude brought a sob to her lips. She covered her mouth with her gloved hand.

Go, she told herself. *Now.* She maneuvered her body into a nearby area where there was space enough here to sit upright, a narrow column among the stacks of debris. Her entire body was cramped with pain. Too much time constricted into unnatural positions. Sam straightened her shoulders and leaned her head back, examining the layers above her. Was that snow she could see overhead? A patch of sky between the shattered layers?

She moved the flashlight beam over the area above. In the lowest layer, she saw broken sheetrock and wood paneling—maybe a wall, maybe part of the ceiling. The paneling seemed to be mostly held in place by a tall metal shelving unit in front of her, and cabinets off to the left. A microwave stood on end a short distance away. This had probably been some sort of storeroom or prep area next to the kitchen.

A low moan seemed to be coming from beneath her. That wasn't possible, was it? She hoped she was imagining the sound.

Swaths of pink fiberglass insulation dangled overhead, dripping moisture into the corner where the shelves and cabinets met. Cedar shingles spilled down from the top of ragged-edged plywood. A streamer of tar paper fluttered in a puff of cold air that whistled in from above.

She was reasonably sure she was looking at the collapsed roof. A flurry of snow gusted in. After crawling through the dust containing God knows what, Sam was grateful for fresh air. But this frigid vertical wind tunnel was doing no favor for the people trapped here.

Sam checked her watch. She'd been inside this time for seventy minutes. Was that the rumble of an engine she heard, or just the roar of her blood in her ears? She might be able to crawl back the way she'd come, but that would take a while and even if someone could follow her route back here, they still wouldn't be able to get the victims out.

She heard the moan again. Or was it a groan of the settling wreckage all around her? Was the building moving again?

The panic enveloping her made it hard to formulate any sort of plan. She forced herself to close her eyes and slowly inhale, exhale, then do it again. What were the alternatives?

Did she dare try to claw her way through the layers to the top, like a mole surfacing for air? Or would that bring the remaining structure down on top of Chase, Nicole, and Daniel? Were they all going to die anyway?

Her shoulder and ribs shrieked. Her face burned, rubbed raw by snow and tree bark. She was so tired. This day would not end. Through the gap above, she could see a single star. So maybe the snow had stopped. The way up promised a potential way out.

"Nicole, I'm climbing up. I'm going for help."

"Hhh . . . ur . . . ry."

Sam crawled again to Chase, and pressed her lips to his ice-cold mouth. She fought the desire to wrap herself around him.

"Chase, you cannot die," she murmured. "You hear me?" She laid her hand on his cheek. "You will not die."

No response. If he and Nicole and others were to have any

chance, she had to go now. Addressing the feet behind her, she said, "Daniel, hang on. I'm going for help."

She wanted to add *Forgive me if I kill you*, but didn't think that would be inspirational to anyone, including herself.

Pushing herself to her feet, she crab-walked, hunched over, beneath the overhang of paneling, moving as far sideways as she could, her right hand following the metal shelves, her left pushing against the obstacle overhead. In the gap in the corner, she could stick her head through. The metallic shade of a broken ceiling light, still attached to a length of chain, glittered in the beam of her flashlight. She used a gloved hand to sweep glass shards away from paneling. Higher up, mammoth wooden beams crisscrossed at crazy angles, like the frame of a giant teepee. Snow swirled down into her face.

Now or never, Westin. Sliding her foot onto a shelf, she pulled herself up, using the edge of the shelving unit. The shelf held. She climbed up three more shelves, wedging her shoulders through the opening above, nudging a couple of bags of coffee out of her way as she ascended. She scraped her forehead against a splintered edge of plywood, then twisted around, tested an elbow on top of the plywood layer. It sank an inch, making her gasp, but then stopped in place.

So far, so good. She stepped up the shelves, pushing herself through the plywood layer, holding gingerly onto the edges of sheetrock and plywood, trying not to put too much weight on them. She spied a pale object at the end of the shelving unit. Was that a human hand?

She sidestepped in that direction until she could peer around the edge of the metal shelves. The object was indeed a human hand, bent at the wrist in an unnatural angle. The arm vanished into a tangle of debris, and it took her brain a moment to recognize the shape. The body, that of a man, was upside down, smashed between a massive upended countertop and the shelves. She couldn't see his head.

"Jerry?" That was the name the woman outside had been screaming. Sam made herself touch his fingers. They were unnaturally white. And ice-cold. She pulled back her hand in horror. Nothing could be done for that poor soul. Taking a deep breath, she continued her climb.

When her feet were finally on top of the shelving unit, she found herself wedged into a narrow tunnel, strands of itchy fiberglass dangling against her neck. The crisscrossed timbers loomed overhead, and beyond that, a final layer of ceiling materials and shingles before an opening to the sky.

She couldn't quite reach the beams above. Every muscle in her body tensed, and she stepped onto a canted sheet of broken paneling. It issued a cracking sound beneath her feet.

Then the stack of rubble she stood on abruptly gave way, collapsing beneath her.

25

As the support fell away from beneath her feet, Sam launched herself toward the nearest beam, grabbing onto it. From beneath her, she heard a scream, abruptly cut off. Sweet Jesus, had she just crushed three people?

The pain of hanging from her damaged shoulder and stretching her sore ribs brought tears to her eyes. She flailed her feet, trying to find purchase. Everything was tilted at crazy angles. She didn't know how long she could hold onto the slanted beam, dangling at an angle, her left hand a foot above her right. Her grasp was tentative, only by fingertips, the six-by-twelve much too broad to wrap her fingers around.

She couldn't maintain this position for long, and she couldn't let go and crash back down through the layers of debris. Gritting her teeth and gripping as tightly as she could with her fingertips, she kicked up several times and finally managed to swing her right foot over the beam, jamming her calf onto an exposed nail. She yelped as the jolt of pain shot through her entire body.

Clenching her jaw, she ripped her leg away from the nail so she could slide the rest of her body on top of the beam. Gasping and moaning, she then lay on top of the rough wood, hugging the beam tightly to keep from sliding down into God-knows-what.

As she panted through waves of pain, she felt blood streaming down her leg, an unwelcome rivulet of warmth in the bitter cold. At least the injury was to her calf, not her thigh, so she was unlikely to bleed to death anytime soon.

There'd been only one scream when whatever she'd dislodged had crashed below. But that could mean anything. That the crash had only frightened Nicole or Daniel. Or that everyone was now dead.

No. She couldn't think like that. *Chase, when we first met, you told me that a macho FBI agent couldn't drown in a flooded canyon. Well, you can't die in a collapsed building, either. Nicole, you have to continue to make me feel like a gawky hick. And Daniel, you're just a kid.*

She inched up the slanted beam, gripping it tightly with her hands and thighs, trying to remember how she'd climbed a tree as a child. Unfortunately, this was a square tree. The beam's edges dug into her legs. Her progress was painfully slow. Emphasis on the painful. She tried not to focus on her distance above the ground, measured by the bright red drops of blood that fell to spatter the debris beneath her.

Finally, she reached the point where one beam crossed another, and she was able to put a foot into the top of the X where they crossed. She yelped as the new beam shifted a few inches with her weight, jarring her injured leg, but then the timber stuck in its new position. The final layer of plywood overhead, she could see, was actually a small section of the roof that was still intact, sitting on two trusses at the back of the building. The front of the lodge had completely collapsed from the impact of the avalanche, but some upright structures remained in the rear of the building.

After pulling herself up, she wormed her way out onto the slanted roof on her stomach, blinking snowflakes out of her eyes. She was thrilled to see that she had indeed heard an engine. In fact, there were two machines nearby now, a huge snowcat around which some of the injured were gathering, and even more miraculous, a track hoe with a bucket attached to its long, jointed arm, parked near the edge of the collapsed lodge. Volunteers were carefully extracting pieces of debris from the pile, loading them into the track hoe bucket. In the distance, a small squadron of snowmobiles buzzed around the buried parking lot.

The star she had seen occupied only a small patch of clear night sky, and as she watched, a large bird silently flapped its wings through that space, white against the black expanse. An owl. A snowy owl. Could it be? Out of the species' common range, but not unheard of. So strange to think of all the other species going about their normal lives, oblivious to the human drama here. She'd give anything to be that owl right now.

The owl was gone in seconds. As the magical creature vanished into the night, Sam's senses abruptly returned to the disaster surrounding her.

"Hey!" She waved her headlamp in the air. "Up here! Up here! I found three survivors."

Heads pivoted. A few bystanders raised their hands and pointed in her direction. She slid on her backside over the snow on the roof to the ground. Even though she landed in soft snow, a jolt of pain from her injured calf nearly caused her to pass out. With a squadron of blackflies buzzing across her field of vision, she limped toward the track hoe operator, a ski patrol employee trotting at her elbow, asking her over and over if she was injured.

Duh. Hell yes, she wanted to say. But she needed to stay focused.

Waving at the track hoe operator in the cab, she told him, "Three people are trapped in the back of the building there, beneath where I came up." She pointed.

"Alive?" he asked.

She grimaced. "They were when I left them. And I thought I heard moaning from under the floor, but that doesn't make sense."

He pursed his lips for a second, then told her, "It might. There are bathrooms below the main level."

"Oh God." Did anyone buried down that far have a chance? "I believe we could—carefully—lift out pieces and clear a way to get the people on the main floor out."

Clumps of ice in the track hoe operator's beard moved along with his lips as he said, "Not *we*. Let *us* take care of it."

"You need to be fast. They're all hypothermic, and at least one is unconscious."

Ice-Beard nodded. "We got it. You need to look after yourself now." He cast a meaningful glance at the man who stood beside her.

The ski patrol guy wrapped a thermal blanket around her shoulders. "Let's get you warm."

"But—"

Blake appeared at her other side. "I'll take care of her."

"But . . ." Sam gestured toward the building, where several red coats were climbing up to her exit hole, gesturing the backhoe closer. The machine pivoted, dumped its load, moved toward the building and extended its bucket toward the ski patrol crew on the roof.

"Sit." Blake pushed her down onto a stack of wooden pallets and handed her a bottle of water. He pulled a long splinter of wood from her hair. "You look like you just dug your way out of a grave."

"I did." She didn't want to think about the girl who hadn't moved, or the man's cold hand. "But I found Chase, and Nicole, and a kid named Daniel." She clutched her housemate's arm. "But, Blake, they are in such a bad way. Nicole has this huge shard of glass in her head, and Daniel is sandwiched, and Chase—" Her voice broke, and she had to take a big swallow of water before she could continue. "Chase was unconscious. When I left him, he was completely unresponsive."

"But alive."

"Yes, alive." She abruptly remembered that she had just described Claude's condition as well as Chase's. "How's Claude?"

"Also still unconscious, but also still alive. They're getting ready to evacuate the worst cases on the big snowcat. There are ambulances waiting down the mountain."

Sam surveyed the bystanders, didn't see anyone familiar. "Blake, have you seen my friend Gina? Two ski patrol guys went to find her a couple of miles away."

Blake shook his head. "But all the resort personnel have come down from the Heather Meadows area now, so it's confusing."

Oh, sweet Jesus, what if they hadn't found Gina? What if there was another avalanche? What if none of them came back?

Another red-coated ski patrol person appeared at Sam's side, a dark-haired woman this time. She elbowed her way in front of Blake. "I'm Kristi, I'm an EMT. Let me have a look at you."

Lifting Sam's chin, she shone a penlight into her eyes. "I'm okay," Sam complained, blinking.

"I don't think so," Kristi argued. "How about this leg?"

Kneeling, Kristi gently wrapped her hands around Sam's right ankle beneath her blood-soaked pants and raised Sam's injured leg onto her knee.

The world started to spin. "Uh," Sam heard herself say. She felt Blake's hands on her shoulders just before everything went black.

* * * * *

When Sam opened her eyes, the world was moving again, the ceiling above her shifting back and forth. Another earthquake? Panic flooded her veins. She had to get out of the building before it collapsed in on her. She tried to sit up.

"Whoa there, hon." An unfamiliar voice accompanied the dark face that leaned over her. The woman's arms pressed Sam back into a sleeping bag. "You're in the snowcat. Sorry to put you on the floor, but it was the best we could do right now. We should be back to the road in a few minutes and the ride will smooth out."

Snowcat. The machine was crawling over the avalanche debris on its caterpillar treads. No wonder everything was rocking back and forth. She tried again to sit up. The woman tried again to push her back.

"I'm okay, really," Sam assured her.

"No, you're not, but I guess you can sit up. For now. I've got other patients who are more urgent." She moved away.

Sam leaned back on her hands, felt something tear in her shoulder, then sat up straighter, cradling her arms against her stomach. Her right leg hurt like it had been bitten by a rattlesnake. The nail.

Chase. Nicole. Daniel. Had they made it out? Gina? Claude?

She blinked, peering around the dim interior of the vehicle. Bodies were strapped into ski patrol sleds and some onto stretchers, more lying on the floor. She was sandwiched between a man she'd never seen before and a woman she didn't recognize at first. On second glance, it was Gina.

Sam laid a hand against her friend's shoulder, on top of the sleeping bag Gina had been slipped into. "Oh, thank God! Gina?"

Opening her eyes, Gina licked her chapped lips before

answering. "Hi."

"I saw a snowy owl," Sam murmured. Her friend would appreciate the miracle of that.

"Awesome." Gina's sigh was more of a low moan.

"You okay?" Stupid question. Nobody on this ride was okay right now.

"Hanging in. Gotta live so I can kill that wolverine guy." She grimaced. "Or gal. I didn't dream that, did I?"

"No," Sam said. "There were two different people, a man and a woman. Boy and girl, whatever." At least she thought they'd seen a man snatch up Feisty, and then they'd uncovered that young woman buried in the snow.

Ice mask. Imprisoned, drugged, buried wolverine. Climbing up a tree, clawing out of a grave of snow. Digging out Gina. Scratching her way out of the icy creek beneath the broken snow bridge. Crawling through the collapsed lodge, again and again. Could that all have happened in one day? It seemed like months had passed since the ski competition.

"Chase?" Gina asked.

Sam's gaze searched the stretchers. The blood-soaked head bandage peeking out from a blanket two stretchers away was most likely Nicole. And next to her, with an attendant pumping up a blood pressure cuff on his arm, lay Chase. Still unconscious, if the way his arm dropped limply back to his side was any indication. The EMT or nurse or doctor or whatever he was wore a grim expression on his face. What did that mean?

She wanted to shout the question across the row of wounded, but the grinding noise of the snowcat's treaded tracks would drown out her words. To reach Chase, she'd have to crawl over other victims.

Was that Daniel in the far corner? At her feet, a dark form bent over a ski patrol sled she believed was occupied by Claude. Blake straightened, then spotted her. "Sam!" His voice was hoarse. "You're awake."

"I think so," she told him. "Are you all right, Blake?"

He nodded. His eyes glistened in the dim light. "They let me ride along because I know four of you."

The front tracks of the snowcat rose up a hill, then the vehicle careened sideways before bumping down onto more level ground. Many of the inert forms surrounding her moaned and gasped at the shifting movements. Sam grabbed the edge of Gina's sled for stability, pressing her own jaws tightly together to keep from shrieking; her ribs felt like they were grinding against one another. A surge of nausea burbled up her esophagus, and she closed her eyes, swallowing hard to keep from vomiting. She slid down to lay flat again.

Blake encircled her upthrust foot with his hand on top of the sleeping bag. "There's nothing you can do right now, Sam. It's not your job. Help is here. Get some rest."

Help is here. Gina, Chase, Nicole, Claude, and—she was reasonably sure—Daniel had been rescued and pulled out of the wreckage. Maybe others, too. Had there been others still alive inside? Others she hadn't found?

It's not your job. She welcomed the darkness and the opportunity to simply lie still in a warm place. And although every inhale reminded her that she was injured, breathing felt pretty great, too. She'd never take warmth and air for granted again.

26

"How do you know the owners of that house?" the female police officer asked Maya for the tenth time.

"Owner," Maya corrected. "Summer Westin. Blake just lives there. He pays rent."

"And you live there, too?"

She sighed. "Sort of. I have—had—a tent in the backyard. Eaze or James destroyed it. And my sleeping bag."

The officer glanced up from her notepad on the table. "Are you currently experiencing homelessness?"

Maya grimaced at the politically correct phrase. *WTF, just say homeless already!* She was currently experiencing frustration and boredom, and she was working up to experiencing fury. "Yeah, I guess. Although I have the tent. And Sam—Summer Westin, the homeowner—and Blake let me use the toilet and shower and wash my clothes, etcetera, etcetera. So that's sorta home, isn't it?"

Her brain swelled with flashbacks to the cozy apartment she'd shared with the other counselors at Wilderness Challenge, and then to the next one with her college roommates. They'd all abandoned her. Now all she had was the tent. *Had been* the tent. She toyed with the Coke the cops had given her, twisting the half-empty can around on the table. "Hey, I'm not the criminal here."

"We are looking for the others, er"—the officer referred to her notepad—"James and Eaze. Now, how do you know Eaze?"

Maya raised her chin to glare at the annoying buzzing, flickering light overhead in the police station interview room. Hadn't those fluorescent tube monstrosities been outlawed years ago? She'd been through this whole story at least an hour ago with a male officer. She knew the officers had access to her juvie history, the burglaries, the thefts. That history was supposed to be erased, now that she was twenty-one. They might be invisible to the public, but her crimes were still there in the files for cops to see. They never cut her a break. "Eaze is what he calls himself. His real name is Ethan Zeran. And his buddy James Winnow was destroying the place with him."

"Were you in your tent when this break-in started?"

Maya explained again about being at the community college library and seeing the two driving by. She left out the whole attempted rape scenario.

"Why did you think they would break in?"

Maya fiddled with the cuff of her shirt sleeve. "I knew they wanted money, and they saw me, and Eaze knows where I live, and he'd been by earlier, so he knew Sam and Blake were gone. He knew I wouldn't be home, and he and James thought Sam and Blake had money."

"So you suspected they might break in. But you didn't call the police?"

Maya snorted and frowned at the ceiling-mounted camera in the corner of the room. "Like you'd do something if I said someone *might* break in?"

"*Umm-hmmm*," the officer hummed noncommittedly. "Do you know where the owner of the house is?"

Leaning back in the hard wooden chair, Maya clasped her hands behind her head. If she wasn't under arrest, could she just stand up and leave now? "I tried to call Sam. I know they all went skiing today."

"Skiing?" The officer's eyebrows shot up. She raised her chin. "At the Mount Baker ski area?"

"Yeah. Listen, right now you need to take me back to the house so I can go find that cat. He might need a vet." Maya chewed the inside of her cheek, trying to distract herself from the thought that Simon might be dead.

The officer's worried expression didn't change.

"What's with the face?" Maya asked, annoyed. "You don't like cats?"

"There was a major avalanche at the Mount Baker Ski Area today. It collapsed one of the huts. Dozens buried. Lots more injured."

Maya pushed herself upright in her chair, her hands gripping the chair arms. "Was Sam hurt? Was Blake?"

The officer shook her head. "They're bringing everyone down now. The hospital will know about survivors soon. The others . . . might take days."

"I need to go." Maya stood up. "Give me back my cell phone."

A commotion in the hallway caught her attention.

"Fuck, man! I don't care what that bitch told you, I was nowhere near that place!" Two officers flanked James as they walked past the doorway. When he spotted Maya inside, he narrowed his eyes, throwing shade at her from the hall.

She shouted at him, "Where's Eaze?"

"Wouldn't you like to know?" he sneered. Then, apparently remembering that the officers were listening, he faced them. "I don't know where her boyfriend is."

The officer on his right grasped James's arm to urge him farther down the hallway. She heard him snarl, "Lawyer! I want a lawyer. Now!"

"Chill," one of the cops told him. "We just need to hear your story."

Maya sank back into her chair. James Winnow came from a rich family. His family probably had lawyers on standby. He would be back on the street in ten minutes. And Eaze was still out there somewhere. And now, James would remind him that she'd ratted them out. *Shit.* She'd only stabbed him in the shoulder; probably just enough to make him red-eyed furious.

How could she have ever cared for that sleazeball? How could she ever have thought Eaze cared for her? Life was so messed up. She'd probably end up shot or stabbed or run over and die in a ditch somewhere like her druggie mom had. With her luck, that ditch would be filled with six inches of icy water and those plastic bags of dog poop that people left beside the trails. Could her world get any worse?

The cops wouldn't hand over her phone, holding it hostage to keep her there for another hour. She didn't want to leave without it, and they kept saying they'd check on it, but they never did. They went back and forth between James and her, checking her story over and over again. What the hell was he telling them about her?

Finally, the female officer came back in and handed over her phone. "You're free to go," she told Maya. "I'll have a patrol car take you. But where?" Her expression softened. "How about a shelter?"

Maya shuddered. To be locked up inside a building with druggies and schizophrenics? No thanks. "Let me call the hospital and find my friends."

The officer waited while she did that. The only thing the hospital would tell her was that neither Sam nor Blake nor Chase were currently patients. She didn't know Claude's or Nicole's last names, so she couldn't ask about them.

If her friends weren't at the hospital, maybe they were on their way home. Next, she tried to call Sam's cell phone, then Blake's. Straight to voicemail. Cell service was spotty in the

Cascades, and she didn't know where they were. If they were buried under six feet of snow, there wasn't anything she could do about it, was there? Sighing, she pushed her phone into her back pocket.

"No luck?" the officer guessed. "So, the shelter?" She checked the watch on her left wrist. "Although it might be hard to get you in right now."

Maya checked her phone. 2:32 a.m. "Take me back to the house that I called from. Sam and Blake will let me stay with them. Besides, I need to find the cat."

The woman's expression was skeptical, but she finally recruited a patrol officer to take Maya back to Sam's house. The officer's hair was gray, and he looked old enough to be her grandpa, if she'd ever had a grandpa. Maya guessed he was a retired cop brought back to help out during the labor shortages, but he had a uniform and a gun, so she hoped he'd know what to do if Eaze suddenly slithered out of the shadows.

The officer opened the back door of a police cruiser for her. That made her feel like a criminal until she saw that the passenger seat in front was occupied by a computer and a notebook. As he shut the door and walked to the driver's side, she saw James walk out of the police station, another man at his side. Lawyer? Father? It didn't matter. James Winnow, a drug dealer, house wrecker, thief, and wannabe rapist, was back on the street to do as he pleased. And he knew where she lived.

When the police cruiser arrived at Sam's cabin, the officer insisted on accompanying her inside. The lights were still blazing and the doors were unlocked.

"Stay here," he instructed, unsnapping the strap on his gun holster and then leaving her on the front porch.

Maya squinted her eyes, trying to see into the backyard between the trees. "Simon?" she murmured softly.

The cop was back. "All clear," he reported. "Nobody home."

Examining the empty house, Maya fretted. She dreaded the moment that Sam and Blake saw this destruction. Where were they? And Simon? Focusing on the blood spatter around the broken window, she caught her lower lip between her teeth. She had to find Sam's cat. It was the least she could do, wasn't it?

"You got something to board up that window?" the old cop asked, tilting his head toward the utility room.

She considered. "There's cardboard in the carport. And I know where there's tape."

He nodded. "I guess that'll have to do for tonight. But tomorrow, get some plywood if you can't get the window fixed."

"I'll do that," she said. Like she had more than three dollars in her pocket to buy a sheet of plywood, or any way to cut it if she bought one. People were so clueless.

Striding to the kitchen, she pulled a flashlight from the drawer where she knew Sam kept them. "I'm going to go look for the cat."

"I'm not supposed to leave you here alone." The officer hooked his hands in his belt.

She flicked the flashlight on, making sure it worked, then flicked it back off. "I know this place; they're my friends. I'll take care of the house and the cat until they come back."

The officer glanced around the room at the ripped cushions and overturned furniture and the distinct lack of a cat anywhere in sight. Maya worried that he would insist on dragging her to a shelter.

But then the radio on his shoulder erupted to life, emitting a string of number codes she didn't understand. His brow furrowed into even more wrinkles. "Well, crap. When it rains . . . We got a multi-vehicle accident on I-5, and half the crew is up at Mt. Baker."

Maya did her best to assume an earnest expression. "Then you should go. I'll be fine, sir."

He turned toward the door. "Don't get into any more trouble."

"Of course not, sir." She gave him what she thought was a Scout salute.

And then, jamming his hat on his head, the officer was gone.

The backyard was dark, the sky shrouded in clouds. Drizzle began to fall. Using the flashlight, Maya examined her tent. The main support pole that arched over the top had been bashed in and now supported nothing. Unzipping the front flap, she surveyed the interior, searching for her raincoat. Only a few items of clothing were strewn across the floor, and when she spotlighted the area around her tent, she saw her sleeping bag and most of her possessions scattered across the damp ground. She found her rain jacket snagged on one of the back tent poles, and was relieved to see that it seemed undamaged.

The fiberfill guts of her sleeping bag bled out onto the ground like a caterpillar someone had stepped on. The sad remains stank. Pee, she determined, sniffing at the wetness as she picked it up. Human pee. A few feet away, she found her quilt square. The embroidered fabric was marred by a big yellow stain as well as the filth Eaze had smeared on it this morning. She imagined James and Eaze laughing as they pissed on her possessions. They probably wrote their names with their dicks. *Yuck, yuck. Hilarious. Fuck you!* She slid on her rain jacket, then slung the ruined bag over her sagging tent.

Walking toward the woods that lined the back of Sam's property, she called, "Simon! C'mere, boy. Here, kitty, kitty, kitty!"

Every few minutes, she stopped to listen, hoping to hear a meow or mewling noise. The only sounds that came to her were the pat-pat-pat of raindrops falling on the rhododendron leaves. The intermittent rain sounded like muffled footsteps. That was creeping her out. Her imagination leaped to Eaze, out there in the dark somewhere, his thirst for revenge burning a hole in his gut.

27

The hospital emergency room was total chaos. Sam kept trying to sit up and slip off the gurney, only to be pushed back down by a stranger wearing scrubs who insisted, "Wait! We'll get to you."

She tried to explain to several people that she needed to go with Chase and Gina, but the last guy in blue scrubs threatened, "You don't want us to put you in restraints, do you?" as he wheeled her into a curtained alcove. His expression was irritated enough that he'd probably do it.

Her leg was bleeding all over the clean white sheets, and her ribs and shoulder and ankle and face hurt like hell. Truth be told, she'd welcome some help with all that, except that her injuries were nothing compared to the others who'd been with her on that snowcat, and she felt guilty taking up anyone's time.

Not to mention, hospitals gave her anxiety attacks. People died in hospitals. How many had died right here of COVID in the last two years? How many times during her childhood had her father dragged her to the hospital in Kansas to visit her mother during her multiple crises? Sam scanned the room for a window, didn't see one anywhere. Even if she was exhausted, even if she was injured, she wanted to be outside in the fresh air, where she could see the sky and trees.

Restraints, she reminded herself, forcing her lungs to take in three deep breaths. *Get a grip, calm down.* Not everyone died in hospitals. Her own mother had died at home. She didn't want to think about that, either. She didn't want to think about dying at all. The purple shoes. The upside-down man. The girl and the bearded guy on the mountainside. Feisty, locked up and suffocated under the snow. All dead. And the others who might be dying now. Oh God, Chase! Claude. Nicole. That boy . . . Daniel, was that his name?

She whimpered aloud, and was immediately ashamed of the pathetic sound. She was not dying. Taking another long breath, she willed her imagination to go back to her cabin. She pictured her cat Simon curled up on her lap, purring as she read a good book and sipped a glass of red wine.

"Well, then, you settle her down," an irritated male voice said from behind the curtains.

Blake clomped in, still wearing his ski jacket and pants and ski boots, but now holding a paper cup of coffee or cocoa or something. His face was drawn, and his dark hair was tousled.

Eyeing the steaming cup, Sam asked, "Is that for me?"

"I'd give it to you if I could. But they said no." His voice changed as it emulated one of the hospital staff, "Miz Westin might have internal injuries, she might need surgery, she might need anesthesia."

"None of that is true," Sam reassured him. "Just a sip."

The cup held coffee and cocoa, she discovered. Mocha. Sam licked her lips, feeling the chapped skin rough against her tongue. "What's the update on Claude and Chase and Nicole? And Gina?"

Her housemate shrugged. "They wheeled them all away and wouldn't tell me a damn thing."

Blake was giving her a third sip when the curtains parted. He yanked the cup from her, catching a drip with his other hand as he stepped back from her bed.

The woman who entered was small and dark. Her badge

identified her as Dr. Singh. She was accompanied by a bearded assistant who was nearly a foot taller and wore a nametag that said only Olson, so Sam had no idea whether he was a nurse or orderly or whatever. He helped Sam out of her filthy, damp coat and then took her blood pressure, pulse, and temperature as the doctor watched, asking her what hurt in a lilting accent. East Indian? Pakistani? South African?

Everything hurts, Sam wanted to say. But she pointed to the gash on her leg. "That, obviously, and my shoulder and my ribs. And maybe my ankle."

The doctor cupped Sam's cheekbones in her blue-gloved hands and pressed her thumbs against both sides of her nose. "The bridge of your nose is most likely broken."

"I agree," Sam told her.

"But it seems to be in place," Singh said, pressing a finger gently on the swollen area.

Sam sucked in a sharp breath, then coughed painfully.

"How'd you get this rash on your face?" With two fingers, the doctor pushed gently against Sam's temple, causing her to tilt her head.

She explained about being buried in the snow and climbing out against the tree. Blake's eyes widened as she spoke. Oh yeah, this was the first time Blake heard that she and Gina had been caught in a different avalanche in the mountains.

The doctor leaned forward to shine a penlight in her eyes. "Did you lose consciousness?"

"No."

"That's not true," Blake interrupted. "You were completely out of it after you climbed out of the hut for the second time."

"That was because I just tore up my leg and it was killing me. And I was exhausted. I wasn't unconscious; I was only asleep," she argued, then yelped, "Ow!" as the doctor probed her ribs. Next came her shoulder, as the doctor pushed her arm backward. Sam couldn't decide which hurt more. Unwelcome tears streamed down her face as she clenched her teeth together. By comparison, her ankle merely felt fat, dull, and sore.

Her leg came next, and her calf felt as if it were being ripped anew as the doctor prodded and flexed her foot. Then Dr. Singh instructed the other guy about an X-ray, stitches, tetanus shot, antibiotics, plus future appointments, and turned to go.

"Wait!" Sam leaned forward, amazed by how much that simple motion hurt. "I need to know about Chase Perez, Nicole Boudreaux, Gina Canfield. They came in on the transport with me."

"And Claude Gagnon," Blake added.

The doctor hesitated. "Are you family?"

"Fiancée," Sam lied.

When the doctor focused on Blake, he nodded. "Likewise."

The doctor grinned. "To all of them?"

"Chase Perez," Sam clarified. "Friend to the others."

Blake matched the doctor's inquisitive stare. "And I belong to Claude Gagnon."

"Well," Dr. Singh said hesitantly, "I have no information to give you right now. I'll ask the attending staff to fill you in as soon as they can."

Blake took a step back. His ski boots clacked against the tile floor.

"Olson." The doctor tilted her head toward Blake. "Slippers, please."

When both the hospital personnel left, Blake commented, "I so hate hospitals."

"Likewise," Sam responded, echoing her housemate's earlier response and causing both of them to chuckle. She hugged an arm across her ribcage. "Don't make me laugh. It hurts."

A new staff member parted the curtains, this one a young

man in navy scrubs, identified as Dr. Remien.

He carried a tray of implements. Setting it down, he pulled a pair of packaged slippers out of his pocket and handed them to Blake, who disappeared behind the curtain with them.

The new doctor's face was so unlined that Sam had to ask if he was an intern. "Yes," he admitted, his cheeks coloring. "I am a new doctor, but I am fully qualified to attend to your injuries." He pulled up a stool next to her leg and then picked up a syringe, holding it in the air as he said, "I'm going to numb this area before I stitch up your leg."

"I appreciate that," she told him.

An unlabeled guy in blue scrubs slipped back into the cubicle as well, holding a tray with three syringes, folded towels, and other medical paraphernalia Sam didn't want to identify. As the doctor worked on her leg, Blue Scrubs injected her three times, telling her what he was giving her. The shot for pain was the only one she really appreciated, especially when he tilted the bright light onto her face and began to clean it, picking bits of bark and dirt out of her skin with tweezers.

The pain medication was downright magical. She envisioned herself as a race car in the Indy 500 as the two men overhauled her like a team of expert mechanics. Blake briefly excused himself, leaving her in their hands for a few minutes before returning.

When he finished stitching and bandaging her leg, Remien said that Sam should spend the night in the hospital.

"No way," she said. "No frickin' way."

"All right, then," Remien said wearily, glancing toward Blake. "You'll take care of her?"

"Of course. We live together."

After Blake nodded to emphasize his promise, the young doctor told them, "Truth be told, with all the avalanche victims and new admissions in the COVID unit, we're full up, anyway."

He rubbed the back of his neck. "I've been here for forty-six hours now."

"Sorry." To Blake, he followed up with, "I shouldn't have told you that."

Returning his attention to Sam, he said, "X-rays tomorrow. Your ribs are probably only cracked, but a few might be broken."

"And our fiancés?" Blake asked. He repeated Chase's and Claude's names.

"Ask at the nurses' station on your way out," Remien told them. "Have a good day."

"Right." Blake helped her off the gurney and into her coat. They'd cut open her pants leg, so now the blood-soaked material flapped against the bandage around her calf. The stroll down the hallway seemed to have a time delay, images and sounds crystalizing a moment after they should have.

The nurses claimed to have no information about either Chase or Claude for them at this time. Sam asked about Nicole and Gina. "We'll do our best to contact relatives. And we'll let you know when we have updates on Perez and Gagnon." A volunteer dutifully took down their phone numbers.

"Right, have a good day," Blake muttered under his breath as they exited through automatic sliding doors. With one arm around Sam, he shuffled in the thin hospital slippers, awkwardly carrying his ski boots in his other hand.

He waved his boots at a blue sedan and then opened the door for Sam, helping her into the back seat before getting into the passenger seat beside the driver.

In the back seat, the world seemed a bit fuzzy. "This is not my car." Sam felt stupid the second after the words emerged from her lips. It had to be the damn pain meds.

"Not mine, either," Blake told her. "Mine's at home, and yours is at Chase's. This is Finch, and he's with Lyft."

The driver's gaze met hers in the rearview mirror.

Thank God her housemate was here to keep track of details. "You're my rock, Blake."

"Pain meds talking," Blake told the driver in a barely audible voice.

"No, it's not," she mumbled, closing her eyes. "I mean, they're not. I love you, Blake, I really do."

Her housemate turned his head to speak over his shoulder. "Likewise."

On the short drive home, Blake obsessed over Claude. He needed to inform someone in Canada, but who should he call? And say what? It was nearly four in the morning, and he couldn't marshal his thoughts into any coherent order.

Claude couldn't die. That was unthinkable. They'd endured the pandemic and the border closures. They were on the verge of starting a good life together in one country or the other, or perhaps straddling both. The EMTs on the snowcat had told him that based on the lump on the back of Claude's skull and his continued unconscious state, they suspected a hematoma, a hemorrhage in the brain under the skull. Blake had heard that the only cure for that was cutting a hole in the skull to relieve the pressure, and if the surgery wasn't done in time, brain damage could result. And then there was the hypoxia from being without air for so long; that could cause brain damage, too.

Whether it was fast or slow, he would help Claude in his healing process. Claude could move into the cabin with him and Sam, or maybe Blake could go to British Columbia to Claude's home. But there was no way he could help Claude with finances, so he had his fingers crossed that Claude had great medical insurance with his profitable job. Canada had universal health care that all their citizens could afford. But that was obviously only available in Canada. He'd read stories of Canadians being bankrupted by needing emergency medical care while vacationing in the United States.

Finch pulled into the driveway of Sam's cabin. All the lights inside were blazing, which was disturbing at four in the morning. Both he and Sam tried to conserve energy as often as possible, turning off the lights as soon as they exited a room. His first thought was that Maya had decided to throw a party in their absence. But he heard no music, and then he remembered that they were originally scheduled to return yesterday evening, by eight or nine o'clock at the latest if they all decided to go out to dinner.

A deer stood at the front of the driveway, blinking uncertainly in the headlights for a moment. When Blake opened the car door, the doe finally made up her mind and trotted away into the darkness. He picked up his ski boots, then tugged Sam's good right arm around his shoulder, as he pulled her out of the back seat. They both stumbled toward the front door. He wondered if his favorite leather shoes, imprisoned in a dressing room locker in the ski lodge, would ever be returned. Maybe the authorities would organize some sort of lost-and-found system for all the possessions that were now under the snow. Claude had given him those shoes.

His slipper clattered against something metallic. In the porch light, he noticed the object that spun away was a kitchen knife. Was the blade covered in blood? *What the . . .?* Biting his lip, he wished that Finch hadn't already left them. Should he dump Sam on the porch steps and call 9-1-1? But the police would take forever to answer a vague call about a knife found in a driveway.

As soon as they lurched inside, Sam nearly sank to her knees. Blake deposited her on the only cushion remaining on the couch. The others were lying on the floor, ripped to shreds.

They both surveyed the room, wide-eyed. The recliner had

been slashed, too, and the television screen was bashed in. In the kitchen, drawers were pulled out and contents dumped on the floor, along with what appeared to be maple syrup and ketchup, forming a crazy Jackson Pollock design on the tile.

Sam finally asked, "What the hell happened here?"

He had no answer to that. Striding around the cabin, he quickly checked all the rooms, feeling as if he should yell "Clear!" when he discovered each was empty. After making the circuit, he reported to his housemate, "Looks like they didn't damage the bedrooms, although they dumped out all the drawers in our dressers."

"I didn't have much to steal." Sam sank into the cushions, resting her head on the back of the couch.

"Me neither." He sighed. "The utility room window is broken, and there's blood." He decided not to tell her about the bullet hole in the wall and the light moving around in the back woods.

He could tell that exhaustion had completely overtaken his housemate by how long it took Sam to register his words. After a long moment, she raised her head. "Blood? Simon?"

"I haven't seen him."

"Maya?"

"Her tent is still out back, but seems like someone bashed it in with a baseball bat."

"Jesus Christ, just shoot me now." Sam feebly tried to sit up but flopped back against the cushion.

"Sorry, no bullets. No gun, either."

"I can't," she complained in frustration, struggling to sit up again. "I need to go look for both Maya and Simon, but I just can't. Not today." Tears streamed down her cheeks. "Is it still today?"

"I'm going to go out back and see if I can find them." He found his running shoes in his room, one under the nightstand

and one in the closet. After lacing them up, he checked the kitchen drawer. No flashlight. Had the intruders taken that as well? Pulling the largest remaining knife out of the butcher block, he slipped it into his jacket pocket and then located the spare flashlight on a utility room shelf.

28

"Simon!" Maya's beam caught a flash of light-colored fur, but the creature quickly ran out of the circle of brightness, dashing into a snag of blackberry vines. Maya knelt and peered into the thicket, searching through the thorns and intertwined hoops of greenery.

Red eyes stared back at her. A rabbit.

A coyote howled somewhere close by. Another answered, and then a chorus of yipping ensued, the laughter-like sound making chills run down her spine. Sam didn't allow her cat out after sundown because coyotes were always on the prowl in the dark. What if a pack of them had cornered the poor injured cat now? She swallowed hard, knowing Sam would never forgive her if Simon was killed that way. And she didn't deserve forgiveness, did she? She was such a fuck-up.

"Simon!" She pushed herself to her feet and continued the search. "Kitty, kitty!"

Why didn't Sam have a dog, for God's sake? A dog would come when you called it. Cats? No way. Especially one that had been shot. But you couldn't blame any animal for that, could you? Maybe Simon couldn't come at all. Sniffling, Maya moved her flashlight in another sweep through the trees.

A flash of white. There was the cat, crouched in a heap between the gnarled roots of a Douglas fir, a mound of white and black and red. His green eyes glared at her suspiciously, but he didn't run when she knelt and extended her hand. "It's me, Simon. You remember me, right? I'd never hurt you. Really, I wouldn't. Are you okay?"

The cat allowed her to place her hand on his head and then gently run it down his backbone. He hissed and spat when her fingers neared his tail. When she pulled her hand away, her fingers were wet with blood. "Shit, boy. I'm sorry. How bad is it?"

She could tell that the blood came from his back, near his tail, but the dim flashlight and Simon's curled position didn't allow her a good look. "I've got to get you back to the house."

When she curled her hands around him to pick him up, he yowled and stiffened, but she quickly stuffed him inside her rain jacket, closing it over him. Simon dug his claws into her stomach, causing tears to leap to her eyes, but she was determined to keep hold of him. Leaving the flashlight on the ground, she staggered toward the cabin. The back porch light was on. Had she switched it on when she'd left the house? She didn't remember.

Then the figure of a man moved into view, silhouetted by the lighted windows behind him.

Fuck! Was that Eaze? James? Maya had no weapon, and she didn't want to let loose of Simon. She'd never catch the cat again. Plastering herself against the rough trunk of a tree, she froze as the beam of light swept around her.

The cat struggled beneath her coat, forcing her to clutch him tighter. Then he yowled his outrage and extended his claws farther into the tender flesh of her stomach. She clenched her teeth and squeezed her eyes shut to keep from crying out.

"Simon?" a man's voice called. "Here, kitty, kitty, kitty."

Not Eaze, she knew his voice. But she didn't know James's well enough to say it wasn't him. She peeked around the tree trunk. Was that a knife in his hand?

"Who is out here?" the man asked next. "I saw your flashlight."

The voice sounded vaguely familiar, but Maya's heart was pounding so loudly that she could barely make out the words. As his footsteps neared the right side of the tree, she slid around the trunk to the left.

And then she was blinded by his flashlight beam. "Don't stab me," she begged, freezing in place. Her legs threatened to buckle as the cat struggled against her trembling belly. "Kill me later if you have to, but please let me save this cat."

The flashlight beam moved away from her eyes. "Maya."

The man held the beam under his chin. Although the light gave him a creepy Halloween-killer aspect, she recognized Sam's housemate. "Blake? Where have you been?"

"To hell and back." Focusing the flashlight beam on the ground ahead, Blake led her to the house. After entering through the back door, she noticed that he made a point of closing the door between that utility room and the living area. Sam was on the couch, her head back on the top cushion, her legs extended to the floor. Her pants were ripped and covered in blood on the right side. A sling cradled her left arm. She looked like she'd been in a horrible accident.

"See who I found sneaking around the backyard," Blake said in a loud voice.

Sam's head snapped up. Her eyes were bloodshot, and her face was raw and red. Across the bridge of her nose was an odd bandage, like one of those stop-snoring devices advertised on television. "Maya. What the hell happened here?"

Maya struggled to control the sobbing that began instantly. "I—I'll tell you in a minute, but first, Simon's hurt." Opening her jacket, she bent over Sam and dumped the bloody cat into her lap.

Sam's arms enclosed her cat immediately, partially trapping him beneath her sling. "What happened to him?"

"He got shot." Maya collapsed into the shredded remains of the recliner.

"Shot?" Sam's voice was incredulous.

In her lap, the cat struggled to be free, yowling. Sam grabbed the scruff of Simon's neck with her right hand as he dug his claws into her thigh.

Blake knelt beside Sam, placing one hand around the cat's front legs and running the other gently over the animal's back. "It looks like a graze, right above his tail."

"Shot," Sam repeated, in a dazed voice. "Who shot him?" She examined the wound as best she could while holding onto the struggling animal.

"Eaze."

"Eaze had a gun? In my house?"

Maya protested, "It wasn't my idea. I wasn't even here to start—"

Sam cut her off. "I don't care."

Maya had never seen Sam so angry. But she deserved it. "I don't have any money, but I'll take him to the emergency vet. Maybe they'll let me clean cages or something to pay—"

Pinning the cat under her sling, Sam held up her free hand in a stop gesture. "Go find some peroxide and gauze and antibiotic cream in my bathroom closet."

Maya let out another sob. "I don't know how to explain—"

"Maya, now!" Sam snapped.

Wiping her nose with the back of her hand, Maya stood up and stumbled through the litter of objects scattered across the living room carpet. She stepped in something sticky. After rummaging in the bathroom, she found the first aid supplies and brought them back.

"Not too bad," Sam was telling Blake. "Lots of blood, but I

think the bleeding's stopped." She instructed Blake to pour some hydrogen peroxide into the gash.

When the peroxide hit his skin, Simon nearly levitated off Sam's lap, but Sam managed to restrain him until Blake wiped a fingerful of antibiotic ointment into the wound. Then she let go, and the cat leaped from her lap, dashed under the dining room table, and sat there, frantically licking the wound on his back.

"So much for antibiotic cream," Blake observed.

"Maybe it'll work from the inside," Sam commented wearily. "Could this day get any worse?"

"It was Eaze," Maya began. "And this other guy, James. They trashed your house."

Wincing, Sam pulled her left arm back into the sling and waved her right hand in the air. "I don't want to hear it. I can't take anything more right now." Her voice cracked after the word "more."

"I'll be right back." Blake grabbed a dish towel from the mess on the floor and then disappeared out the front door. When he came back, he was holding a knife in his towel-wrapped hand.

"Care to explain this?" he asked.

Maya groaned. "When Eaze pulled out his gun to shoot Simon, I stabbed him. But don't worry, when I called the police, they took off."

She looked from Sam to Blake. "Are Chase and Claude okay?"

Sam's face crumpled. Blake's expression was agonized, too. Neither said anything for a more than a minute, then Sam repeated, "I can't take any more . . ."

Blake extended a hand to his housemate. "Bed." He pulled her up from the couch.

Maya stepped forward. "I'll help."

"Get away from me," Sam growled.

Maya froze in place, letting her arms drop back to her sides. Tears slid down her face. From the corner of her eye, she saw Simon dash from beneath the dining room table through Sam's bedroom door.

One arm around Sam's waist, Blake helped her toward her bedroom. "Maya's tent is ruined," he murmured in a soft voice.

"She can sleep on the couch. What's left of it."

Neither Blake nor Sam spoke another word to her, but simply left her standing amid the ruins of the living area as they worked their way to their respective bedrooms and then turned out the lights.

Staring out the back window into the dark as she wiped the wetness from her eyes, Maya saw the dim glow of the flashlight she'd left behind. Did the beam seem to waver, or was that just the blurring effect of her tears? Was Eaze out there? James? Would they try to kill her next?

What a small loss that would be. Her mentor Sam and all of Sam's friends hated her. Maya's own friends hated her, not that they'd ever been real friends. And she'd nearly gotten Simon killed. She didn't even have a tent or a sleeping bag now. Could things get worse? Her life was over.

She lifted the ripped cushions back onto the couch and curled up on top of them as best she could. Yes, Maya suspected, with dawn, things might get much worse.

29

Sam sat on her bed, propped up against the headboard with pillows. She was so exhausted that she could barely move, but she had no idea when she could get to sleep. Even with painkillers wrapping her in cotton batting, her body was one huge ache, both inside and out. Rain spattered against her window, adding to the dismal atmosphere. Somewhere in the woods behind her home, a barred owl hooted.

"C'mon out, Simon," she crooned. "I need a kitty to hold. I need my buddy."

Nothing. Continuing in a soft murmur, she told him, "Simon, the world has gone to hell. Well, you know that, don't you? You must have been terrified last night. I'm glad you survived. But I really need to see you. I really need my best friend right now." She wiped her nose.

A black-and-pink nose emerged from beneath the overhang of the quilt, and then he crawled out and sat on the floor, his solemn green eyes fixed on her face. She patted her thigh under the blanket. "C'mon, Simon. I'm sorry you got shot."

Just saying those words made bile rise into her throat. She'd never trust Maya to take care of her pet again. Or her house. Or anything else.

The cat slunk toward her in a crouch, his belly close to the ground as if he were hunting, but she rejoiced when he was able to leap onto the mattress and then crawl into her lap. She could feel the tension in his small warm body. The divot on his back was raw, an insulting bloody slash through the fur and skin just above his tail. She stroked Simon's head, moving her fingers over the soft velvet fur behind his ears, then massaging his shoulders, careful not to move her hand too close to his injury.

"Oh, buddy, that has got to hurt. You deserve a Purple Heart. And some raw chicken liver. If the bastards didn't dump that on the floor, too." She always checked for his favorite treat at the grocery store. It was surprisingly difficult to score these days. Had people given up eating chicken livers?

He gazed up at her, and she moved her hand to his throat, gently scratching him under his chin. Slitting his eyes, he purred.

"I'm amazed that you can do that after all you've been through. If I could go back in time, I would, Simon." She'd make an excuse not to go to the ski area yesterday. If she hadn't gone at all, Chase and Nicole would have left before the avalanche. Claude and Blake might have, as well. Her house would not have been invaded. "I'm so sorry I wasn't here." She caressed each of the cat's rose-petal ears. "I love you, buddy."

They sat that way, comforting each other, until they both fell asleep, she with her free hand on Simon's soft fur, the cat purring, his small body warming her legs.

She couldn't breathe. Snow smothered her face and imprisoned her arms and legs. But something urgently scratched at the back of her thighs. Something hot and alive. With claws. Whimpering. The wolverine! Feisty had fallen into the same hole Sam had. She had to get them both out before the wolverine shredded her, clawing her way up her imprisoned body to get to air.

The whimpering transformed into small cries, a man's voice saying "Sam, Sam, Sam." Clawing at her. Chase? Chase!

With a gasp, Sam woke up. She was tangled in her bedsheets and quilt, a smaller hot body wrapped up in the bedcovers with her. Simon mewling to be freed. Above her stood Blake. He pulled the quilt from beneath her bandaged leg. The cat slid out with a yelp of indignation and leaped to the top of her bookcase headboard.

Blake's fingers grasped her shoulder. "You okay now, Sam? You were moaning."

"Wolverine," she explained, licking her dry lips. Then, "Transformed into Chase."

"Uh-huh." Blake straightened. "Of course."

"Bad dream. I'm okay now." Surveying her dresser, with drawers pulled out and contents on the floor, she amended that. "Well, as okay as I'm going to be for a while."

"Good." Her housemate slipped out through the bedroom door. Sam took a deep breath, alarmed at the daylight streaming in through her bedroom window. Her bedside clock read 10:32 a.m. How could she have slept so late? She needed to call the hospital, find out about Chase. And Nicole. And Claude. Was everyone still alive?

Had Feisty been buried with her?

No. Buried, yes, and so had she been, but not together. Reaching an arm above her head, she touched soft fur. Simon gave a feline chirp of response. "You okay, bud?"

The cat chirped again. She wanted to twist around to look at him, but she didn't think she could manage the twisting part. She pushed herself up with her free hand, and immediately regretted changing position. Every part of her body hurt. Ribs, left shoulder, left ankle. Right leg. Face. She needed a drink of water, but she wasn't sure she could make it to the bathroom. She swung her legs over the side of the bed. Simon shifted from her pillow to her side, and rubbed against her hip.

Blake knocked on her bedroom door. "Permission to enter again, Captain."

Sam waved a hand in the air. "Whatever."

He handed Sam a cell phone.

"Oh good. I was going to ask if I could borrow yours."

Pointing to the cell phone, he said, "That's not yours. Or mine. I made Maya go get another like yours first thing this morning. They put your old SIM card in, so most everything should be there."

She checked the screen, discovered she had two texts and a phone message from the editor at *Out There*. He probably wanted to know when her article about the aerial ski contest would be done. She was too tired to search for her notes and videos, too fatigued to even think about finishing that job. Surely they'd cut her some slack. There should be some special dispensation for being buried alive.

There was also a call from her father in Kansas, less than an hour ago.

"If you don't like that phone, we can find another one for you." Her housemate gave her a tentative smile.

Blake's kindness made her throat close up. "I know you thought I was out of it last night," Sam told him. "Or this morning, or whatever. On the way home. But I remember what I said; I was totally coherent."

He shot her a skeptical look.

"Well, maybe not totally. But I meant it when I said I love you. And you *are* my rock, Blake. I don't know what I'd do without you."

Her housemate dipped his chin, his lips pressed tightly together as if he were trying not to cry. She noticed he was unshaven, and the bags under his eyes revealed his exhaustion. He probably hadn't slept at all.

She was almost afraid to ask. "Any news from the hospital?"

"They did emergency surgery on Claude to relieve the pressure from the hematoma. Now he's in a medically induced coma until the swelling goes down. They won't know about brain damage until he wakes up."

She wrapped her good hand around his wrist. "He'll be okay."

"Of course, they wouldn't tell me anything about Chase. Or Nicole."

"Of course, they wouldn't. I need to go to the hospital."

Blake nodded. "Let's go together after you get dressed and we get some breakfast."

"I'm not sure I want to leave the house unattended right now. Sometimes they come back, you know." It gave her a chill to think Maya's thuggish friends were still at large. "I'll go after you come back."

Her housemate shook his head. "No. You go first. I know what Claude's condition is right now; you don't know about Chase."

At the reminder of what they were both going though, Sam's throat threatened to close up again. "Thank you, Blake," she murmured.

The bathroom seemed so far away. She stared glumly in that direction, willing her body to rise onto her feet.

Maya strode into the bedroom. "I'll help her."

Simon streaked off the headboard and vanished under the bed.

Throwing an arm around Sam, Maya lifted.

When Sam yelped in pain, Maya dropped her back onto the mattress. "Sorry! I'm so sorry!"

Recovering, Sam told her, "It's okay. Just get me to the toilet—gently—and find me some clothes."

Maya looked from Sam to Blake. "And *I'll* stay and guard

the house while you're gone. And clean up however I can." She pulled her cell phone from her back jeans pocket, then, after checking it, said. "Well, I do have to go somewhere in about three hours, but I'll stay until then."

Both Blake and Sam hesitated.

Maya held her right hand in the air. "I solemnly swear that if I see any sign of Eaze or James, I'll call the police immediately."

"Okay," Sam said. "I'm holding you to that."

Blake ducked out of the bedroom. "I'll make French toast and coffee."

"Extra strong coffee, please," Sam told him. "A gallon." She felt like it would take that much caffeine to get her body parts synchronized again.

"Coming up," he answered from the kitchen.

After Maya had helped her walk to the toilet, Sam said, "That's enough. I think I can handle it from here. Can you find me some jeans and a sweater?" She couldn't bring herself to say "thank you" to Maya right now. She could barely keep from screaming at the girl who'd helped to wreck her home and shoot her cat.

Sam pulled off her sling. "I'm going to take a shower. Then you're going to tell me everything you know about what happened last night."

The pressure of the shower hurt nearly as much as the warm water helped, but she was reasonably certain that she smelled better afterward, and her hair was free of clumps of sheetrock and pine needles and dirt. That was progress.

As soon as she was dressed and had taken a cup of coffee in hand from the kitchen counter, Sam grilled Maya, asking the girl who James was, why he had been with Eaze, and why they decided to destroy her home.

Maya kept her eyes on the floor as she answered. "Eaze

owed James Winnow money, and Eaze thought there might be money in your house."

"Winnow?" Sam asked Blake. "Isn't there a Winnow Construction here in town?"

"If you mean the Winnow Construction Corporation whose name is featured on banners all over town and who is building the new elementary school, the new hotel, and the new apartment complex, then yes," Blake answered as he deftly flipped a skillet full of French toast.

Smart aleck. Sam focused her attention back on Maya. "Why did Eaze owe this guy? And how much?"

The girl shrugged her shoulders, not lifting her gaze from the floor. "I called the police."

Sam narrowed her eyes, sure that Maya was not telling the whole story. "Are they in custody?"

Again, Maya simply shrugged. "They weren't last night. The cops didn't seem too worked up about it."

Sam's jaw already ached; she'd been clenching her teeth throughout the conversation. When the *Out There* offices had been burglarized last year, the police admitted that they didn't have the manpower to investigate burglaries. Although this was more of a home invasion—that should qualify as a serious crime, shouldn't it?

"We'll have to talk to the police, Sam," Blake suggested. "And give them a complete list of everything stolen and damaged."

It made Sam tired just to think about it. Staring at the ruins of her living area and kitchen was too much to endure right now. She limped back to her bedroom, furious with Maya, and completely outraged at the intruders. How dare they trash her home? Did homeowner's insurance cover vandalism and theft?

How about attempted murder of a pet? Was that a charge that would stand up in court? Probably not.

Sweeping along with the wave of fury was a cold prickle of fright. Where were Eaze and the other sleazebag, James, right now? Would they be back? Eaze seemed like a harmless-but-worthless loser, but she'd never heard of James Winnow before.

Blake brought her a plate of French toast, which she ate off her dresser in between putting on her socks and slipping into her shoes.

Her cell phone buzzed just as she was following Blake out the front door. Michael Fredd, the editor. "I'll get the article on the contest to you tomorrow," she promised on answering.

"Excellent," he said, "But we'll take minimal, just stats and a few photos."

Sam wondered if she had all the information she needed to finish even a minimal job. She and Gina had left before the contest was completely finished.

"But that's not what I'm calling about. We want you to write about what it was like."

"What the contest was like?"

"Duh. No, Sam. Crawling around inside the lodge, searching for survivors. What it was like to be there."

Not memories she really wanted to revisit. "Uh . . ."

"As quickly as you can, Sam. Five hundred dollars, okay?"

That was two hundred and fifty more than *Out There* typically paid her for articles. Could she type with her left hand? She'd left off the annoying sling but held her arm close to her chest. Now she wiggled her fingers. Stiff, but not especially painful. She raised that hand into the air. Yow! Tears sprang to her eyes as an ice pick jabbed into her left shoulder. But yes, she could probably type, as long as she could keep her shoulder still.

"Okay?" Michael asked.

"I'm not sure I have a computer." She glanced at Blake. He shook his head.

"What happened to your computer?"

"It got stolen last night."

"Bummer. I could drop a laptop by your place in an hour or so."

"I'll be at the hospital checking on my friends."

Maya appeared in the doorway. "You can borrow my laptop."

That figured, that the girl had kept her own laptop while allowing Sam's to be stolen. When Sam hesitated, the girl added, "Please. It's the least I can do."

"I've got a loaner here," Sam told Michael.

"Great. So call me when you're done, okay? Okay?"

Sam couldn't focus on anything except Chase and Claude and Simon and how much she hurt right now. She exhaled heavily. "I'll try to have it done by tomorrow."

"This afternoon would be even better."

Sam snorted. Could she pull it together to write an article? It seemed like an insurmountable task. "Do you remember that I was involved in that avalanche? And that was *yesterday?*"

"Of course. That's what the story will be about, right?"

After a moment, she reminded him again, "I'm not exactly one hundred percent today."

"We don't expect you to be Superwoman. All right, tomorrow afternoon would be fine. And, oh, I'm glad you survived."

30

Sam lurched down the corridors of St. Joseph Hospital, moving like one of the undead. She probably looked like a zombie, too, with her face swollen and scratched under her mask, and her left arm in a sling, limping on her sore ankle. Patients were exempt, but all the visitors and staff she passed in the hallway wore masks, most the ubiquitous disposable paper version, but some wore cloth coverings in various patterns or with embroidered teeth or smiles. Her own was a red-and-black Native American Northwest design that Chase had given her. The COVID-19 pandemic had peaked, but new mutations of the disease were still out there. Nature's way of getting rid of surplus humans in an attempt to save the planet?

She could definitely name two humans that deserved to be permanently removed: Ethan Zeran and James Winnow. After such a major violation, she hadn't wanted to leave the house unattended this morning, but they'd already boarded up the broken window, and against her better judgment, had trusted Maya to stay and guard the house for a few hours.

Simon was limping as much as she was this morning, and like Maya's criminal cohorts, Sam was no longer sure that the girl could or should be saved. Given multiple choices to redeem herself over the last year, she'd chosen wrong every time.

Sam had refused the scheduled X-rays. Her ribs ached with every breath and her whole chest was sore, but she knew what broken ribs felt like, and her pain didn't seem that sharp or that deep. Not to mention that she doubted her health insurance would cover the cost.

Taking a seat beside Chase's bed in the Intensive Care Unit didn't do much to improve her grim thoughts. Chase lay inert beneath the blankets, connected to two different IVs. There were also electrodes leading to monitors, with oxygen tubing wrapped around his face and inserted into his nostrils. She'd never seen him like that, not even after he'd been shot. When she picked up his hand, he did not respond, not even to curl his fingers around hers.

"Chase, I'm here." She tried to enunciate through her mask, make her tone cheerful. "You're not on the mountain anymore. You're in the hospital in Bellingham, and you're going to get well soon. Remember that FBI agents have to go out in a blaze of glory. I don't think getting squashed in a building counts, do you? There weren't even any criminals involved."

The slack expression on his face didn't change. His familiar, lean form was stretched out on the bed, but the Starchaser Perez she knew didn't seem to be there at all. A sob escaped her lips, and she clapped a hand over her mouth, hoping he hadn't heard it. Unconscious people could often hear, she'd been told.

A doctor and nurse came in to check on him. The doctor, a handsome man with Asian features, faced her. "I'm Dr. Ishimoto, Mr. Perez's doctor here. You're the fiancée?"

"Yes," she lied. "How long will he be unconscious?"

"He's not," the doctor told her. "He's just heavily sedated. Only hours ago, he had emergency surgery to remove his ruptured spleen and repair a laceration to his liver and a tear in his large intestine. He lost a lot of blood. It's amazing that he survived with those injuries."

"He's a strong man." Sam wanted to believe Chase could overcome anything.

"It seems so. We'll hope for the best."

Sam fixed on the doctor's tired gray eyes above his mask. "What do you mean, *hope*?"

His face was solemn. "The next thirty-six hours or so will be determinative."

"Determinative?" She understood the word, but not the prognosis.

"In the hours that come, we'll see how well his organs are functioning. We need to guard against infection, especially because of the intestinal injury. If there are relatives to inform, you might want to do that."

Oh God, was this doctor was saying that Chase could die? She realized that she didn't know if Chase's parents were living. He had a sister, Rae, or Raven, actually; Sam had met her once in passing when Chase had been in the hospital in Utah. Sam thought Raven might live in Boise. She was married; was her last name still Perez? And he'd mentioned a brother, Wolf, that she'd never met. Could she find them? Perez was a common name in many communities.

"Do you have his cell phone?" she asked the nurse.

She shook her head. "But one was found a short distance away from him. The wallet identified him as an FBI agent, so we turned that cell phone over to them."

The FBI would probably know Chase's relatives' contact information. They wouldn't share that information with her, but they might call the relatives. Nicole would probably know how to get that information as well. She was most likely in this hospital, too.

Before the doctor left, he told Sam, "Mr. Perez is doing as well as can be expected. Keep a positive thought."

Anxiety clawed at her gut. A vision of her mother lying in a hospital bed rose in her memory. Susan Westin had died of ALS, becoming more of a zombie every year until death claimed her when Sam was nine years old. She had more recollections of a bedridden, wasting, skeletal body than of a mother.

Sam leaned over her lover. "Chase, if you die, I'll never forgive you. Keep that in mind." Pulling down her mask, she kissed his cheek above the oxygen cannula. "And I love you. And I told the staff that I'm your fiancée, so if—when—you wake up, you'd better remember all that."

How had her father dealt with her mother's illness all those years? Chase had to be okay, because Sam couldn't do what her father had done, what so many other selfless people had done. She wasn't that strong. She didn't want to sit by the side of a man who was now only a body. *Coward.* She clutched at her throat with her right hand. There wasn't enough air in the room. She had to find a restroom, wash her face, get a drink of water. *Escape.*

Her phone chimed when she was halfway down the corridor. She ducked out a door onto an outdoor balcony to answer it, blinking in the spring sunshine.

"Dad, I was just about to call you."

"Thank the Lord, you're okay, Summer." His voice was warm. "We saw the news about the avalanche, and Zola and I knew that you sometimes go snowshoeing or skiing up there. Thank God you weren't there yesterday."

"I *was* there, Dad. And so were Chase and Blake. And Nicole and Claude; you don't know them, but they're Chase's FBI partner and Blake's"—she hesitated about what to call Claude to her conservative preacher father—"close friend. And my friend, Gina."

"Well, thank heavens they are all okay. God must have been watching out for you all."

Why did he always automatically assume the best-case

scenario? Sam sucked in a deep breath, trying to tamp down her frustration. "They aren't all okay, Dad. Chase is in the hospital right now, fighting for his life. So is Claude. And Gina and Nicole are in bad shape, too."

A measure of silence passed before her father responded, "I'm sorry to hear that. But you're fine, right?"

A young man in green scrubs joined her on the balcony. After a quick glance at her, he turned his back to light a cigarette.

"I was buried in an avalanche, Dad. And I watched two other people get buried. They killed a wolverine. Gina and I managed to dig ourselves out, but they didn't. They're dead. And then, when we returned to the ski area, we discovered another avalanche had hit the ski lodge."

"Oh, Summer." That, followed by a sigh, was his only response. He was no doubt confused by the mélange of events that had just spilled out of her mouth.

Cigarette smoke wafted her way, and she moved to the other side of the young man to be upwind of the air pollution. Shooting her an apologetic look, he slid down to the far end of the balcony. At least he was a polite polluter.

Zola, her father's wife, came on the line. "You poor dear, you've been through so much."

"Yes." She couldn't bring herself to add the news of Maya and the wreckage of her home. Yesterday already seemed like some sort of over-the-top disaster movie script.

Her father recovered enough to ask, "Would you like me and Zola to come?"

Having her father and his wife here would add a level of stress she couldn't take right now. He'd probably insist on praying over everyone and saying that God didn't give anyone more than they could endure. Like that was a comforting thought. He'd suggest that she should give up trekking around the mountains seeking wild animals, give up living with her gay housemate, find a normal job, marry Chase, and settle down.

But she also knew her father was kind-hearted—a truly good Christian, as opposed to the many fakers who abused that label these days—so she softened her tone to answer, "Thanks, Dad. But I can't imagine what you two could do to help right now. And I know you've got the congregation to consider."

After promising to keep them posted about what was happening, she ended the call and went back into the building.

A short distance down the corridor, she stopped in the doorway of a room that held Gina Canfield. Her friend was asleep and also had a nasal cannula taped to her face and an IV running to her arm. It was painful to see the athletic woman reduced to this state. Sam vowed to call the other members of the wolverine study group and find out whether Gina had family who should be here. She was ashamed she didn't know. A monitor showed a steady heartbeat and other numbers Sam couldn't interpret. Nothing appeared alarming. She turned to go.

"Hey!"

She pivoted back toward the bed. Gina cleared her throat, but her voice was still hoarse as she croaked, "Zeke."

Sam told her, "It's me, Sam Westin, Gina."

"Duh."

Sam waited.

"Did you really see a snowy owl?"

"I think so."

"I need a favor."

Unsure if she was supposed to be following a thread of logic that didn't seem to exist, Sam asked, "Because of an owl?"

Gina rolled her eyes. "No!"

"Okay."

Gina cleared her throat again. "A big favor."

"Of course, Gina. What can I do?"

"I need you to take care of Zeke. He'll be frantic by now." Gina coughed and gestured toward a water cup on the bedside table. After Sam handed it to her and Gina had taken a sip, she was able to explain that Zeke was her pet bird. "I'm sorry. There's nobody else. My insides got sort of . . . rearranged by the slide. They say I'm going to be here for a while."

"They have no clue how tough you are." When her friend's concerned expression didn't change, Sam added, "No worries, Gina. I'll be happy to take care of your bird." How hard could it be to care for a bird?

Gina's brow creased, and she seemed to roll her eyes before telling Sam how to get into her house. Sam patted her shoulder. "You just get well."

Next door, Sam found the room where Claude Gagnon lay, still unconscious. Beside him sat Blake, his back to the door as he held his lover's hand. She watched as Blake unhooked his mask from behind his ears, leaned close to Claude's ear saying softly, slowly, as if trying to persuade Claude, "You *will* live. You will be *fine*. We *will* have a future together."

Sam squirmed in the doorway, uncomfortable at observing such a personal moment. She shouldn't be listening to her housemate's intimate soliloquy. She moved on.

Next in the Intensive Care Unit was Nicole Boudreaux's room. At first, Sam wasn't sure the patient was Nicole, as her head was swathed in bandages and her eyes were shut, but she checked the door and saw her name. Sam stared at Chase's former partner for a moment. Nicole didn't wake up, but her cheeks were rosy and naturally, she didn't have a mark on her beautiful face. Her eyelids were a delicate shade of mauve and her lips were pink.

Sam ran her tongue over her own chapped lips. Her envy of

Nicole had remained over the years, maybe had become even deeper as she'd gotten to know Chase's FBI partner and realized how sharp and competent Nicole was. But Sam was glad that Chase hadn't been alone in the collapsed hut, that he and Nicole maintained a supportive relationship although they rarely worked together now. Chase had Nicole to confide in; she had Blake.

As she pivoted to exit the room, she nearly collided with a man and a female nurse. The man's jacket stretched tight over his muscular arms. His head was shaved. This had to be Oscar, Nicole's husband. He certainly looked as if he sculpted rock and could lift vats of molten brass.

Both Oscar and the nurse appeared startled at her presence in Nicole's room. At least, that's how Sam read their postures. With faces half-covered in masks, it was difficult to tell for sure what anyone was feeling these days. She probably was not supposed to be in this room.

"I'm a friend," Sam explained. "I'm the other FBI agent's fiancée." She cringed inwardly at the lie, but she needed to keep up the pretense, didn't she?

The nurse's gaze morphed to surprise. "FBI?"

Sam immediately wondered if she should have said that. Was it a secret? Chase's medical team had seemed to know. "Uh, yeah," she mumbled.

"I'm guessing you were involved in the incident yesterday," the nurse observed, scrutinizing Sam's face and sling.

Sam started to raise her right hand to her forehead, but then thought better about touching her raw scratches and dropped it down to clutch at her sling. "Yeah, I was there, but I'm doing okay."

Oscar's expression softened, and he held out a hand to Sam. "Oscar Fielding, Nicole's husband. And you must be Chase's Summer."

Sam couldn't sort out whether she was pleased or annoyed to be referred to as Chase's. "How is Nicole?"

Oscar nodded at the nurse, who explained, "She's doing well, all things considered. Lots of bruises and torn ligaments in one ankle, but no broken bones. Her skull and dura mater were pierced by a sharp object, so she had emergency surgery to clean and repair the injury. We need to keep her here for a couple of days to be sure there's no infection, but there shouldn't be any brain damage. She'll probably have a whale of a headache, though."

"The whale has arrived," Nicole murmured from behind Sam. They all focused on the bed. Her eyes were only partially open, as if the light were too bright in the room. "This headache is a blue whale." Fixing her gaze on her husband, she added, "That's the largest creature on earth."

The nurse murmured something about pain control and headed off down the hall.

Oscar stepped forward and took Nicole's hand. "Darling."

Nicole glanced at Sam. "Summer, how's Chase?"

Like Chase, she always called her Summer, her birth name. "He's still out. The doctor told me he's heavily sedated."

Nicole pursed her lips for a moment, then asked, "What's his prognosis?"

After taking a deep breath to steady herself, Sam said, "The next thirty-six hours are determinative, according to the doctor." Her throat threatened to close up.

Nicole's attempt at a smile crumpled into a wince. "He'll be okay. Special Agent Starchaser Perez is the toughest man I know."

"Hey!" Oscar objected.

"I'll leave you two." Moving toward the door, Sam said, "I'm sorry you were caught in the avalanche, Nicole, but I am glad that Chase didn't have to go through that experience by himself."

Mentally replaying her crawl through snow and debris brought on an oppressive feeling of claustrophobia. She needed air. Continuing down the hall, she passed into an area with two patients per room. How many of these people had been involved in last night's disaster?

One of the names on the doors was Daniel Olfanger. The patient in the bed by the window appeared to be in his teens, or maybe young twenties. "Daniel?" She walked closer. "Raven Hut Daniel?"

"Busted." He grinned at her. Aside from a black eye, he appeared healthy. "You're my hero, the one who was crawling around in there, right?"

"I don't know about the hero part, but yeah, that was me."

"I recognize you." He waggled a foot under the sheets. "I bet you'd recognize my boots, 'cept I have no idea where they are."

"I'm glad to see all of you, Daniel." She introduced herself. "You're looking good."

"Not bad, considering." Snagging a finger in the neck of his hospital gown, he pulled it down to display purple and black bruises on his chest. "Mashed, but not broken. I'm getting out this afternoon. You saved me."

She snorted. "Hardly. It was a group effort. I'm glad you're going to be okay."

"How about the others?"

She shrugged, unsure who he was asking about. "You know hospitals. They won't tell you anything."

"Stay cool," he said.

"I'll try. You too." She hoped Daniel hadn't known the girl with the purple shoes. Or the upside-down man. Or any of the other people who died yesterday. How many were still buried up on the mountain?

Abruptly, she remembered the dead wolverine poachers.

She hadn't told anyone about them. And she was certain that Gina hadn't, either.

At the information desk in the main lobby, she learned that a police officer was always on duty in the emergency department. She told the officer about the dead man and girl in the backcountry miles away from the ski area.

His attitude seemed a bit uncertain, as if he wasn't sure she was telling the truth, but he took down her name and number and wrote a brief note on the small notebook in his chest pocket. "I'll relay that information to my commander."

The doctors told Blake that Claude would live, but that they'd placed him in an induced coma while his brain recovered from the hematoma, the hypothermia and asphyxiation in the snow, as well as the subsequent surgery. Any or all of those could result in brain damage. The extent of the damage would not be known until Claude woke up.

The news left Blake feeling numb with uncertainty. What would happen now? He didn't know what to do with himself until Claude woke up. He strolled outside to process the information, trying to decide how he would deliver the news to Claude's relatives. He'd removed his lover's cell from Claude's jacket before they arrived at the hospital, and now he scrolled through Claude's phone contacts, knowing that he needed to tell someone in Canada what had happened.

The spring wind was brisk and cool. Two kids zipped around on skateboards, zigzagging among the pedestrians, their boards clackety-clacking on the sidewalk joints.

He paced, thumbing through the list of names. None of them meant anything to him. *Home*? No, Claude lived alone. *ICE*, that would be it. Surely not the US Immigration and Customs Enforcement agency, but "In Case of Emergency." He punched the Call icon.

After three rings, a woman answered. "Claude? When are you coming home?" Her accent was vaguely French, or, Blake guessed, French Canadian. "You'd better not miss David's party. He'll never forgive you. *I'll* never forgive you. Do *not* tell me you have to stay longer because of work!"

"Um," Blake stuttered. "This isn't Claude. My name is Blake, and I'm using Claude's phone. We're both in Bellingham, Washington."

The woman's voice took on an anxious tone. "Why do you have his phone? Has something happened to Claude?"

Blake couldn't just blurt out the state of affairs without knowing whom he was telling. "I found your number on his phone as an emergency contact. Are you Claude's mother?"

"What?!" The woman sounded insulted. So maybe she wasn't a senior citizen.

"Or his sister, Marie?" Blake suggested.

"I'm guessing you are a client of his, correct?"

Blake didn't respond, dismayed that Claude hadn't told his family about their relationship. But then, there could be all sorts of reasons for that. For all he knew, this woman could be homophobic.

The woman continued, "You probably do not have any reason to know much about Claude's home life. Yes, er, Blake, was it? My name is Marie Gagnon."

The sister.

"I'm Claude's wife."

The word sliced through his mind. *Wife?* Claude had told him he'd never had a serious relationship before. *Wife?* Claude had said he was single.

Blake made himself take a breath. He turned back toward the building, nearly colliding with one of the skateboarders, who gave him the finger as he glided past. Blake had been married to

Hannah's mother. It was not an uncommon history for men their age. Maybe Claude had not yet been ready to reveal his whole self.

"You're Claude's ex-wife?" He hated how squeaky his voice sounded now.

"*Wife*," Marie said firmly. "As in right now. As in the mother of his children, David and Miranda. You are scaring me, Mister . . . um . . . Blake? What has happened to Claude?"

Blake took another deep breath, trying to keep his thoughts on why he had called in the first place. "There's been an accident, Marie. Claude is in the hospital here in Bellingham."

When Blake left the hospital with Sam an hour later, they walked side by side in ponderous silence for several moments.

Finally, she said, "I don't know what to do, Blake. How can I help Chase? The doctors don't know what comes next. I can't stand this waiting."

Blake nodded, his mood similarly morose. "It's the same with Claude."

"What am I supposed to do? I can't lose him, Blake." Sam choked off a sob.

Blake stopped and took his housemate in his arms. "You'll get him back, Sam."

She inhaled shakily, and her eyes filled with tears as she met his gaze. "You'll get Claude back, too."

"No." His voice broke on the word. Averting his eyes, he swallowed, then reiterated, "No, I won't get him back."

He shifted his eyes toward the horizon, but he could feel her staring at him. She knew him too well. "Tell you later," he muttered, struggling to regain control of his emotions.

"Whenever you're ready." After giving him an extra squeeze, Sam let go, and they continued to the parking lot.

"Change of subject," he announced. "Hannah's supposed to arrive in two days. It's still spring break for her." Typically, Blake looked forward to his teenage daughter's visits, but this time, Hannah would be walking into chaos, both in the house and in his emotions. "Should I tell her not to come?"

Sam considered that for only a second before saying, "She'd be a happy distraction, wouldn't she? We'll make it work. Bigger change of subject. I need to go to this address." She showed him Gina's address on her phone.

At the small house in the Lettered Streets neighborhood, Sam found the spare key under the rock where Gina had explained it would be. When she and Blake walked in the front door, a raucous squawk preceded a loud greeting.

"*Hello! Hello!*"

Blake groaned. "You're kidding me."

"Gina's pet bird."

Sam had pictured a tiny budgie or a songbird, but Zeke turned out to be a handsome blue-and-gold macaw, dancing on a perch in a large cage. He squawked again, made a croaking noise, then screeched, "*Alexa, play NPR!*"

An Echo Dot on the kitchen countertop flashed and Alexa's female voice said, "*Okay, here's KUOW.*"

Zeke bobbed his head and screeched again, drowning out the device's commercial message that followed.

"Alexa, stop!" Sam ordered between the parrot's squawks.

Blake put his hands over his ears. "Be quiet, Zeke."

The macaw bobbed his head. "*Be quiet! Be quiet! Shut up!*"

Sam frowned at Blake. "He's obviously heard that a few times. And he's obviously hungry and thirsty." The bird's water bottle was empty, and his food dish had been flipped over.

From the hall closet, Sam pulled out a bag of parrot chow. If the photo on the front was accurate, parrot chow consisted of balls of seeds and some kind of processed pellets. "And Gina told me there's a container of fruit in the refrigerator."

Pulling out a handful of the chunky parrot chow, Sam opened the cage door and inserted her hand to upright the food dish. With an ear-piercing shriek and a flash of feathers, the parrot attacked, biting the back of her hand.

"Bastard!" She dropped the handful of seeds and yanked her bleeding hand back.

"Shut up! Here's KUOW!" Zeke excitedly bounced in place for a second, then picked up a wad of seeds from the cage floor and cracked the chunk with his beak.

Blake stood behind her, a large plastic container in his hands. "Oh, this is going to be fun."

"Gina says he'll settle down when his cage is covered." She sucked the blood from the back of her hand. "Let me just give him a drink and then we'll take him."

At least she could remove the macaw's water bottle and fill it from the outside of the cage without putting any digits in danger. After the parrot had eaten the handful of chow and tongued a drink from his water bottle, she pulled the canvas cover over the cage. *"Bye for now!"* Zeke chortled as the cover came down.

Then the parrot was blissfully quiet as Blake carried his cage to the car.

"Zeke is probably so loud because he's distressed," Sam commented. "He's been alone for two days now. And we're strangers to him. He's probably frightened."

"Uh-huh. Maybe we can keep him covered," Blake suggested. "At least until tomorrow morning?"

After Googling James Winnow on her cell phone, Sam shared the Instagram photos of him zooming around Bellingham on his Onewheel. There were also a couple of photos of him in a hardhat at one of his father's construction sites. James didn't appear too happy in those. Another bored privileged kid, choosing to share the thrills of homewrecking and drug dealing with Eaze. It was creepy to think they were both still on the streets.

"I'll be on the lookout for both of them from now on," Blake told Sam.

"Likewise." She limped into her office with Maya's laptop in hand. Simon parked himself below Zeke's cage on a stool next to the kitchen counter, staring at the canvas cover, swishing his tail. Blake hoped the cat wouldn't try to stick a paw through the bars. He could lose a toe.

Maya was nowhere to be found. The young woman had left a note, saying, simply, *Out*.

Blake wasn't sure how to take that. It might possibly indicate a step in the right direction. Maybe Maya was *out* searching for work. Jobs were plentiful now; Maya could probably find one easily, even with her juvenile record and bad habits. Or maybe she was *out* finding another couch to sleep on. It was about time; she'd been sponging off Sam's goodwill for way too long. But he was worried that she might be *out* searching for the two criminals who'd torn up the house, or *out* trying to hide from them. Maya was the lure that had brought them here.

The Bellingham police had confirmed that neither Eaze nor James was in custody, and Maya was right: The officer he spoke to didn't seem too concerned about the situation, telling Blake to keep the police informed if the pair showed up again.

Peering into the backyard, Blake saw that Maya had done her best to straighten her bent tent poles and had patched one of the poles as well as the nylon tent walls with duct tape. The sleeping bag had vanished. When he laundered the filthy kitchen towels the invaders had trampled on the floor, he found a few strands of polyester fiber in the lint trap of the dryer, so most likely, Maya had dried her sleeping bag and stuffed it back inside her tent.

It was probably a good thing that Maya intended to stay outside, even if it was a cold and damp spring. With luck, that Eaze character would be arrested and put in jail. How Maya could ever have taken up with him was a complete mystery. Blake had no idea how the James mutt fit into the picture. He shook his head. If his daughter Hannah ever hitchhiked down the same self-destructive roads that Maya had recently taken, he didn't know what he'd do.

Maya's efforts to clean up seemed to be limited to sweeping and mopping the floor and doing her own laundry. He busied himself trying to set the house back in order, taking photos and making a list of destroyed items, taking the discards out to the trash, saving the things that could possibly be salvaged. Maybe the sofa cushions could be covered again with new fabric? Or would that cost more than a new sofa? A broken chair leg could be glued back together. He mourned the loss of cherished books, their pages stuck together now with maple syrup. He'd miss the green wine glasses and the blue ceramic platter, now shattered on the floor; he had purchased those. His renter's insurance might cover them if Sam's homeowner's didn't.

Attitude of gratitude, he thought, grimacing at the triteness of that phrase. So Claude had eaten a hole through his heart, like a worm in an apple. That was at least half his fault, wasn't it? He had a daughter and a good friend and housemate he loved, a decent place he could afford to live, and a job he enjoyed.

He and Hannah could tour the local thrift stores and search for new treasures. And he had his health, no small thing these days.

Eaze and the other scumbag had emptied the maple syrup, but they'd overlooked a bottle of molasses. Maybe he'd make his molasses cookies. Sam loved those. So did Hannah. Blake pulled out an unbroken bowl and the mixer.

Claude had adored his special recipe, too. Blake laid his head on the kitchen countertop and cried.

31

The next day, Sam read over the draft of article she'd thrown together for *Out There*, determined to finish so she could get back to the hospital. It was embarrassingly evident how absent her brain had been the day before. The story contained so many errors; *their* for *there*, *its* for *it's*, missing pronouns, misspellings. The editor would probably change all the instances of *he* and *she* to *they; her* and *his* to *their*. Although she had to admit that *they* and *their* was efficiently non-gender-specific, to her those terms sounded like an individual had multiple personality disorder. Maybe English needed to create some new words for possessives and pronouns, the way the kids on her Wilderness Challenge expedition had made up new swear words when they weren't allowed to utter the typical ones.

She fixed the typos but decided to leave all the politically correct challenges to the editor. She'd just clicked Send when her phone chimed. She expected Michael Fredd to be asking yet again when she'd be finished with the piece.

But the caller ID on Sam's new cell displayed the name Adam Steele. Did she want to answer? Before Chase, the ambitious reporter had been her lover. Years later, on several occasions, he'd been her collaborator in reporting stories that needed to be told. But Adam was often her nemesis when it came to publicizing details she'd rather keep quiet. Sam hadn't heard from Adam since the nightmare of the search for Maya's half sister, Jade Silva, at the Arizona-Mexico border wall.

"Hello?" she finally answered.

"*Hello! Hello!*" echoed Zeke from the kitchen, followed by "*Alexa, set re-eyender.*"

Reminder? Maybe lips were required for *M* sounds. Thank God she had no smart device in the house. Lucky man, Blake had left for work before she uncovered the parrot's cage.

"I can't believe you *still* don't call me!"

"Hi, Adam. And how are you?" She failed to keep the note of sarcasm from her voice.

"After all the stories we've done together. Utah, Galápagos, Arizona. And now you've been involved in the biggest avalanche disaster to hit the Western US in a decade, and you *still* don't call me."

This greeting was so typical of Adam Steele. Everything was about the next exciting news story. "Frankly, it didn't cross my mind."

"Didn't cross your mind? You've got to be kidding! I bet you're writing that story right now!"

Sam stared at the words on the screen, a thread of needless guilt weaving its way into her brain. How dare he make this sound like some sort of game! "People died, Adam."

"Nine, I heard. So far."

Nine? *So far?* Would there be more? Sam rubbed a thumb across her lips. The purple-shoe babysitter, the upside-down man ... How many others had she not discovered in the collapsed building? Were they alive when she crawled out? If they had been, she didn't want to know; she already felt guilty enough for surviving. "You shouldn't sound so eager, Adam."

"Sorry." He didn't sound remorseful at all.

"*Gonna trade you for a dog,*" Zeke yelped. That was a new one. But maybe a good idea.

"What's all that noise in the background?"

"Radio." She rose from her chair and closed her office door, muffling the parrot's chatter. She continued, "Dozens are injured. A whole ski lodge was destroyed. They haven't even accounted for everyone yet."

"Yes, I heard that people are still missing and they're not finished digging out."

She could tell that Adam was trying not to sound too enthusiastic, but of course he would be thrilled at the chance to cover a developing story instead of summarizing one that had already been wrapped up.

How many bodies were still buried on the ski slopes? How many in the parking lot? She was relieved it wasn't her job to account for everyone who had been at the ski area that day. "It's a major disaster, Adam," she emphasized.

"Well, yeah." Now *his* tone was sarcastic. "The phrase 'if it bleeds, it leads' pretty much sums up the news biz." He didn't admit it, but of course that was the reason he called her. A hotshot reporter would not be interested in her private disasters. At least Adam was honest about it.

"And you were there, Avalanche Angel, rescuing victims right and left."

She snorted. "Hardly. I crawled through a collapsed building and located a few people—"

"Exactly!" She heard muffled sounds in the background— people talking, shuffling noises—and she pictured Adam gesturing to his film crew as he spoke to her.

"I just told the real rescuers about the victims I found and where they were."

"You brought out a baby!" Was that a faint whoop of excitement in the background? Who else was in the room with him?

How could she have forgotten about Baby Emma? "Yeah, I

guess I did do that. That was the easiest part."

"You were *there*, throughout it all."

"Hardly a major accomplishment, being in the wrong place at the wrong time. Along with dozens of other people."

"I want the whole story, babe. *Your* story."

"I'm not your babe. And actually, I wasn't even there when the avalanche hit the ski hut. I and a friend were miles away, on another mountain, buried in another avalanche."

"You were *buried*? In *another* avalanche?"

"Yes."

"Even better!" he chortled.

Pulling the phone away from her ear, she stared at it with dismay. How could she have ever dated this man?

"What was that like?"

Sam felt a piece of ice slide down her spine and shook her head. She didn't want to dwell on that memory. "I managed to get myself out."

He laughed. "Obviously."

She put the phone back to her ear, miffed that he was making light of that horrendous experience. "My friend survived, too. But we barely made it out alive. Two other people who were there didn't, and neither did a wolverine."

"Really? There were others buried in your personal avalanche?"

"Two people. And a wolverine," she reiterated.

"And nobody else knows about this?"

"I told a cop yesterday. I don't have a clue what he will do with that information."

"*Ummm.*" She heard him mumbling something to someone close by. After a moment, he said to her, "Good. There's nothing online about that. As far as the hut thing goes, there are plenty of others who were at the ski area when the avalanche hit, so I can get their stories."

She frowned. *The hut thing?*

"But your story is unique, right?" He sounded eager.

"I suppose. I already promised a story to *Out There* about crawling into the collapsed building. I just delivered it a few minutes ago."

Adam sighed dramatically, then, after a brief pause, said, "*Out There* is only a print 'zine, right?"

"*Out There* is my employer. There's an online version of the magazine, too."

"Okay, internet too." More muffled sounds in the background. "I'm reading their stats now. Pretty small subscriber base. Local."

"But important, Adam. Especially to me. Covering outdoor stories for them is my only regular income."

"That's fine. You haven't signed any sort of exclusive agreement, have you?"

She was pretty sure a contract like that would never have occurred to the staff at *Out There*. "No. We have a pretty informal arrangement."

"Good. I've seen the article in the *Times*, obviously, Avalanche Angel."

That was the second time he'd called her that. "What?"

"*Seattle Times*," he repeated, sounding impatient. "Your deal with *Out There* is just to write about the ski hut, right?" He didn't wait for her response, but she could hear the faint echo that signaled that he'd put the conversation on speakerphone when next he asked, "Now, what about the two other people you say are buried up there? Who were they?"

"Adam, take this off speaker, please."

She waited for the click that indicated he'd switched back before she continued, "A young man and woman, or really, just a girl. I don't know their names. They were in the same avalanche that Gina and I were caught in. Along with a wolverine."

"I want it, Sammie. I need this story. You've got to give me an exclusive for a TV special."

She could hear Adam speaking in a muffled voice to someone. He'd either covered the microphone or lowered the volume on his cell as he murmured, "Bellingham. Washington State. W-A, not M-A. Yes, I think there's an airport."

Was he coming up here? Adam and his crew would poke their noses—and their cameras—into everyone and everything she knew. Would that include Blake? Claude? Chase and Nicole? Maya?

Then he was back. "I can give you two thousand dollars."

"I don't know, Adam. We have to come to an agreement about what you can cover and who you can talk to. This is a sensitive subject, and the story is still evolving. Like you said, they're still digging out up there."

"I'll make it three. Three thousand dollars, for a couple of days work. Only hours, really. You can't turn that down."

He knew her too well. She hadn't managed to find any new contract work this month, and *Out There* had promised her only a few short assignments. Three thousand dollars could make a world of difference in her life, especially with all the replacements the house needed now. As soon as the thought streaked through her head, she felt like an avaricious money-grubber, eager to take advantage of a tragedy. She chewed her thumb as she considered.

Putting aside his attitude about tragic stories and his seeming callousness to survivors and his too-frequent omission of clarifying details, Adam's reporting had always been factual. Sam admired that. The same could not be said of many news stories these days.

If Adam didn't cover the story, the odds were that someone else would, and who knew how it would come out? The way the news was reported in the current political climate, the wolverine poachers might be portrayed as heroes saving the world from dangerous wildlife, and the avalanche victims deserving of their deaths for some obscure political reason Sam couldn't even imagine right now.

"Do we have a deal, Sammie?"

He'd bulldoze his way into the situation, no matter what she told him now. "We need to talk, Adam. And you have to promise to include the wolverine."

"Great! We'll be in Bellingham tomorrow." He ended the call.

Sam glared at her phone for a long moment, wondering what she'd just gotten herself into.

As she purchased a copy of the *Seattle Times* in the grocery store, Sam was grateful that nobody gave her a second look. In the hospital, she sat in Chase's room, listening to the beeps of the cardiac monitor and his quiet breathing.

"Chase, your sister Raven called me this morning," she told him. "The FBI told her that you're in the hospital here. She said to tell you that she loves you, but she can't come visit. She has COVID. A mild case, but she's in quarantine. And she doesn't know where your brother Wolf is right now. And your parents are somewhere in the Mediterranean on a cruise, believe it or not."

She hoped that news didn't make Chase feel as if his family had deserted him.

"I'm sorry I don't know more about your family," she told him. "And if you want me to call other people, you've never told me about them. You have so many parts of you that are private, Chase. I, on the other hand, am an open book. I've told you everything."

She hesitated there, knowing that wasn't true. She'd never told anyone about the day of her mother's death, about how she'd found her father standing over her mother, his gaze fixed on his wife's finally serene expression, his arms clutching a pillow to his chest. Sam had never asked him about that pillow in all these years. She never would.

She told him about Nicole doing well and Claude still comatose a few doors down, about her wrecked house and Maya's criminal friends. "I should have stayed at the ski area, Chase. If I hadn't gone with Gina to rescue Feisty, all of us might have left before the avalanche."

Even without anyone to tell her so, Sam knew she was babbling.

"Feisty's a wolverine, by the way. Gina's my friend who volunteers on a wolverine research project. I've gone with her a couple of times to set up cameras. But this time Feisty had been trapped."

She thought about describing how the poacher had been buried, how she'd been buried, but decided Chase he didn't need any more stories of snow and injury filling his thoughts. If he was actually listening.

"Wolverines aren't on the endangered species list, Chase. But they should be. We can't afford to lose a single one. And it's illegal to trap or kill one unless it's self-defense, and in this case, only Feisty would have the right to claim that."

There was no indication that he heard a word she said.

"And the worst part is that we didn't save Feisty." She stopped there, imagining the cage entombed in a concrete bunker of snow, only a few puffs of air left.

At this point in her soliloquy, it would have been nice to hear something like, "I'm sure you gave it your all, Summer." Even if that wasn't true.

Chase did not respond when Sam stroked his arm or

pushed his hair away from his forehead. His beard was growing quickly; he'd hate that. He often had a five o'clock shadow, and sometimes shaved twice a day.

Was he just heavily sedated, or was he well on his way to dying? She watched his chest rise and fall. No, not dying. At least not yet.

She scanned the newspaper article about the avalanches caused by the earthquake in the area around Mount Baker. The article also called the volcano by its native name, Koma Kulshan, and she wondered if using two names confused readers. Many small slides had been observed in areas surrounding the mountain, but as most of the terrain was wilderness and the popular trailheads were still inaccessible in the spring snow, the only known casualties had been near the Mt. Baker Ski Area.

The front-page photo was of the destroyed Raven Hut, with trauma-stricken bystanders huddled around the structure, a few in the act of pulling pieces of debris from the edges, and others embracing one another.

Then she spied a smaller section heading, An Avalanche Angel. That section of the article detailed how Summer Westin had crawled into the collapsed building and extricated the baby, and then how she'd alerted the equipment crews and ski patrol about three survivors inside.

Blake must have told someone her name. The article included a photo of one of the ski patrol guys handing Baby Emma off to her mother as Blake yanked Sam from the debris tunnel like a wad of wet washing. That was embarrassing.

Another photo depicted her waving from the top of the collapsed hut. Fortunately, neither photo was good enough quality to recognize her face. She had never been photogenic, but exhausted and injured, Sam was sure she'd been more bedraggled than usual that day.

Her new cell phone buzzed from her jacket pocket on the back of the visitor chair, and Sam snatched it up quickly to stifle the sound. She walked quickly to the window before answering, remembering warning signs about cell phones.

The voice on the phone identified himself as Whatcom County Sheriff's Deputy Ben Ortiz, then said, "I hear that yesterday you reported avalanche victims beyond the boundary of the Mt. Baker Ski Area?"

An unwelcome image of Purple Parka's frozen face rose in Sam's imagination, along with a crushing memory of being buried under the snow. Icy slush crowding her back, the metallic taste of adrenaline in her mouth—

"Miz Westin?"

She forced her thoughts back to the present. "Um, yeah," she said in a quiet voice. "Two victims, I'm pretty sure. A boy or young man, and a girl. And a wolverine."

Silence filled the airwaves for a beat, as the deputy no doubt tried to untangle those phrases. Then, "You're *pretty* sure there were two people?"

She wondered if the deputy thought she'd hallucinated the wolverine, and if so, he believed her whole story was in doubt. Straightening her posture, she jerked her thoughts back into line as well. "Let me rephrase. I'm certain there were two people. And the wolverine. But there may have been others we didn't see before the avalanche hit."

"We?"

Sam gave him the whole spiel, Gina and the wolverine trap, the earthquake, the avalanche, discovering the girl, not finding the boy or the wolverine. The tranquilized wolverine smothering in that cage.

"Hmm. It's odd that we haven't received any missing persons reports for two individuals like you're describing."

So maybe he did think she was making it all up. "I don't

know what to tell you."

After a pause, he added, "All the cars in the parking lots have not yet been dug out, though. It may be several more days before we locate them all."

"I know. My friends are missing two vehicles." Claude's BMW was under the snow somewhere, and so was Nicole's car. Gina's old Ford Escape had been found and would eventually be towed to a lot in Deming. Sam would have to get the keys from her friend, if Gina still had them, and rescue the SUV for her. She doubted that Gina would be in shape to drive for several months.

Her own RAV4 was out at Chase's cabin. Sam was glad to have Blake's old Outback to borrow until she could get him to drive her out there. Blake, although he was physically present right now, was mentally absent, wandering from task to task in automaton style, obviously in mourning.

"Can you give me the GPS coordinates of the burial site?" the deputy asked.

"Gina might have those for the camera, but I don't. She's in the hospital. I can show you the approximate location on a topo map."

"Just a minute." She heard indistinct conversation as he conferred with someone else, and then he was back. "Can you join us tomorrow to show us where the bodies are?"

Hadn't he just said that cars in the parking lot were still buried? "Is the road clear now?"

"Partially."

"I don't think I'm up to hiking for miles right now."

"I've been told you are ambulatory."

That was annoying. Who had he been talking to? Probably the hospital cop. She had walked up to him, after all, she reminded herself, so of course he'd know she could walk. "Yeah, I'm uh, ambulatory. I'm not in great shape, but—"

"No worries. We'll get a chopper ride as close as we can. I promise we won't make you dig." He gave her the meeting place and time in the morning. "We'll probably be out there for hours. I don't have to tell you to dress for the weather, do I?"

"I'll have on all my winter gear. You'll need extendable avalanche poles."

There was another brief silence on his end. "Ah, okay. I guess those two would be buried, right? I expect the forest service guys will probably bring everything we need. See you at the airport tomorrow."

After hanging up, she called Blake to give her a ride home, where she organized her gear, already dreading the next day. She didn't want to see that dead girl's face again, and she definitely didn't want to find a frozen wolverine. The boy/man; she wasn't looking forward to that, either, but at least maybe finding him would prove that he wasn't a figment of her imagination.

Although she hated to admit it to herself, she was relieved that she was needed up in the mountains rather than in that hospital chair by Chase's side.

32

As the helicopter lifted off from the strip at Bellingham International Airport the next morning, Sam fought the urge to fling herself out the door. The last time—the only time—she'd been on a helicopter had been in Utah when she and Chase had been in a desperate search to find a missing boy while gunshots rang out all around as government hunters searched for cougars to shoot. Helicopters had never promised happy rides for her.

She'd almost lost Chase on that trip, too. They'd both come close to drowning in a flooded slot canyon.

And then there was the time he'd been shot in Arizona by anti-immigrant vigilantes. And now, again, she felt close to losing her lover. He had to pull through. She didn't know what she'd do without him.

The pilot distributed two headsets to the deputy and the male ranger, leaving Sam and the female USFS ranger to suffer with the racket inside the bird. Across the aisle, the female ranger rolled her eyes in sisterhood at the slight.

Sam had to admit that the scenery was stunning from above, though. The day was sunny and the North Cascades were etched in stark relief against a cloudless blue sky. The mountains seemed to roll on forever to the north, ridge after ridge of wilderness, extending up past the border into British Columbia. Her heart always rejoiced at the sight of so much roadless, townless land dotted by crystal-clear lakes, thousands and thousands of acres reserved for wildlife and a few human explorers.

The closest the helicopter could land was on a reasonably flat area in the valley crossed by the Lake Ann trail. "Hover" was a more accurate term than "land"; the pilot explained that the snow was too soft for the weight of the helo, so he had to keep the blades rotating. Sam, Deputy Ortiz, and two USFS rangers, Selah and Wayne something-or-other, bailed out into a flurry of flying ice pellets. Under the bright sun, the snow had softened to six inches of slush on top of several feet of hard pack. Even with her borrowed snowshoes strapped on and poles in hand, Sam sank in up to her ankles, her boots vanishing beneath the muck, grunting in pain from her injuries.

Shielding their faces with gloved hands, all four of them kick-stepped their way out of range, and then the chopper lifted and abandoned them to a winter wonderland. Or wasteland. Or graveyard, depending on how one chose to think about it.

Sam snorted bits of wet snow out of her nose and pulled off her knitted hat to shake the ice pellets loose from it, then squinted at the bright sun. "I should have worn a ball cap like you guys. Or at least remembered my sunglasses."

Deputy Ortiz dug in his pack, and pulled out a black-and-white cap bearing the embroidered six-point star of the Whatcom County Sheriff's Office. "Here."

"That'll help, thanks." Taking it, she jammed it on top of her knit hat and pulled the bill down low over her eyes. Then she pointed to the southeast. "This way."

The slippery wet snow slowed their climb. She'd abandoned her sling, but her ribs and shoulder and injured leg were all singing a chorus of misery by the time they approached the disaster scene. The bandage on her calf felt tight and wet, and she feared she might have popped some stitches there, but she didn't bother to check.

Spring snow flurries had hit the area overnight several times since the avalanche, with clumps hanging heavily on the limbs of the evergreens. The area appeared serene now, the broken and fallen trees coated in white velvet.

Sam thought she spied the tree she'd clutched as she climbed out of her icy tomb, but she couldn't even be sure about that, because recent snow had obscured any hole she'd left behind. The wind and new flurries had also covered the trench she and Gina had dug out around the girl's corpse. Mother Nature was not into memorials.

She led the group out onto the hillside and spread her arms to encompass the clearing. "They're somewhere in here." After taking a dozen steps up the hill, she waved a gloved hand in an arc around her feet, indicating the more uneven snow in the center of the avalanche chute. "I think the girl is about here."

Ranger Selah shrugged off her pack and removed an extendible pole from it. After snapping it out to its full length, she then plunged it into the snow a few feet away. Deputy Ortiz set his pack down to emulate her.

Sam gazed up the slope. The line where the avalanche had broken loose was obvious, a horizontal scar in the ground cover, visible even beneath the new snow. Below the tree line, the wolverine trap was visible, canted now, its short, stacked logs twisted into a trapezoidal shape. She pointed. "The boy, or man—the poacher—pulled the wolverine he'd drugged out of the trap there, stuffed her into a carrier, and was carrying her across there when the earthquake and avalanche happened." Moving her hand in a flat line, she indicated the sideways movement of the poacher.

She faced downhill. "I have no idea where he ended up. Or the wolverine. Probably the snow carried them both down the slope quite a way." Her head was beginning to ache at the memory of the guy stuffing Feisty into that plastic coffin.

Wayne extracted his avalanche pole, climbed up a few yards away from the broken trap, and began to jab the long pole into the snow. Positioning himself between Wayne and Selah, Deputy Ortiz copied their motions.

The simple act of shrugging out of her pack hurt her ribs and shoulder, but Sam pulled out her own pole and snapped the sections out to the full length.

Ortiz paused in his actions to frown at her. His black moustache glittered with snow crystals, giving him a somewhat comical appearance. "You're recuperating," he told Sam. "Take it easy. We'll do the rest."

"I can do this much." Using her right hand, she stabbed her avalanche pole into the snow, about where she expected the girl's corpse to be. After a brief stutter as it transitioned through wet snow to hard pack, the pole glided in smoothly. No impact.

She pulled it out, stepped sideways a foot, jammed it in again. As she extracted the pole, she glanced up the slope, trying to envision the scene again as it had been that day. A glint at the edge of the trees above caught her eye. Gina's wildlife camera lay on its side, caught in a bare-twigged shrub about six inches above the snow.

Sam climbed up to it, shook it free of the brush it rested in, peered at it. The lens was dirty and had a couple of scratches, but otherwise, the camera seemed okay. Without power, though. The nylon loop that had attached it to a bough was still intact, and judging by the broken branches littering the ground, the camera had been dislodged from a snapped limb. The battery was dead. The cord that had snaked up to a small solar panel in the treetop had been jerked out of the camera. Peering up, Sam couldn't tell if the panel was still up there or not. Unlikely, she decided, given the shaking of the earthquake. She zipped the camera into her pack so it wouldn't be lost or stolen. She'd tell Gina; maybe there'd be footage of the poachers recorded inside.

It took nearly twenty exhausting minutes of thrusting poles into the snowy slope before Selah made a strike. Leaving their avalanche poles in place, the two men joined Selah and Sam, uncovering the girl's corpse with small folding shovels they'd packed in. All four of them were sweating by the time the purple parka came into view.

Deputy Ortiz halted the excavation long enough to take photos of the scene, measure the snow depth to the corpse, and record the precise GPS coordinates, using a Garmin navigational device. Then the rangers hauled the stiff body out of the snowy grave and laid it on a black vinyl body bag. The time had long ago passed for rigor mortis; the girl's body had to be frozen clear through by now.

The body was slender, dressed in black skinny jeans and a blue turtleneck under the purple parka. Selah went through the girl's parka pockets, pulling out a Chapstick, a hair barrette, and a wad of tissues, and finally summarizing, "No ID."

The female ranger sat back on her heels. "Well, damn." She placed the items she'd extracted in the outstretched palm of Deputy Ortiz, then regarded the ice-shrouded corpse sadly. "What is she doing up here? Why isn't anyone missing her?"

After a glimpse at the deputy, Selah zipped the body bag closed. They began the probing process again.

After another half hour, Wayne jabbed his pole repeatedly in the same spot, shouting, "I think I got something." They all moved to his position. Leaving the pole upright in the snow for a marker, the two rangers shoveled, digging a hole around it. They uncovered a collapsed blue plastic carrier.

The carrier had been torn nearly in half, the plastic sides crushed and broken and its wire grill twisted out of shape. A bloodied tuft of hair was caught in a crack, clearly torn away from an animal. More blood, now more brown than red, darkened the snow around the carrier.

"That's what the guy stuffed Feisty in," Sam told them. Poor tortured creature. She hoped that the wolverine had stayed unconscious after being drugged, that the wolverine's last moments were not filled with terror.

Ortiz raised his eyebrows. "Feisty?"

"The wolverine. Her official name is F3, for the third female in the North Cascades."

Wayne stated the obvious. "Looks like the carrier was crushed. The wolverine's body was probably ejected and slid farther under the snow." He straightened. "If the man you saw was carrying this, he's probably not too far away." Stepping sideways, he forced his avalanche pole into the snow again.

Selah took up her pole and performed the same actions. Ortiz joined them, moving out in a slow circle from the location of the carrier.

Picking up her own pole and stepping higher up the slope, Sam chewed on her lower lip, trying to eject the scenario of a trapped, drugged, buried, crushed wolverine from her brain.

A loud whump sounded above her. Every muscle in her body froze. Her heart pounding, Sam's gaze raced back and forth over the trees and ridge above her, scanning the surface of the snow as far as she could see. The branches of one tall Douglas fir swayed against the sky.

"Are you okay?" Wayne shouted.

Sam realized she was trembling, and her lips were open, about to shout a warning before a deadly wave of snow rushed down the slope. She closed her mouth, licked her lips, sent a message to her heart to stop its galloping.

Another avalanche was not imminent. The shimmying tree had just dumped a load of heavy wet snow from its topmost branches. Normal in this warming weather.

Taking a steadying breath, she twisted to give her three companions a thumbs-up. "I'm fine." *Just a little PTSD.* Not wanting to turn her back to the ridge above, she watched until the tree limbs stilled, making sure the snow stayed in place on the ground.

She stepped closer to the trees. Were those paw prints around the crater caused by the snow dump? Wolverine prints? Wouldn't it be wonderful if she found evidence that Feisty's kits had survived? She kept hearing the cries of hidden, starving babies beneath her feet, but that was only her imagination. She studied the marks. The prints were not clear. They had been sheltered from recent snow by the tree limbs above, but they'd melted and frozen several times over the last few days. Large clumps of snow falling from the limbs above had obliterated most of the impressions.

It was impossible to tell when the tracks been made. Maybe before the avalanche, perhaps when Feisty was scouting out the trap, which had no doubt been baited with something irresistible to a wolverine nose. Bait that would lure Feisty to her eventual death.

Was that a boot print? The round impression could be the heel of a shoe. And farther on, she found several more. Whose boot prints, and when had they been made? More hunters, maybe looking for other wolverines?

Stepping back down to the others, she stabbed her pole into the snow with ferocity. Damn that girl, and damn the guy she was with. What did it matter if they were young? If they hadn't been trapping Feisty, they wouldn't be human popsicles right now. Feisty wouldn't be dead. Wolverine kits wouldn't have starved and frozen to death alone in the snow. Gina wouldn't be in the hospital. Her own shoulder and ribs wouldn't be screaming for painkillers right now; her forehead and cheeks wouldn't look like she'd used a cheese shredder to give herself a facial.

She thrust her pole in again, leaning on it, using her weight to pierce the layers. If it hadn't been for this damn poacher, she would have left with Chase and Nicole when the aerobatic competition was over. Chase wouldn't be fighting for his life in the hospital. Claude and Blake might have left before the avalanche, too. *Damn it!*

Her pole abruptly stopped two feet down, sending a jolt that radiated up her right arm and echoed all the way across her neck into her injured left shoulder. She had to close her eyes and grit her teeth for a moment before she could shout. "I got a hit."

They first uncovered what appeared to be a black frozen tree branch, but after more digging, it was clear that a hand was attached. Following the arm, they dug out the corpse. His head was face down in the snow, his neck twisted unnaturally. Ortiz brushed off the frozen face.

A few yards away, a small evergreen abruptly sprang upright from the snow that had bent it over. Sam startled at the sudden snap of motion.

"Okay?" Ortiz asked.

"Yeah." She forced a chuckle. "Just surprised me. Springtime in the mountains." Would she be this jumpy on steep slopes from now on?

A helicopter buzzed overhead. They all raised their faces to the sky. The machine circled above them, the reverberation of its blades shaking the tree limbs on the slope above, causing them to dump their loads of wet snow. The rapid clomping sounds sped Sam's heart rate into a trot again.

"Why'd the pilot come back so early?" Selah asked Ortiz.

"That's not ours." Ortiz frowned, switching his gaze from one face to the next. "Did any of you tell the media we'd be out here?"

They all denied it.

Sam had a bad feeling about who might be in that helicopter. Adam Steele was a sleuth, after all. He'd be questioning where she'd gone instead of meeting him when he arrived today in Bellingham.

Frowning skyward, Deputy Ortiz made a slashing gesture across his throat and then angrily gestured to the horizon. After a few more seconds of circling, the helicopter thundered away, moving north toward the ski area.

The team of four focused again on the body they'd uncovered. She'd been wrong that the young man had a beard. Beneath his chin was a wadded black neck gaiter. Some people called them buffs. He was clean-shaven, and his face was very young. One diamond stud gleamed from his right ear. His eyes were partially open, and his mouth was filled with snow. One boot was missing. The black down jacket and the flannel shirt underneath were torn off his shoulder. His jeans were intact, held on by a web belt with a leather sheath at his side. A large hunting knife with a bright-orange handle was secured in the sheath by a leather strap, still snapped into place.

Sam stared at the knife. Why did he need a weapon like that? Had he tranquilized the wolverine, or had he slit Feisty's throat? Was the blood they'd found around the crate from a fatal knife wound?

The deputy patted down the corpse. "No wallet," he reported. "But the back pocket of his jeans is torn, so maybe it got ripped out."

"Or maybe they left their IDs in the car, and we'll find it buried somewhere down below," Wayne murmured, leaning on the handle of his shovel. "Poor kids."

Sam clenched her fists. "I hate them both."

The other three stopped to stare at her.

She felt the blood drain from her face. Yeesh, had she said

that out loud? "Well, I don't mean that I actually *hate* them," she backpedaled. "I don't know either one of them. But they're stupid kids," Sam explained. "Selfish, mean kids."

The deputy raised an eyebrow.

"The boy was trapping a wolverine," she told them. "He had no reason to do that. He killed himself, that girl, and an innocent animal."

Selah shrugged. "True."

Wayne jammed his hands in his pockets and made no comment.

Sam had no idea what either ranger felt about the whole incident. The stated mission of the US Forest Service was a mishmash of everything from facilitating hunting and logging to wildlife conservation. Its rangers were dedicated to following all the regulations, and wolverines were not a protected species. And, of course, she reminded herself, the earthquake caused the avalanche, and the avalanche caused the death of both humans and wolverine.

Ortiz busied himself taking photos and then told the group, "We got what we came for. Let's pack it up, gang."

He jammed the remains of the plastic carrier into his pack, while the rangers threaded climbing ropes through the handles on the sides of the body bag and then attached the ropes to the hip belts of their backpacks. If it seemed slightly disrespectful to drag the corpses down the mountain, it was more efficient and practical than carrying them.

By the time they slip-slid down the mountain to reach the plateau again, Sam was totally drained. Her entire body ached, thrumming so badly she couldn't identify any pain as coming from any specific place. Her face burned like it had been scoured with sandpaper, likely the sting of salty sweat that she'd worked up during the corpse-hunting process. For the first time in her life, she was grateful to hear the *whop-whop* of an approaching helicopter.

As he had earlier, the pilot hovered his craft a couple of feet off the ground instead of actually touching down. The rangers tossed the body bags into the helicopter bay and then stepped onto the skid and jumped in. Deputy Ortiz stood in back of Sam as she climbed in. A sudden pain shot through her ribs, making her pause as a surging black cloud dimmed her vision.

"Let's go," Ortiz ordered.

She felt the deputy's hands against her thighs and then Ranger Wayne grabbed the front of her parka and hauled her inside like a sack of potatoes. She landed on one of the body bags. That felt macabre, but she was too tired to move. Deputy Ortiz climbed in, slammed the door behind him, and they lifted off.

The men donned headsets again, but for the second time, nobody offered her or Selah one. She managed to shift away from the cold body bag, leaned back against the wall, and closed her eyes against the thunder of the rotors overhead.

She could barely believe that she slept all the way back to the Bellingham airport, waking only when the helicopter rotors changed to a whine as they slowed to a stop.

Deputy Ortiz leaned over her. "Welcome back."

Sam sat up, embarrassed, and wiped a thread of drool from her cheek with the back of her hand. She slid out of the helicopter, her shoulder and ribs still aching, and then accepted her pack, snowshoes, and hiking poles as the rangers handed them out to her.

"Thanks for taking us up there," Selah told her.

Ortiz nodded. "We would never have found that location without your assistance."

Sam surveyed the area around the landing pad, half expecting to see Adam Steele lying in wait for her. Happily, he was nowhere in sight. "Are you going to find the parents now?"

she asked Ortiz.

He nodded toward the two body bags that still lay inside the helicopter bay. "We've got no ID to start with, but we'll do our best. I don't remember any teenagers on the missing list, but there are several dozen college-age kids. It could take a while."

There had been twenty-somethings entered in the aerobatic competition, but it hadn't seemed like that many. "Several dozen?"

Ortiz ran his fingers through his hair. "They probably aren't all actually missing. It's spring break all over the country, after all. Last year, my own daughter made that last for two weeks. She still hasn't told me where she was or who she was with."

He sighed at the memory, then glanced at the body bags. "Maybe these two are older than they appear. I've got some arrangements to make and paperwork to do, and then I'll see what I can find out." His expression was grim as he gestured to the driver of a sheriff's department van to drive closer.

"When you locate the parents, can I come for the notifications?" She didn't really want to be there when the parents were told about their dead children, but she had to know why two teenagers might want a wolverine.

Ortiz's wrinkled brow showed his confusion about her request.

"I could tell the parents about finding them," she said.

"Not now." The deputy shook his head. "We have to ID them first. But even after we do, it's not a good idea for you to come. I need to find out where the parents thought their kids were, and why these two haven't been reported missing."

"Can you ask why they wanted a wolverine?" she queried.

"I'll give the families your name and number if they want to know anything about the circumstances, as long as you promise to inform me if they contact you."

"Of course. And you'll let me know what you find out,

right?"

She wasn't surprised when his expression let her know that he probably wouldn't do that. Chase rarely told her anything about any case he was working on. That was law enforcement for you.

Oh God, Chase. She needed to get to him.

"We appreciate your help," Ortiz said. "Now go home and rest."

33

As soon as she stepped into the small airport terminal, Adam ambushed her. He was wearing designer jeans and a soft leather jacket that probably cost more than she'd made all last year. "Sammie! You're darn lucky we got some good footage of your guys at the site. Why didn't you tell me?"

She was too tired for this. "I said we needed to talk first, Adam."

"That's why I'm here." He grinned, as handsome as ever. Perfect teeth, primed for the camera. Blond hair, styled in an expensive cut, and startling blue eyes. Not really her type.

She was more attracted to the dark looks—Hispanic, Native American. To Chase. Just thinking of her lover still lying in the hospital caused a sympathetic twinge in her side. Or maybe that was just her sore ribs after the strenuous day in the mountains. She yawned, painfully stretching the scratched skin on her face.

"Nice hat," Adam commented. "Joining the force?"

She reached up to realize she hadn't given back the deputy's ball cap. "Why not?"

Whisking it off, she stowed it and her knit hat in her pack, then ran her fingers through her sweat-dampened hair. Why hadn't she even packed a comb today?

"Yep, major hat hair," Adam observed. He slashed a hand through the air. "But never mind that; we need to make a plan.

We can get Makeup to fix your face if you're worried about that."

She met his gaze with a frown.

"No?" He fingered his chin, considering, then nodded and aimed a manicured index finger in her direction. "Actually, you're right. You should look like you clawed your way out of an avalanche. More authentic. We got some decent aerial shots today, but tomorrow we'll get up close and personal with the wreckage, okay?"

"No." The last thing she wanted was to get "up close and personal" with the collapsed hut again.

Adam leaned close. "Three thousand," he said in a low voice.

Sam winced. She could definitely use that money to restore her house and her computer, but this was making her feel like a low-level drug dealer. "Let's talk this evening. Right now, I need to go to the hospital."

A flicker of concern flashed over his face. "Did you get injured today?"

She scowled at him.

"I mean, more injured?"

She pulled a tube of lip balm from her pants pocket and snapped the cap off. After she'd applied the moisturizer to her lips, she told him, "I need to visit some of the avalanche victims."

The concern on Adam's face was replaced by interest. He looped a hand around her arm. "I'll take you there. I should interview some of them, too."

She should have said she was visiting a COVID patient. "You can't. They're in the ICU. The staff won't let you in."

He studied her for a moment. "So, FBI man? Lover Boy was on the mountain with you?"

"Leave it, Adam." She turned away, sounding like a dog owner reprimanding her poodle. "Lyft is waiting for me."

His expression darkened. "Okay then. I'll pick you up at seven for dinner and that talk. You have to eat."

She sighed. "Six thirty. My address is—"

He laughed. "I know where you live." He walked her outside the terminal and then pulled open the door of a waiting car that matched the description on her phone.

The Lyft driver was a young woman. "Wow!" she said after Sam slid into the car and Adam had closed the door. "I know him from somewhere, don't I?"

"Adam Steele. Roving reporter. You've probably seen him quite a few times on television. Internet, too."

"You're with him? Lucky you!"

Leaning back in her seat, Sam touched her fingers to her aching forehead, then realized that rubbing it would only hurt more. "Please take me to the hospital. I'm not with him."

The young woman smiled at her from the rearview mirror. "Then can I have him?"

"You have no idea what you're asking." Dealing with Adam Steele was like lighting a sparkler on July Fourth. All bright flashes and sizzling fun for a brief time, then reduced to ashes and gone.

She had to live in this town. She hoped Adam wouldn't do anything to alienate the locals or damage her future while he was here. She didn't want to be recognized as an avalanche angel or anyone other than Summer "Sam" Westin. Actually, she'd prefer not to be recognized by anyone except her friends, period.

At the hospital, Chase remained inert in his bed. Sam caressed his hand and arm as she told him about excavating the two frozen corpses with the deputy and rangers. Not the type of conversation you'd want to have with a regular civilian, but Chase would normally be interested. But with zero response from him, she soon found it depressing as well as boring to sit with an unconscious man.

Admitting that to herself, she then added guilt to the disturbing turmoil of her emotions. She loved Chase, so she shouldn't be feeling depressed or bored at all, should she? Was there something wrong with her? The lyrics of "Stand by Your Man" kept ringing through her head, as if Tammy Wynette were challenging her loyalty. "Sit By Your Man" just didn't have the same *umph* to it. After half an hour, she was so exasperated with herself that she caught a Lyft back home and took a shower and a nap.

In the now-vacant living area, Blake measured spaces and sketched notes and surfed the local websites to determine which pieces of the furniture advertised for sale on Craigslist might work there. Sam was relieved that he had taken the initiative to deal with the house problems. She certainly didn't have the energy right now.

At the restaurant that evening, Adam continued his cheerful monologue, blithely assuming that Sam would be interested in everything he had done recently.

"The ski patrol told me they have some camera footage of the inside of the collapsed ski hut." Adam paused in the recital of his day to take a swig of Merlot. "It's being delivered to my hotel as we speak."

Sam considered. "I guess they could have some. I started off wearing a helmet with a GoPro camera on top."

"Fantastic." Adam flashed his trademark smile. "Handheld—or in this case, head-held—video is always more authentic. So we have video of the whole thing."

"Hardly." She took a bite of her salmon and chewed, reliving her crawl through the building. "There was a cave-in, I nearly got crushed, and I had to leave the helmet and camera behind."

Adam speared a forkful of his steak. "Damn it!"

"Thanks for your concern." She took a swig of sauvignon blanc to wash the memory of wallboard dust and insulation fibers from her throat.

He raised a shoulder. "I guess we'll have to fake it, then. Maybe use a crawler robot, see how the camera can get around inside that building. The place looked pretty well pancaked, though."

"Yeah, it was fun slithering between pieces of furniture and parts of the roof."

He paused with his fork in mid-air, his expression curious. "Was it?"

She jerked her chin up. "Well, hell no, Adam! It was terrifying. Not to mention painful. I told you I'd just climbed out of my own snow tomb and hiked for miles to get there."

"Good." He focused on his food again. "You worried me there for a minute, saying it was fun. Drama's always better. Survival stories are always hits with the public."

"Not everyone survived, Adam. What I wouldn't give to live in your world, where every tragedy is just another story." Her thoughts turned to the two corpses she'd come across in the collapsed hut. The two buried teens on the mountain slope. The wolverine. Involuntarily, she shivered.

"People died," she reminded Adam. "Others, like Chase, are fighting for their lives."

His expression solemn for a change, he chewed for a minute before answering. "I know. We'll do little vignettes for each of the dead. I will do a few interviews with the injured. Families and friends always appreciate those things, and it shows that we care." After taking another sip of wine, he asked, "Any word on identifying those two kids you were digging out this morning?"

Had that been *this* morning? No wonder she could barely hold a fork. "The deputy said they had no IDs, and so far, they don't seem to match the owners of any cars they've dug out. But they have a long list of missing people, and they still have a long way to go to uncover everything. And of course, those kids could have been driving a borrowed car."

"Yeah," Adam agreed regretfully. "This may take longer than I expected."

"Sorry to disappoint you with such a problematic avalanche and recovery." She signaled the server for a second glass of wine.

"No, that's okay." He reached for her hand, patted it. "There's a lot we can do already. I got some great aerial film today—your guys in the snow and the body bags and all. And I'll set up an interview with one of the major stations."

"Interview?" She wrapped her fingers around the new glass of wine that the server placed in front of her.

"Everyone wants to hear from the Avalanche Angel."

She rolled her eyes. "Then you'd better find that poor woman. In the meantime, I'll put together some facts and figures on wolverines and other threatened wildlife."

The blank expression on Adam's face told her he'd forgotten his promise to include the wolverine. Always light on his feet, he quickly recovered, though. "Sounds good."

From the coat folded beside her on the padded bench, her cell phone dinged. She extracted it from a pocket. The text was from Chase's nurse at the hospital. Mr. Perez's vitals much improved. We are reducing his sedation. He seems likely to wake up within 24 hours.

"Yes!" Sam clenched a fist in celebration.

"Let me guess." Adam picked up his wine glass. "FBI Guy."

"A text from one of his nurses. Chase is better."

Their server, a pretty young woman with long dark hair swept back into a neat bun, hovered at the side of the table. "Dessert? Coffee?"

Sam declined both. What she wanted right now was ibuprofen and a bed and a purring cat. With luck, she'd wake up looking more presentable for Chase tomorrow.

"Guess not," Adam told the server.

When the server returned with the bill, Adam signed it with a flourish, and as soon as he'd lifted the pen, she slid a blank sheet of the restaurant's stationery onto the tablecloth. "Could I have your signature on this, too, Mr. Steele?"

He gave her his best charming smile. "Of course."

"Are you working on a story here?" she asked. "I'm a journalism major myself, at Western Washington U."

"I'm staying at the Bellwether." He named the priciest waterfront hotel in Bellingham. "I'll be here for a few days, doing a special report on the avalanches up near Baker." After signing, he handed her the paper and pen, still grinning. "Spread the word."

34

Sam spent the next morning battling phone calls from Adam, her insurance company, and the editor at *Out There*. Hannah had arrived the evening before on the Amtrak train from Seattle, and it seemed like Sam's phone dinged every few seconds with endless photos from Blake, who was now out thrift-store shopping with his daughter for items to replace their possessions that had been trashed during the rampage.

Sam's RAV4 was still out at Chase's house, so she was forced to call Lyft again for a ride to the hospital.

She couldn't wait to peer into Chase's brown eyes again. Peat-bog brown, tea-brown eyes, she called them, not hazel but a clear brown, not the dense chocolate of most brown eyes. On this afternoon visit, she carried a potted orchid. The frilled flowers were pale yellow with vivid purple dots. In Chase's normal life, the plant would probably die of thirst when he was on the road doing some top-secret FBI investigation, but his current condition would give him some time to enjoy the blossoms. If he recovered quickly, that would be even better, and she'd gladly take the orchid back to her house. Her pocket held a bar of Chase's favorite dark bittersweet chocolate. She couldn't wait to share it with him.

As she rounded the doorway to his room, she nearly collided with Dr. Ishimoto, who stood with his back to her, conversing with a nurse who was checking Chase's IV. Sam was disappointed to see that Chase's eyes were still closed. Above the oxygen cannula wrapped around his face, his cheeks were flushed. Apparently, the chocolate sharing would have to wait until he woke up.

"Ah," Dr. Ishimoto murmured in a quiet voice. "We were just about to call you."

An alarm bell clanged in Sam's head. She tried to head off the doctor. "Last night, I heard Chase was better. The nurse told me he might be awake today."

"I'm afraid Mr. Perez has developed an infection."

She was afraid to ask, but she did, anyway. "Is it bad?"

The doctor nodded. After glancing at her frightened face, he added, "It's not COVID. No problems breathing, which is a positive thing. But the lacerations to his liver and intestines and spleen released toxins into his abdomen. We hoped that we'd handled that risk with antibiotics."

She waited, her jaw tight, braced for bad news, her eyes focused on the orchid in her hands.

"We'll try different medications, but Mr. Perez is currently a very sick man."

Sam wanted to grab the doctor by the arms and shake him. She glanced toward the nurse. "But you said he was fine yesterday."

The woman crossed her arms over her chest. "I said he was improving."

Dr. Ishimoto regarded Chase's still form in the bed, his expression somber. "Yes, he seemed better yesterday. Good thing we didn't move him from intensive care. The nurses will monitor him constantly, and within twelve hours at the most, we'll know if these new antibiotics are working."

Twelve hours. An eternity. A chill made the hairs on the back of her neck stand up. "And if they're not?"

"Then we'll switch to another type." Ishimoto gently touched her forearm with an index finger. "We'll take the best possible care of him. I promise."

Sam felt like she might shatter into a hundred pieces at any moment. She knew the hospital staff at St. Joe's, like hospital personnel everywhere these days, were overworked and stressed out. She questioned if it was even possible for them to take the "best possible care" of any patient right now. "Thanks," she said, for lack of anything more intelligent. "Do you know when he'll wake up?"

"He's pretty heavily sedated at the moment. So most likely, that won't happen until tomorrow at the earliest."

"After he does wake up, what's the prognosis?"

"Reevaluation of his situation."

She must have looked dissatisfied with that answer, because the doctor sighed and added, "I'm not going to sugarcoat the truth here. Internal injuries are difficult to assess. Mr. Perez could end up gravely disabled, or he could eventually regain his full health. We won't know until he's fully conscious and able to cooperate with our tests."

That sounded grim. Sam bit her lip.

"Try to stay positive. The nurses will keep you posted on his condition." After a quick glance at his watch, the doctor walked out of the room.

Sam collapsed into the visitor chair, clutching the orchid in her lap. "Oh, Chase," she sighed, staring at her lover's horizontal form through a blur of tears.

The nurse tapped a few keystrokes into a tablet she carried, and then focused pointedly on Sam. "You can put that plant on his bedside table."

Sam placed the orchid there, pushing it close to the wall where it wouldn't be accidentally knocked off. It seemed too small and delicate to survive in this sterile environment.

The nurse straightened the sheet over Chase's chest. It seemed an intimate movement, but then, so many nursing procedures seemed overly intimate to Sam. Taking temperatures, dealing with IVs and catheters. She couldn't imagine performing any of them herself.

"I'll only stay a few moments," Sam promised from her chair, struggling to keep her voice from breaking.

"That would be good." Picking up her tablet and a tray laden with a syringe and antiseptic wipes, the nurse walked around the bed toward the door. "Chase is a strong man, but he needs rest right now."

Sam stared at her lover, her emotions tangled into a painful knot. How much more rest could Chase get than being unconscious?

Before leaving, the nurse softened her tone. "I'm sorry he's had a setback."

Sam wanted to close the door after the nurse had gone, but she guessed that might set off some sort of alarm bells. Leaning forward, she placed her hand over Chase's and gently stroked the skin of his wrist. "Chase, I'm here." She wet her lips, trying to think of anything that might be comforting. "I'm so sorry you're still sick, but I know you're going to get better fast."

Please God, make it true.

He'd always had a fast-growing beard, and now black whiskers darkened his lower chin and neck. He was religious about shaving each day, and she'd never seen him with more than a two-day growth of beard. If he were conscious, the first thing he'd ask for would be a razor. She ran a gentle finger along his jawline to feel the uncommon rasp of his skin there.

"Chase, you need to shave soon, but I sort of like this look, too. You're rocking it. You know that Nicole is going to be fine, and she'll be so angry if you're not. Are you hearing me?" No response. "Hey, you survived an avalanche and a building collapse, for heaven's sake. You have survived being shot."

Sam suddenly realized that she didn't know if Chase had been shot more than once in his FBI career. She paused for a moment, wondering what other life-threatening experiences Chase might have endured before they'd met. There were still so many things she needed to learn about this man she loved. Would there be time? "So, as you've often said yourself, you can't die now. That would be embarrassing, wouldn't it?"

There was no reaction from the body in the bed. No movement, not even a sigh or an eyebrow twitch. A tear ran down her cheek and dropped onto the bedsheet. She jiggled his arm. "Chase, fight this. We've got so many more adventures to have together. I need you."

Did his lips move? Maybe. Or maybe that was just her imagination. She stood up. Leaning over him, she slid down her mask and gently pressed her lips to his forehead. His skin was hot. She straightened, blinking away tears. "I'm going to leave now, but I'll be back tomorrow, and you'd better be on your way to recovery then. I love you, Chase."

At noon, the Seattle news featured a short report by freelance reporter Adam Steele about the avalanches near Mount Baker, mentioning the nine dead at the main avalanche area, with aerial footage of crews working to find more victims and dig out buried cars. Then the video switched to show Sam, Ortiz, and the rangers above the ski area as they stood over the young man's corpse, one black body bag zipped shut and off to the side; another one open and awaiting contents.

"If you have any information that might help to identify these two young people," Adam said earnestly to the camera, "Please contact the Whatcom County Sheriff's Department."

Sam could tell that last bit had been filmed at the Bellingham airport, the wind a whistling background in the microphone clamped onto Adam's jacket collar as he stood in front of a helicopter. Behind him, Mount Baker poked its triangular head up in the distance, beyond the Chuckanut Mountains.

After a respectful beat, Adam added, "More coverage of this disaster will follow as news develops in the coming days. This is reporter Adam Steele, coming to you from the rugged North Cascades."

Following the news, she received a text message. Did you see me on the midday news? We need to schedule the filming of your crawl-through, and then I will do a face-to-face interview with the Avalanche Angel. Getting bids in on both; working out details. Call you tomorrow.

Crawl-through? Avalanche Angel? Bids? She'd been thinking Zoom or maybe the phone; he hadn't said anything about a face-to-face. *Adam Steele strikes again,* Sam thought grimly. And he didn't even mention the wolverine.

35

In the afternoon, Blake drove her to Chase's cabin. During the half-hour drive, they were both quiet. Blake had told her about Claude's wife, and beyond the sympathy she'd originally expressed in the form of multiple swear words, she couldn't think of anything to add. She knew her housemate had been hoping for a future with Claude. She had no idea how to comfort him.

When she checked in with the sheriff's office, she discovered that nobody had called with any clues to the identities of the two wolverine kidnappers. How could nobody have noticed them missing? Or maybe their families didn't watch the TV news? She had to admit that she rarely did. Bellingham didn't have its own station, so the reports were mostly about Seattle or the endless COVID stats or the ongoing political battles in the national news. She didn't need any more depressing issues taking up space in her brain.

She couldn't stop fretting about her own future. Would Chase recover? She couldn't face the prospect of his death. No, he couldn't die. He wouldn't die. But how long would it take for him to get back to normal? Would he ever again be the man she'd fallen in love with? Could she still love him if he wasn't the same strong, virile, sharp-witted man?

In no way could she picture Chase as an invalid. And in no

way could she picture herself taking care of an invalid. She still had nightmares from growing up during her mother's decline from ALS. Every year, as she grew taller and older, her mother shrank, until Susan Westin finally died when Summer was nine.

Her thoughts naturally shifted to her father, Reverend Mark Westin, and how devoted he'd been to her mother after the poor woman had been diagnosed, how tenderly he'd cared for his wife during nearly a decade of Sam's young life. Now, from the wiser viewpoint of more than twenty years after her mother's death, Sam realized that her perception of her parents' relationship was derived only from her experience as their young daughter. The external actions did not necessarily reflect the internal reality of the participants. Who knows what struggles her poor father had gone through but never shared with his wild little girl? As a minister, he was accustomed to listening to the tribulations of members of his congregation. But who did *he* have to confide in? He'd never admit to resentments, to feeling oppressed or burdened, at least not to her. Who had counseled him?

Maybe his best friend, Martin Heath, another minister. She hoped her father had been able to talk to Martin, had his support through the years. And maybe Zola, the current Mrs. Westin. She'd been part of the community as long as Sam could remember.

Her housemate drove between tall firs into the gravel driveway of Chase's cabin. Three mule deer watched from the other side of the clearing as he parked near the house. The does were fat, probably close to giving birth. Would Chase be here to see the new fawns? Sam, lost in her thoughts, blurted, "I don't think I could do it, Blake."

Thankfully, he didn't need to ask what she was referring to. Blake said simply, "Let's hope it doesn't come to that." After putting the gearshift in park, he reached over, squeezed her shoulder, and then changed the subject. "Do you think Zeke talks to himself all day long?"

"Probably. I now understand why Gina spends so much time outdoors with wildlife."

"I hope she gets better soon and can take him back."

"Amen to that." She slid out of Blake's car.

Her old RAV4 was coated with sticky, olive-green pollen from the surrounding cedar trees. To her relief, the engine started as soon as she twisted the key in the ignition. She left it running for a minute to talk to Blake.

"Follow me home?" he asked through the open window.

"I'm going to stay for a little bit," she told him. "Make sure everything's okay out here."

"Need help? Those deer might be ferocious. Are you sure it's safe? Want me to defend you against the raccoons?"

"No, thanks. We got rid of them." After a brief hesitation, she told him, "I need to be alone for a while."

Blake nodded, his eyes sad. "I get it. I need to go back to let the workmen in, anyway." The front door-frame, utility window, and new deadbolts were all on the schedule for the afternoon. "See you later." He backed out of the driveway.

After clearing the bits of bark and needles and old leaves from her windshield, she turned off the engine, stepped over the broken porch step that needed to be replaced, and used her key to go into Chase's cabin. From the clawed handprints on the front porch and the muddy paw smudges on the front window, she knew the raccoons had been back. Chase had been locked in a perpetual struggle with the masked bandits ever since he purchased the cabin. The raccoons had happily lived there in the attic, probably for generations, and even after more than a year, they still regarded it as unfair that they'd been barricaded out with metal flashing under the eaves. Sam had no doubt they were working on finding a new way in.

The interior of the cabin had the stale air of having been abandoned. The kitchen and living area were spotless, in Chase's typical sparse, tidy style. The small autumn-colored quilt laying across the couch was the only element not neatly tucked or folded, and that was because it was hers. She'd left it like that.

Upstairs, in the small bedroom, she stretched across the queen bed on the comforter she'd given Chase, one of the several handmade bed coverings her grandmother had quilted. Burying her face in the pillow he normally used, she inhaled. If this were a romance novel, she'd smell her lover's unique manly scent. In this reality, she could only detect, at best, a whiff of laundry detergent, and she wasn't even sure of that. Both she and Chase always used unscented products.

Sitting up again, she picked up her cell phone and called her father. He'd likely be in his home office at this time in the afternoon.

"Summer!" He sounded cheerful, as usual. "How are things going today?"

"Not so good. One of the things I didn't tell you yesterday was about Maya. You remember I've told you about Maya?"

"Of course. Your young protégé."

"Don't call her that."

"Why not? You've mentored her for years."

"That makes it all my fault."

Paper rustled in the background, and then he said, "Tell me."

She explained how Maya had gotten mixed up with bad company, had given up on her job and education and seemingly, had given up on life in general. She concluded with the tale of Maya's friends trashing her house and shooting her cat.

"Good gracious! Sounds like Maya is so depressed that

she's a danger to everyone, including herself. Are you helping her with that?"

Was he kidding? "She shot Simon, Dad! Well, *she* didn't, but—" Sam cut off her tirade before it could gain too much momentum. "I told her she had to leave."

After a brief but weighty silence, her father said, "I hope Maya finds the help she needs. Now, how is Chase today?"

"He's very sick with an infection. If he's not going to completely recover, Dad, I don't know what I'll do. I don't know how you took care of Mom all those years. I'm sorry that I never thought about how difficult that must have been." She stared at the ceiling.

"You were a child, Summer. You weren't supposed to think about things like that."

A spiderweb was growing in the corner. She watched as the spider added a new strand.

"Do you still love Chase?" her father asked.

"Yes." A gnat was struggling, snared in a dangling thread of the spider's web.

"Then you'll do whatever you need to. That's the way it works."

Stifling a sarcastic response, she said merely, "Thanks. Bye, Dad." Rolling over, she slid the phone onto the bedside table. She doubted that "it" would work that way, whatever "it" was supposed to be. She wasn't strong, and she wasn't particularly kind. And she was *not* a caregiver. She'd never wanted children for that reason. Her own biggest fear was being dependent on anyone else.

She rolled back onto the pillow again. The spider was now efficiently wrapping the gnat into a small bundle of sticky strands. Should she let the industrious arachnid take over the corner, get a broom and clear out the cobwebs now, or wait until she knew when Chase would return? *If* he would return. Would he be able to climb upstairs to the bedroom? Her mind flashed back to lying here with him, listening to sounds overhead in the attic, something rolling heavily from one side to the other.

"Bowling squirrels?" Chase had guessed.

"Thirty pounders, with masked faces and bushy, striped tails," she'd told him, laughing. A city boy, he'd been raised in the Boise suburbs, while she'd grown up in rural Kansas.

"Oh, Chase," she murmured now. "You've got to be okay. *Please* be okay."

A clatter from outside the window caught her attention. She sat up to investigate, pulling aside the curtain. A young woman riding a bay horse was making her way up the gravel driveway, leading another saddled horse, this one a paint.

Weird. As far as she knew, Chase had never had any interest in horses. When the young woman dismounted, Sam slid out of bed and dashed down the stairs just in time to answer her knock on the door.

The surprise on the face of the other woman probably mirrored her own. She was attractive, with long chestnut hair gathered into a ponytail. The lack of lines anywhere on her face indicated youth.

"Hi," the stranger said. "I'm Bethany, from down the road. Is Chase home?"

"I'm Sam. Are you a neighbor?" Sam wasn't sure how she felt about Chase having such a pretty young woman living so close.

The girl's face relaxed into a smile. "I guess, although I live about a mile away. Is he here?"

"Not right now," Sam said. Was it dangerous to let her know that Chase might not be home for some time? Would that be an invitation for robbery or vandalism? "Was he expecting you?"

The paint horse rubbed his head against the deck post, jingling the rings attached to his bit, and Bethany glanced back at him before returning her gaze to Sam.

"We had a schedule set up," she said. "I called him to confirm, but I didn't get an answer."

"I think his cell phone's not working." As far as Sam knew, Chase's cell was either still missing or in the hands of the FBI. "What was on the schedule?"

Bethany twisted sideways to flick a hand at the horses. "Riding lessons."

"Really?" Although Chase knew she'd owned a horse in her Kansas youth, Sam had never heard him express a desire to ride.

"Yeah." Bethany chuckled. "He didn't want to make a fool out of himself when he took this woman named Summer to a guest ranch in Canada in a few months. I guess it wouldn't be too romantic for your hero to fall off his horse, would it?"

Chase was planning to take her to a ranch in Canada? That would be a dream trip for her, a sweet reminder of her happiest times growing up.

The pain from the lump that formed in Sam's throat must have shown on her face, because Bethany's smile abruptly faded. "Oh shit." She took a step back from the doorway. "I mean, shoot. You didn't know about Summer."

She raised a hand to flick a strand of hair from her forehead. "I'm sorry. I'm an idiot. Shit." She backed up toward the horses.

"*I'm* Summer," Sam told her. "Sam is a nickname I use sometimes."

Bethany stopped, her cheeks flaming now. "Then I guess I should be doubly sorry. I let the cat out of the bag, right? This was supposed to be a big surprise. Please don't tell Chase."

It was Sam's turn to chuckle. "You thought I was 'the other woman', didn't you? And I was afraid *you* might be her."

"Me?" the girl squeaked. "Chase is a handsome dude, but I think he's probably as old as"—Bethany's words faded for a second as she considered who she was talking to, then she finally concluded with—"my dad."

After an uncomfortable silence, the girl said, "I guess we'll have to reschedule. Tell Chase to call me, would you?"

"Come in for a minute, Bethany." Sam opened the door.

Then, when they were both seated at Chase's kitchen table, Sam told the girl about the avalanche.

"Omigod, everyone heard about that. Chase was in that? Is he gonna be okay?"

Sam sniffed and wiped a tear away from her eye before it could escape down her cheek. "We hope so. But he might not be back for a while."

"I'll tell the other neighbors. We'll keep an eye on this place."

"Thanks." Sam accompanied her back to the porch, and while Bethany untied the bay, Sam untied the paint, but before handing the reins back to Bethany, she buried her face in the horse's neck. He was a gelding, like her old horse, Comanche. His winter fur, still long and thick, smelled slightly sweet in the cold air, like fresh grass.

"I had a pinto like this when I was about your age, in Kansas," she told the girl. "I had some of the best times of my life riding Comanche."

"I think Chase must know that." Bethany swung into the saddle on her bay mare. "Tell him I said to get well soon. Bye for now, Summer-Sam."

Tears rolled freely down Sam's face as she watched Bethany ride away with the two horses. Why did it hurt so much to learn about Chase's wonderful plans?

Because it was a promise of the future. And now that future was uncertain.

No, she couldn't think like that. If Chase needed her help to recuperate, she'd move in with him for as long as it took. Or maybe Chase could move into her house. She *could* cook, if she had to. She *could* take care of him, although it was hard to imagine what that might entail. Maybe, like her dad said, it *could* work that way.

"Chase, you and I *will* go to that ranch in Canada," she said aloud.

Going back into the cabin, she went upstairs and packed a change of clothes for Chase. Layers. The spring weather could bring anything. Wool socks. His spare boots; he and Nicole had still been wearing their ski boots when she'd found them, and his shoes were probably lost wherever he'd changed. Jeans. A dark blue long-sleeved placket shirt that showed off his muscular frame. An ivory cable fisherman's sweater she loved. His spare jacket. She stuffed it all into the backpack she found in his closet.

After checking the garage to be sure Chase's car was still there, she didn't have another mission to accomplish at Chase's home. Unlike her, he had no pets waiting to be fed, no plants to water. Across the clearing, the deer had vanished. Sam scanned the edge of the bordering trees for a moment, but spotted only a rabbit nibbling the grass, close to the safety of nearby shrubs.

Everything was so unresolved. Chase's future. Gina's recovery. The identity of the buried young man and woman, their motivation for capturing a wolverine. And oh God, the baby wolverines. She couldn't bear to think about them. She wished that Gina hadn't planted that possibility in her head.

She had to do something to provide an element of certainty somewhere. Anywhere. Provide some forward momentum. All the loose threads were driving her crazy.

Gina had mentioned Anton Priest as a local trapper. Checking the online information service, Sam determined that Priest lived a few miles north of Maple Falls, a drive of approximately forty-five minutes from her house in Bellingham, but from Chase's, probably no more than twenty.

She slid into her RAV4 and instructed her cell phone to take her there. "Navigating," the female voice announced.

Priest lived on a small farm off the Silver Lake Road. A hand-crafted wooden address sign hung from a metal bar at the driveway entrance, along with a sign that read TAXIDERMY.

The house was a nondescript manufactured home with an added deck. A large barn, painted in the traditional red with white trim, was the most attractive feature of the place, set against lush green pastures occupied by a handful of cows. Herefords, if her memories from rural Kansas were accurate.

Nobody answered her knock on the front door of the house, but she heard hammering from the barn, so she walked in that direction. Nothing appeared immediately ominous, and she chided herself for expecting puddles of blood or piles of hacked-off animal parts. It had been Gina's label, *poacher*, that put those pictures in her head.

Pushing open a side door to the barn, she shouted, "Hello?"

"Come on back!" The response came from a far corner.

Although the floor was a mix of dirt and sawdust and there were a dozen bales of hay stacked in one corner, the barn was outfitted to be more of a workshop than a traditional shelter for animals.

She walked past cardboard boxes and glass jars on tall wooden shelves, several containing what appeared, disturbingly, to be eyes of different sizes and colors. Taxidermy, she reminded herself. Any stuffed beast would not be wearing its original eyes.

Feisty. Frozen eyes. Baby wolverines, waiting for a mother who would never come. She made herself pause and take a breath. *Get a grip, Westin.* Killing all sorts of wild creatures was legal in many locations.

Priest, a short thick man with white hair and a close-cut beard, turned from a long wooden counter to greet her. Sam was grateful the counter in front of him did not hold a corpse or any part of one.

"What can I do you for?" Priest asked in the folksy manner of rural folks.

She explained that she knew of several hunters who might need taxidermy services in the near future. "I'm thinking of getting a gift for my husband, and maybe my brother, too. Do you have a specialty?"

Priest shook his head. "Nope, I do it all."

"What sort of animals have you . . . er . . . preserved?"

"Come see." He led her to a walled-off portion of the barn and opened the door on what might have been a museum to some.

The room seemed like a graveyard to her. He gestured proudly around the space. "Some just want the antlers or the head," he explained, pointing to wall mounts of a deer, an elk, a bighorn ram, and saddest of all, a mountain lion. She stared at the magnificent cat's head. Its mouth was open in an eternal snarl.

He noticed. "Usually, when someone gets a cat or a bear, they want the whole animal." He waved a hand toward a group of preserved specimens in different poses: a bobcat walking on a tree branch, another mountain lion with paws in the air, ready to spring from its haunches.

"That one," he pointed to a porcupine, "was tricky."

She forced a laugh. "I'll bet."

"Sorry I don't have a bear right now for you to see. I just sold a grizzly; posed him like this." He held his hands up in a threatening pose and bared his teeth.

Grizzlies were even more rare in the Cascades than wolverines. She had to think for a moment about the right way to ask if he'd shot that bear, finally came up with, "Your own trophy?"

"Yep," he said, grinning. "Got him on a hunt in Canada. Sold him to a museum in Germany, if you can believe that. Museums are some of my best customers. They like to show visitors the wildlife of an area."

"I see." How horribly ironic. They'd rather feature a dead animal instead of protecting the live creature. She was reminded of a stuffed jaguar she'd seen in a museum in Tucson. The display should have been labeled *How humans preserve jaguars in Arizona.*

"'Course," he said, "Sometimes too much gets blown away to restore. You do have to know what a critter originally looked like, after all."

She didn't want to think too much about hunters hauling in horribly mangled bodies to preserve.

"But if I can't save the head or some other part, I can just skin 'em." He waved his hand at a line of skins hanging from clips on the wall. A thick pelt of course dark fur with a blond fringe running along the sides and forming a vee above the tail was tacked to the wall. She pointed at it. "Is that a wolverine?"

"Well, it used to be." Priest laughed, displaying remarkably white, even teeth. "Got him in Canada, too. His head was too ruined to keep. But the pelt is still worth a lot."

She cocked an eyebrow. "Really?"

"Wolverine pelts go for more than five hundred. Even close to a thousand if they're primo and you have the head and claws."

She gulped. "I hear that there are some wolverines in the North Cascades. Does anyone try to hunt them?"

Priest narrowed his eyes. "Not that I know of. Too hard to find here."

Not to mention it's illegal to kill them in this state. She wondered if Anton Priest knew that, or if he would care. Just this morning, she'd read about three critically endangered Sumatran tigers that had been found dead in traps in Indonesia.

The rarer a creature was, the more doomed it was to be slaughtered.

Sam fingered the wolverine fur for a moment, besieged by memories of all the magical wild animals she'd seen over the years. The living creatures, with their liquid eyes and fluid movements, their strength and ferocious beauty. *I am so sorry for what my species does to yours.*

"If you ever hear of a wolverine around here, you tell me first, okay?" he said.

When Hanoi freezes. She swallowed and then managed to mutter, "Sure thing."

She continued to stroke the pelt, surprised by how soft the wolverine fur was. How dense and warm.

"Nice, huh?" Priest put his hand next to hers. "You interested in this pelt?"

Sam jerked her hand away. "Oh God, no!"

He narrowed his eyes at her again, watching her curiously. A frown line creased his forehead. In a minute, he would be asking her to leave.

"It's gorgeous," she stuttered, backpedaling. "But it's too expensive, and too precious. I can't afford it."

She had forgotten her mission. The dead kids. After pondering the situation for a minute, she told Priest, "I have a nephew who might be interested in taxidermy. Have you ever taken on students?"

Priest grimaced and leaned back against the rough plank wall. "Now why would I want to create competition for myself?"

She shrugged. "I think he's interested in trapping. Maybe you've met him? Dark hair, kinda scruffy? Nineteen, I think. Or maybe he's twenty by now. He wears an earring in his right ear, usually what looks like a diamond. About six feet tall?" She was guessing at the height, since she'd only seen the poacher stretched out horizontally.

Priest's expression was blank. "Doesn't sound like any kid I know."

He led her back into the workshop. They stood at his work table as he handed her a business card and a sheet of paper with price ranges. In a series of small cubbies along the wall, she spied various tools that appeared to be a variety of scalpels and scraping devices, tweezers and hole punches, and one large hunting knife with an orange handle. It appeared to be the same model the frozen trapper boy had carried.

"Interesting knife." She pointed. "I think I've seen that kind before."

Priest snorted. "I'm not surprised. Every hunter I know has one of those," he told her.

He ushered her to the door and held it open for her. "Come back whenever you're ready. I'll make you a good deal. Tell your friends."

If she hadn't known what he did for a living, she might have liked Anton Priest. The tools of his trade were creepy, though, designed for removing flesh. And that knife. Was it the same model as the dead kid's? Or was it, like Priest said, just a common brand that a multitude of outdoor types carried?

But the sheriff's department had the knife now. She didn't have any way to compare the knives without telling Ortiz she'd been checking out Anton Priest, and she wasn't sure it was wise to admit that.

The sun was low in the west as she drove back to Bellingham, comparing in her head the live creatures she'd known with the stuffed ones in Priest's display room. Stealthy mountain lions in Utah. Sleek sharks and amazing sea turtles in the Galápagos. Bears she'd encountered over the years. Pronghorns in Arizona. And deer everywhere—in Chase's yard, in hers. Raccoons with their humanlike hands on the windows, begging to get inside.

Taxidermy definitely required skill, and there was even a sort of artistry to what the man did, but each mount began with the violent death of a living wild animal. Had all the stuffed animals she'd seen in museums been murdered just for display purposes? She shivered, thinking about it.

Legal, she reminded herself. Most of the time, for most animals.

Damn.

Though wolverines were not on the federal list of endangered species, they were legally protected in Washington State from being trapped or killed, except in cases of self-defense. But who would know if a lone wolverine was killed? The "skunk bears" were solitary animals, and the few that researchers had found in the North Cascades were mostly well-kept secrets. If caught, a poacher could claim he'd been attacked first. Self-defense. As if wolverines hunted people.

How the hell did those kids know where to find a wolverine?

36

"So."

Maya was cutting willow switches in Sam's back yard to repair her tent poles when she heard the familiar voice behind her. She twirled around.

"Hannah!" Although Blake's daughter was five years younger, Maya had always gotten along well with Hannah. She was the closest thing Maya had to a sister.

"I'm glad to see you!" She threw her arms around Hannah. "Wow! You're taller than I am now."

The girl stiffened in her embrace and twisted away. "Big duh." Hannah's expression was as sullen as her tone.

"What have you been up to?" Maya tried to sound cheerful. "How long are you visiting?"

Hannah stepped back, her face darkening into a scowl. "I can't believe you."

"What?"

"I'm helping Dad and Sam fix the wreck you made of the house. And you shot Simon!" The younger girl made a face to show her disapproval.

"That wasn't me," Maya protested. "It was Eaze. And a freak named James. And he's going to be okay, isn't he—Simon?"

"Who's Eaze?"

"He was my boyfriend, I guess. But not anymore. In fact, I stabbed him."

"What?"

"I stabbed Eaze with a kitchen knife. He and his buddy James wrecked the place, looking for stuff to steal."

"Why'd you let them in?"

Maya waved the willow switch in the air like a baton. "I didn't! They broke in while I was on the bus, before I could get back."

"But they were your friends." Hannah gazed at the ground for a minute before raising her head again. "I was looking forward to doing some of the things we used to do, like making homemade pizzas and inventing crazy lyrics for songs."

"We can still do that, Hannah. I want to do all that with you."

Hannah shook her head. "Not going to happen. My dad is super upset, and I don't blame him. You trashed the house. Now we don't even have a TV. You ruined everything."

Maya stared at her. "It wasn't all my fault."

The younger girl crossed her arms and narrowed her eyes. "You got Sam's computer stolen. Dad says you're a druggie now. Or maybe I should say 'again.'"

Like she needed a reminder of everything she'd screwed up in her life. Maya opened her mouth to protest, but couldn't think of any appropriate words.

"Sam says you're not welcome in the house anymore because you have such poor judgment. You're such a bitch!"

That stung. Maya had never heard language like that from Hannah. She was shocked that Blake's normally sunny daughter was acting like the troubled kids she'd led on trips with Wilderness Challenge. Kids pretending to be tough. Insolent, Troy Johnson called them. Wounded, that's what his wife Kim had said they were. Kim, who had believed in her. Kim, who was now dead. Like all the other people who ever cared about her.

Hannah scowled. "You know, you used to be my friend. I looked up to you. We used to have fun. But not anymore. I'm unfriending you. You're a loser."

The younger girl dramatically pressed the fingers of her left hand against her forehead in the shape of a capital letter L, then, flicking her chestnut hair over her shoulder, she stalked back to the house.

Maya had understood those Wilderness Challenge kids. Like them, she'd been called names, constantly told she was a loser. And now Blake's daughter was telling her she was a fuck-up. Again. She focused on her damaged tent, tears blurring the scene in front of her. *Shit.*

So, Sam and Blake weren't going to forgive her. Nobody was going to forgive her. Nobody was going to give her another chance. She wished Eaze had shot her instead of Simon. She had the gun, buried now under her tent. Maybe she should finish that job herself.

She patched the rips in her tent and splinted the broken poles with the willow switches and duct tape borrowed from Sam's carport shed. Well, stolen from Sam's carport shed, if she was honest. The duct tape came in handy sealing the tears in her sleeping bag, too. She'd replace the roll of tape later, she promised herself. Somehow.

A pickup pulled into Sam's driveway, and Maya tensed, fearing James or Eaze was back. But then Blake and Sam emerged from the cabin. Blake slapped the pickup driver on the back. "Thanks, man. I don't know how we'd have gotten this home without your help."

Together, Blake and the stranger tugged a blue-and-green plaid couch out of the pickup bed and carried it into the house. They emerged with Sam's old, ripped-up sofa and set it down in the driveway. Sam climbed into the truck bed and shoved a forest green recliner to the edge, complaining, "Ugh. This is even heavier than the couch."

She straightened, holding her arm against her ribs.

"Stop that, Sam." Blake leaped in beside her. "Greg and I can handle it."

Maya trotted over, put a hand on the fender of the pickup. "I'm strong. I can help."

Sam snapped, "We don't need you, Maya." She gingerly climbed down from the pickup bed as the two men manhandled the recliner into the house. Hannah held open the door.

The stranger, Greg, glanced in Maya's direction, his expression quizzical. Nobody else even looked at her. Why wasn't anyone worried that Eaze or James would come after her? They might even try to kill her. Small loss, her former friends probably figured. And they were right.

She returned to her tent. Pulling out her backpack, she stuffed in the few possessions she still had, then dismantled her tent and lashed it to the outside. She didn't intend to stick around where she wasn't wanted.

The damn calls just wouldn't stop coming. The first time his phone had sounded, Blake had been at work, and when he went to check the calls, he couldn't sort out his feelings at seeing Claude's number on the list. There was no voicemail message. Should he be relieved to see a call from Claude, or at least from Claude's phone? Did it mean that Claude was now conscious, or was it Claude's wife, Marie, telling him that his lover had passed? Unsure if he wanted to know, Blake didn't return the call.

When the next call came, he was still afraid to answer. What was the point? What could he possibly say to Claude or, even worse, to Claude's wife?

Later, at home, in the middle of chopping vegetables for stir fry, he understood the calls wouldn't stop until he responded. Although she was pretending to read the book in her lap, Sam was watching him from the living room couch. Hannah sat in the new recliner, thumbing through something on her cell. And the damn parrot was starting to imitate Blake's owlish cell phone tone. *Hoo-hoo. Hoo-hoo-hoo.* Screwing up his courage, when the phone hooted again, Blake finally answered.

"Hello, Blake."

In spite of his resolution to be stoic, Claude's voice brought tears to his eyes. He pinched the bridge of his nose to stop the flow as he ducked into his bedroom, closing the door behind him.

"Blake? Blake?"

In the past, he'd always been so happy to hear that voice. He swallowed against the lump in his throat. "I'm glad you're alive, Claude." Every word hurt.

In the thick silence that followed his statement, Blake listened to his own heart beating.

"I don't know what to say," Claude finally murmured. "I'm sorry you found out this way."

This way? Was there another better way? "Did you intend to tell me?"

There was another long pause. "Maybe."

From the other side of the door, Zeke squawked, *"Shut up! Shut up!"*

For a second, Blake felt like echoing the bird's order. But after a breath, he asked, "Do you plan to leave your wife?"

A sigh. "I couldn't do that. And I have the children."

"I know." Blake thought about his own child, Hannah, and how less than a week ago, he had hoped to introduce her to Claude, whom he had hoped to have as a life partner.

"I never meant to hurt you, Blake."

And yet, you did. For years. There was only one thing left to say. "Goodbye, Claude." He ended the call.

"Goodbye!" Zeke echoed from the living area. Coincidence, or did that bird have extra sensitive hearing?

When he finally opened the door and came out of his room, Sam had chopped the rest of the vegetables and was heating up the wok. He took the wooden spatula from her before she ruined their dinner. They didn't exchange glances or words, but she gently rubbed her hand across his back before she retired to the couch.

Thankfully, his daughter never even noticed.

"Hoo-hoo. Hoo-hoo-hoo!" But this time it was the parrot, not his phone.

He'd have to change that damn ring tone.

As Maya slogged through mud puddles, she thought about where she might set up camp. She might be able to camp in the Hundred Acre Woods somewhere out of sight, or off one of the many trails in the nearby Chuckanuts. Just as she was mentally sorting through the spots she knew, trying to pick a location, cold water seeped into her right boot, and then a passing car splashed her with mud.

No, too wet in those places. Much of the area was wetland during the spring months.

She tramped through the Fairhaven neighborhood, then through the dog park behind the water treatment plant, ending up along the train tracks. She paced along the worn railroad ties for a while, searching for a dry location where nobody would call the police to move her along. At least not for a night or more.

A tiny-home encampment loomed ahead, in a parking lot surrounded by a tall cyclone fence. She knew the tiny-homes, shed-sized, all different colors, had been constructed to move the homeless off the streets. Maybe she could score one of those? It would be sweet to be out of the rain and cold, have a real bed, maybe a chair and table. Did those little houses have electricity? She'd never been out here at night to see if there were lights.

In addition to the tiny-homes, a few tents were crowded into a corner. The place seemed reasonably clean. A mountain of trash held up the lid of a dumpster, and several stolen shopping carts were parked next to two portable toilets at the end of a central corridor. Maya stood across the street for several minutes, observing the occupants inside the fence. The majority of people inside were men. Most looked old enough to be her father, if she'd ever had one. Nobody was stumbling around drunk or high, though, that was something. None of them was raving to unseen companions.

She hadn't seen Eaze since the break-in. Was he sleeping on James's couch, or would he move into a place like this? She knew there were several tiny-home camps around Bellingham. Maybe there was some sort of system, and he'd end up in an encampment for younger men. If he was even still in town. She hoped he was long gone; she was tired of expecting to see him or James around every corner.

After a minute, a woman emerged from a tent, carrying a small, curly-haired white dog, probably to keep its feet out of the puddles that dotted the asphalt.

The woman spotted her across the street and made a "come here" gesture, then pointed to an empty space in a corner within the fence.

The sun was already low over Lummi Island in the west. Well, this place would do for one night, wouldn't it? Maya walked inside the gate and shrugged off her pack, grateful for the tall cyclone fence. At least nobody could attack from outside during the night. Maya felt lucky to still have her backpack, her tent and sleeping bag, as well as her outdoor clothes, all accumulated during her Wilderness Challenge summer. She pulled out a sheet of plastic and spread it out on the asphalt, then unstrapped her tent from her backpack and unrolled it on the ground.

Up close, the woman was older than Maya had guessed at first. What was her story? Divorce, drugs, alcohol, a man who ran off with everything? That had been her mother's story, the man who ran off with everything, although Maya couldn't remember ever having anything in the entire time she'd lived with her mom.

What was *her* story—Maya Velasquez's story? A dead druggie mother, foster care, a dead father she'd never known, a dead half sister she'd never known, four dead friends, Eaze and his fucking H. It all seemed so inevitable, that she'd end up with nothing and no one. Nobody wanted her anymore. Not even Hannah.

"I'm Nancy." The woman gestured to herself. "And this is Piquant." She waved one of the dog's paws.

"Pecan?" Maya responded. "That's cute."

"No, *piquant*, from the French." Nancy emphasized the *T* at the end, and then spelled the word. "It means sharp. You'll understand when you hear him bark." Nancy tilted her head toward a larger tent off the central corridor. She glanced at a watch on her left wrist. "Around six thirty, a church group brings us food. You can meet whoever's around then. The manager won't be back until tomorrow. Then you'll have to be approved for temporary stay and fill out an application."

"Cool." Nancy seemed decent, if maybe a trifle snooty with that French comment, and all the approval and application talk.

Maya warily eyed a bearded man who exited the outhouse and then let himself into his fuchsia-painted hut. If they knew

Eaze was looking for her, would the men here rat on her? Were they predators like James?

Time would tell. She had the pistol Eaze had dropped, a lead weight in the bottom of her pack.

Nancy observed from a folding lawn chair as Maya snapped her tent poles together, attached the triangular tent, and then stretched the duct-taped rainfly over the top.

"Home sweet tent," the older woman commented. "No drugs, no alcohol, no weapons. Those are the rules here."

"No problem." After laying out her sleeping bag and tossing her small bag of clothes and possessions into the back, Maya tucked the pistol into the pocket of her jacket before backing out of her tent and zipping the flap closed.

"Here's supper." Nancy lifted her chin toward a small cluster of people walking through the middle of the tiny-home village, clutching sacks and coolers. Piquant barked and wagged his stubby tail.

Doors of several tiny-homes opened, and Maya watched as the occupants spilled out and trailed the church group. Mostly men with unkempt beards and hair, a scruffy mutt that was big enough to swallow Piquant, a few women with faces roughened by outdoor life. All the humans wore jeans and jackets as rumpled as her own.

"C'mon," Nancy urged. "If you want to eat, you're expected to help."

As they joined the flow of villagers moving toward the large tent, a younger man fell into step beside Maya. When she glanced at him, he winked and smiled, displaying a hole where one of his front teeth should be. "Hi, sugar. You're new."

"Yep." She shifted her gaze away from his face, fingering the pistol in her pocket.

The small woman on her right flashed a timid smile at her, and Maya realized that she was actually a kid, probably about the age of Hannah, but with tired eyes that made her appear much older. What was her story?

A boy with greasy hair caught up to the girl, grabbed her hand possessively, and pulled her ahead. Maya's brain coughed up an unpleasant vision of Eaze.

Inside the tent, the food—sandwiches and soup—was tempting. She held out her hands for a stack of napkins and throwaway bowls and then arranged them at the end of the table in front of the inhabitants who lined up.

Another volunteer arrived, carrying boxes of apples and cookies. After he set them on the table and donned an apron, he scanned the line of villagers, and his gaze came to rest on Maya. *Oh God.* How humiliating. She stared at the asphalt beneath her feet. Troy Johnson, her former boss at Wilderness Challenge. Kim's husband, Kyla's father. Kim and Kyla were both dead, and Troy had told her he couldn't hire her for this coming summer. Just because she'd been drinking a little when she showed up at his office.

"Maya," he said. That one word seemed to convey both surprise and disappointment.

Damn him. Why did everyone have to be so judgmental? She raised her chin and glared at him defiantly. He raised an eyebrow. When she turned away, Troy went back to work, opening his box of cookies and setting them out on a tray on the tabletop.

Maya moved forward in the line, picked up a bowl. A plump, gray-haired volunteer wearing an apron and a white plastic badge with a small cross and the name Irma nodded at her, ladled soup into her bowl, and said, "Welcome, dear."

That was the nicest thing anyone had said to her for months. *Welcome.* She'd find a way to fit in here. She'd fill out the damn application. She'd get approved. She moved forward, picked up a sandwich.

These were her people now.

37

"No change," the nurse reported to Sam when she checked on Chase the next day. "But that means he's holding his own. He's fighting. His vitals are not bad, but his fever's still high."

Sam could tell that much from the flush on his cheeks. She sat and held his hand and told him about Hannah and Blake redecorating the house with furniture from Habitat for Humanity and Craigslist. "Blake found these beautiful plates and bowls, too. Bright colors and designs. Really dresses up the place. We can't wait to have you over for dinner."

"Maya's moved out," she said. "I don't know if that's good or bad. I've heard that some people have to hit rock bottom before they straighten up. Maybe the break-in was Maya's rock bottom, and she's gone somewhere to get her life back on track."

Sam hoped that was true. She'd found a wadded-up quilt square in the laundry room trash basket. Maya's first attempt at cross-stitch, a representation of her as a trail builder. The girl had once been so proud of the work she did in Olympic National Forest, and so proud of that quilt square, too, the first for a story quilt like the one Sam had stitched squares for most of her life. Eventually, when she'd created enough, she'd stitch them together in a quilt.

Sam felt a twinge of guilt now, thinking about the quilt squares. Her grandmother had taught her to embroider and quilt as a child. She hadn't created a square for a while now. Surviving an avalanche was worth remembering, wasn't it? When she had time, she'd pull out her graph paper and sketch out a few ideas. Maybe a human hand emerging from a light-blue snowbank? Maybe a wave of snow chasing a woman down a mountain? Should there be a wolverine? No, she thought, that would only be a sad reminder.

Maya had clearly washed her quilt square, but a brown stain remained, marring the white cloth behind the image. Sam had saved the square and marked out a couple of trees that she would add to hide the stain. It was in her embroidery hoop at home right now. Maybe getting that repaired square back would show Maya that mistakes in life could be fixed, or at least forgotten.

Then Sam told Chase about pet-sitting a parrot who wouldn't stop talking. "He says 'Gonna trade you for a dog,' Chase. I'll bet that came from Gina. He tries to talk to Alexa. He probably thinks another bird lives inside Gina's Echo Dot."

There was no response from the man in the bed.

"I'm not making any progress on finding out who the wolverine poachers were." She sighed. "I feel so useless. I could really use your help."

Nothing. Sam couldn't tolerate the situation anymore; it hurt just to sit beside him. She kissed Chase's hot forehead and told him she loved him, then, feeling like a deserter sneaking away from a battle, she wandered down the hall to Gina's room. There, she was pleasantly surprised to find her friend reclining with the head of her bed slightly raised. Gina's eyes were open.

"Girlfriend!" Sam said in greeting. "You're alive!"

"Still not sure that's a good thing," Gina croaked.

"I'm so glad to see you doing better."

Gina used the heels of her hands to try to shove herself up on the pillow, her face contorted in pain.

"Wait." Sam reached for the button clamped to the bedside railing, and pressed it to raise the head of the bed to a more vertical position. "Better?"

"Shit. I forgot about that." Gina licked her dry lips. "Better is a relative term. They say I'm not gonna die, but I won't be able to hike for months. Who's going to track the wolverines? If I can't work, I don't know who I am. And I'll owe three times my life savings to this damn hospital. I wish I'd kicked the bucket up there on the mountain."

"You don't mean that, because you are too tough to be an invalid." Sam put her hand on top of her friend's. "I'll help with wolverine tracking, and your team will, too. As for the hospital, I've heard you can get a lot of the expenses erased, excused—whatever—if you don't have the funds to pay."

"May that be true." Lifting a hand from her midriff only an inch or so, Gina extended a finger toward the water pitcher and glass on the tray table.

Sam filled the plastic cup halfway and handed it to her. Gina slowly raised her forearm and clasped her hand around the cup, and then tucked her chin to drink from it. The process was painful to watch. When she was finished, Sam took the cup from her and returned it to the table. Her friend leaned back and briefly closed her eyes. "I'm suddenly a hundred years old."

"That'll change," Sam promised. "You'll be back to feeling seventy-five in no time."

Gina chuckled, then wrinkled her brow in pain. After swallowing hard, she asked, "Your friends?"

"Nicole's already out of the hospital. She's magical like that." *Stop*, Sam told herself. *That wasn't fair.* "She will have a scar on her head and she's on crutches right now because of a torn-up ankle. Chase is hanging in, but he's got a bad fever. And I'm not sure about Claude."

"And your housemate?"

"Blake didn't get injured, lucky devil." Well, not so lucky. He'd clearly been injured, just not physically, but that was not her story to share. Naming her comrades reminded Sam that she'd never heard Gina mention family. She'd never seen Gina with other friends. "Have you been in touch with your family or your friends at the wolverine study group?"

Gina gestured to a card next to the water pitcher. The cover was a wolf howling at the moon on a snowy night. Sam noticed several signatures inside the card. After licking her dry lips, Gina said, "Nobody's talking to me. What's new on the wolverine killers?"

Sam pulled up the bedside chair. "I went up there with a deputy and two rangers a couple of days ago. We found two bodies." Sam pulled her cell phone from her jacket pocket, thumbed to the photos of the frozen corpses, and showed them to Gina. "Nobody's come forward to identify them. Do you recognize them?"

As she studied the photos, Gina's brow furrowed. "They look so young. What the hell were they doing?"

"So you don't know them," Sam concluded, disappointed.

"Not a clue," Gina verified. "I've never seen them before." Her expression transformed into a grimace, and she placed a hand over her abdomen. "No sign of F3?"

Sam explained about finding the broken, bloodstained carrier, but no wolverine corpse. "I saw some footprints and pawprints above the trap."

"Maybe more than one wolverine up there?" Gina's voice held a hint of hope.

"Maybe. I couldn't tell. Definitely not baby wolverines, though. And the tracks didn't seem too fresh. They might have been Feisty's, there before the avalanche."

"Maybe."

"I went to see Anton Priest," Sam added.

"And?"

"And he had the same knife that the boy poacher was carrying. Think that's a coincidence?"

"Who knows?" Gina croaked.

"He says he doesn't have any idea about who those kids are."

"And you believe him?"

"Yeah, I do, actually," Sam admitted. "He seems like a decent sort, for the most part."

Gina sighed. "That makes it so much harder to hate him, doesn't it?"

"Yeah. Why couldn't he have fangs and drag his knuckles on the ground?"

Gina focused her gaze on the wall beyond the foot of her bed. Sam wished she had better news to impart about Feisty, or saving baby wolverines, or anything, really. Next time, she'd bring flowers.

She continued her news. "Nobody else seems to know the two kids, either. They had no ID on them, and although the Whatcom News ran descriptions of them yesterday and the day before, nobody's called in any clues."

"No photos?"

"They don't publish pics of dead people, Gina."

"Shit," Gina commented, her eyes closing again.

Sam asked, "How did they know where to find a wolverine? Could the photos on the wolverine research site have tipped 'em off to the location or something? You never published the GPS coordinates, did you?"

Gina started to shake her head, but stopped after the first sideways movement, wincing. "The coordinates are not online. But some of the local volunteers have 'em, of course, so they can go and swap out batteries and SD cards. They say they never shared."

"Okay if I talk to them?" Sam asked.

"Knock yourself out. Becca Diehl. Ryan Peralta. Their numbers are on my phone."

Sam didn't respond for a couple of minutes.

"Damn. My cell's under a foot of snow somewhere, right?" Gina guessed.

"Um, yeah. Do you know their numbers?"

Gina frowned. "Shit. No. That's what smart phones are for. Try the info line on the website."

"I'll check in with them, see if they've ever had friends come along with them to visit the site."

"Thanks." Gina's voice was growing softer, her words slower.

"Is there anyone else I can call for you?"

"Nope. And before you ask, all my relatives croaked a long time ago. I grew up in the foster care system. I've never been married or had kids. And my volunteers can't come; you know the hospital won't allow anyone who's not related these days."

Sam nodded. "I lied, said I was Chase's fiancée. I'm probably not supposed to be in your room. I don't think they're organized enough to keep track, but if I get caught, I'll tell them I'm your sister."

"Hey, Sis, congrats on your upcoming marriage."

Sam laughed.

"I'm afraid to ask—"

"Zeke's fine. Although I'm thinking of trading him in for a dog."

The gurgling sound from Gina might have started out as a laugh. "Parrots live too long. My father willed that dang bird to me five years ago. Only thing that old man ever gave to me. Zeke will probably be cracking jokes at my funeral."

"Hannah—that's Blake's daughter—is convinced she can teach him a proper parrot song. 'What Do You Do with a

Drunken Sailor.'"

"God save us," Gina muttered, her eyelids fluttering.

Sam stood up. "I'd better be going." She moved toward the door. "One more thing. I almost forgot. No, two more things. The camera survived. I've got it at home. Maybe there's something useful on the SD card."

"Uh-huh." Her friend's eyes closed.

"And a reporter friend of mine is doing a special television report about the avalanche. I'm going to do a plug for wolverine protection."

The only response was a soft snore from the bed. Sam picked up her jacket and left, feeling downhearted. Former foster kid, no living relatives, no close friends. That sounded too familiar.

In the hall, a woman was speaking to a doctor in an old-fashioned white coat. Sam caught only the tail end of her sentence. ". . . across the border, to a hospital in Vancouver, as soon as possible."

That had to be Claude's wife. Was she aware of Claude's affair with Blake? Most likely not. The betrayal made Sam's heart hurt for her housemate.

As soon as she stepped outside, her cell phone bleeped. Adam was on the line. "We've got to step it up, Sammie. Interest is waning!"

It was fatiguing just to listen to him. "Interest in what, exactly?"

"Interest in the avalanche and everything associated with it. Did you even realize there was a mass shooting in Memphis today?"

"It's so challenging to keep track of all the Americans dying every day, isn't it?"

He either failed to recognize the droll tone of her comment or chose to ignore it as he said, "Never mind. I did some dynamite interviews with the recovery workers up at the ski resort today while you were off doing whatever it is you do, so my crew is busy patching that together. Tonight, I'll interview you to fill in the gaps. We'll just have to do a green screen take and replace the background later. Wear your usual outdoor getup, just nothing green. And don't worry about your face. Makeup and Hair will be there to help."

"Adam . . ." She tried to stop the runaway train of his dialogue.

"You can talk about what it was like to crawl through the collapsed ski hut, and what it was like to be in an avalanche of your own."

"Sounds like a movie, *'An Avalanche of Her Own.'*"

"Yeah, could be, I guess. My hotel room, seven-thirty."

Doing a late interview was the last thing on her mind right now. She'd planned an evening of Ibuprofen, a good book, and Simon in her lap. She hadn't had an opportunity to pull her thoughts together or collect the facts and figures on wolverines in the United States. She'd been focused on Chase and Maya and Blake and her destroyed house. She'd sound like a nincompoop and look like she'd been riding the rails for a decade. "Uh, I don't think—"

"I'll have that check for you after the interview," he interrupted. "See you then."

She walked to her SUV, gritting her teeth. Adam certainly knew how to keep her in line.

38

At home, Sam found Blake and Hannah sitting side by side on the new used plaid hide-a-bed couch, chatting about area rugs they'd seen that day, heads bent over photos in Blake's camera as they discussed the possibilities with the furniture that was beginning to fill the room. The air was redolent with garlic and tomato sauce.

"Lasagna for dinner?" Sam guessed.

"Rigatoni," Blake responded.

Zeke's cage had been moved to a new side table, where the parrot was currently, inexplicably, barking like a dog.

Simon was stretched across the back of the sofa, switching his tail and glaring at the bird. Sam sympathized with her cat's mood.

"*Arf! Arf! Arf!*"

"Be quiet, Zeke," Sam told him.

"*Hello?*" the macaw squawked. "*Shut up!*"

Hannah rose from the couch and walked over to his cage. Bending down to gaze at the bird, she sang, "What do you do with a drunken sailor? What do you do with a drunken sailor?"

Zeke bounced twice on his perch, squawked, and then screeched, "*Why can't you sing?*"

"What?" Hannah straightened, insulted. Sam and Blake burst into laughter.

"Why can't you sing?" Zeke repeated. *"Gonna trade you for a dog!"*

"Gonna put the cover on your cage," Sam retorted, picking up the folded canvas.

Hanna protested, "You're going to confuse him. It's not even dark outside."

"Bye for now!" The parrot screeched as the canvas came down.

"Parrots are smarter than you think," Hannah told Sam.

"That's what I'm afraid of. Don't leave your cell phone close to him. Zeke would probably order pizza."

"Some people say macaws have the intelligence of a five-year-old human," Blake interjected.

"Like the gorillas in that article Dad showed me." Hannah pointed to the magazine on the kitchen island. "Can you believe they understand sign language?"

"I'll trade Zeke for one of those gorillas any day. Sign language would make for a much quieter housemate." Sam stroked Simon from head to tail. The cat closed his eyes and pressed his head and spine against her hand, purring. "Any word from Maya?"

"No." Moving to the kitchen, Blake checked on the pasta. After shutting the oven door, he asked, "Chase?"

"No change yet. They say he's holding his own." She knew better than to ask after Claude.

The place seemed different without Maya, sort of hollow. Empty. Maybe the new furniture gave the house a different atmosphere? Not to mention the parrot. So many changes at once. It felt as if the world was waiting, everything suspended in time. The wolverine poachers were still unidentified; cars and corpses were still buried up at the ski resort; Chase, Claude, and Gina were still in dire condition at the hospital; Zeke was still a visiting pain in the neck in the house; and Eaze and James were hiding in the shadows somewhere. Maya, unaccounted for.

Sam felt like she had been holding her breath for days. She still had no idea what the future held. She glanced at her housemate, who was flipping through photos on his phone. At least Blake had an answer to his situation, even if it wasn't the one he'd hoped for.

After dinner she washed her face and combed her hair and headed for the Bellwether Hotel, fretting about what Adam might ask on camera. Even more worried about what she'd say.

Adam's hotel room was filled with lights and cameras and people, all moving around against a giant green backdrop. A male makeup artist insisted on ratting her hair on top "to give it body" and swiping lipstick on her mouth. Then he swished reddish powder onto the bark rash on her forehead to make the scratches there look "fresher." *Lovely.* Adam, of course, had slightly mussed hair and a bit of blush on his cheeks, making him appear rugged and outdoorsy.

There was a short debate about whether the interview should take place standing or sitting, but since the crew thought it might be best to finally position them on a snowy mountain, Adam decided to question Sam standing up. Both of them shrugged into their jackets, and the makeup guy, who apparently did sound-guy things as well, clipped microphones to their collars. Sam's nerves jangled more loudly with each passing moment, but finally they began the interview, standing awkwardly in front of the green screen with the lights shining in their faces.

Adam's first question: "You were buried in the avalanche yourself, is that right?"

"Not 'the avalanche,'" she corrected, using air quotes, glad to have something to do with her hands. "There were quite a few avalanches caused by the earthquake that day. I and three others and a wolverine were buried in a smaller avalanche miles away from the ski lodge. Only two of us survived. Two young people who had captured a wolverine were killed, along with the poor wolverine."

Please ask something intelligent about the wolverine, she begged Adam with her mind.

"Why would anyone want to capture a wolverine?" he asked.

Yay! "Who knows?" she responded. "Wolverines are very rare. Experts think there are only about three hundred left in the entire United States, and global warming is threatening the habitats for the ones we have. It is illegal to kill a wolverine in this state, but that's not true everywhere. Wolverines are not a protected species in the United States; they're not on the endangered list."

Adam's blue gaze bore into hers, reminding her she had not answered his question.

"People still trap the poor animals," she said. "A wolverine pelt is worth hundreds of dollars, and a whole stuffed wolverine is worth thousands." Abruptly aware that those words might have just enticed ambitious trappers to slaughter more, she quickly added, "Each wolverine killed endangers the entire species even more. Future generations of Americans may never get the chance to see a wolverine."

She quit there, suddenly realizing that not many of the current generation, including herself, had ever seen one, either. Clearly, she was not cut out to be a spontaneous television personality.

"That's sad," Adam replied mildly.

"Tragic," she countered.

"But I'm glad you survived being buried. What's it like to be caught in an avalanche?"

What do you think it's like, she wanted to retort. Taking a breath, she actually said, "It's terrifying. The force of the slide is incredible, and being buried is one of the worst experiences of my life. I'm lucky to be alive, and so is my friend Gina, a wolverine researcher who was there with me."

"And then, after digging yourselves out, you made your way to the destroyed building, Raven Hut, at the ski area."

A little simplistic, but okay. "Yes, thanks to a ski patroller who was out on a snowmobile searching for victims."

"So, he gave you a ride back to the resort." Adam added. "And then, although you were injured yourself, you crawled inside the collapsed building to rescue others."

She scoffed at how heroic and selfless that made her sound. "I was the only person there small enough to fit through a gap in the wreckage."

"Tell us what you found inside."

She related the tale of finding the girl with the purple shoes and then the baby.

"And you brought that baby back to its mother."

"I dragged her carrier outside."

"And then you went back." He took her through her experience of crawling through the maze of debris, finding three live victims and another dead man, and then climbing up through the ruined layers to escape and tell rescuers where the victims were. The interview process was nearly as exhausting as the original adventure had been. Sam thought her voice would crack and her legs tremble before it ended. Inside her jacket, she was drenched in sweat.

"And that's why they call you Avalanche Angel," Adam finally summarized.

At the last second, Sam remembered not to roll her eyes on camera.

"You did well," Adam told her, unclipping her microphone.

"I need a drink."

He walked her to the door, and then pulled a check from his inside jacket pocket. She glanced at it. Twenty-five hundred, not three thousand.

"What—" she began.

He touched a finger to her lips. "The other five when we interview the parents of the wolverine kids."

"If," she said, backing away a step.

"I'll make it happen."

He probably would. She folded the check and tucked it into the pocket of her jeans. Abruptly, Adam stepped into the hotel hallway and shut his room door behind him. Then he swooped in, wrapped his arms tightly around her and planted a hungry kiss on her lips.

She pushed him away. "Adam!"

He shrugged. "You're single, I'm single. Oh babe, we used to be such a hot item."

"Ancient history. Now I have Chase," she reminded him.

He raised an eyebrow. "Are you sure about that?"

That was just plain cruel. "Good night, Adam."

"See you later, Sammie."

She was still smoldering when she arrived home. There had been no updates from the hospital, which she chose to interpret as good news, or at least neutral news. Fortunately, Blake had chilled a bottle of pinot grigio in the fridge. She poured herself a tall glassful.

"So, the interview went well," Blake snidely observed from his television observation post on the couch.

"We have a television again?"

"We do. On sale at Best Buy. Courtesy of my renter's insurance."

"Why can't you sing?" Zeke screeched from his cage. *"Alexa, play NPR!"*

"Who uncovered him?" Sam asked.

"Hannah claimed parrot abuse."

Sam surveyed the room.

"She's in my bedroom Instagram-ing or TikTok-ing or something," he responded. "Her train leaves tomorrow morning."

"We'll miss her. She's been a big help pulling this house back together."

"Okay! Okay! Alexa, what time is it?" Zeke squawked.

"It's bedtime in the Pacific Northwest Amazon." Sam pulled the canvas cover over the bars of the macaw's cage.

"Bye for now!" Zeke added a shriek for the final exclamation point.

"Simon's curled up on your bed, I think." Blake's gaze moved back to the television screen.

Picking up her wine glass, Sam said, "I'm headed that way myself."

"By the way, I like your new look." Blake patted the top of his head and then pursed his lips at her.

"I'll get you back tomorrow," Sam promised.

39

There were few chairs in the dinner tent in the tiny-home village. Maya guessed that the lucky occupants of the tiny-homes had dragged off the majority of them, if they'd ever existed, and now most of those occupants took their dinners off to their private spaces. The others stood, eating from plates on the serving table. Maya and Nancy shared a bench, balancing their plates awkwardly on their laps. Piquant danced at their feet, his eyes bright, hopeful of a handout. Nancy gave him a crust of bread, and so Maya did, too. And they both let the small dog lick their soup bowls clean.

Nancy introduced her to two middle-aged women in the village, Petra and Leanne. Both appeared to be in their fifties or possibly even older, with reddened faces and ragged hair, and although her hands and face were clean, Leanne smelled as if she'd been sorting through garbage all day. Which, Maya knew, was a real possibility. Or perhaps she had retrieved the fleece jacket and ripped jeans she was wearing out of a dumpster.

The women introduced her to the men who remained in the dining tent. Most were so uninteresting that Maya immediately forgot their names. Two men were to be avoided, Petra explained, pointing them out, adding, "Not really dangerous, but creepy."

One, a greasy knit hat pulled down over his hair, was

muttering to the air in front of him. Maya wondered if he actually envisioned someone standing across from him. The other sprawled open-legged in one of the chairs, his right hand moving in his pants pocket as he leered, his gaze so fixed on her that she felt naked. She welcomed the weight of the gun in her own pocket.

After the serving containers were empty of food and the villagers had tossed their plates in the trash, Nancy announced she was taking Piquant for a walk.

"Back in an hour or so," she told Maya.

Lights blinked on around the camp. So, the tiny homes *did* have electricity. Those lucky people. She noticed now that there were also a few poles with plugs on them. She'd use one of those to charge her cell phone.

Petra and Leanne melted away to wherever they'd come from. Careful to avoid Troy, Maya helped the church people clean up and carry coolers and utensils back to their van. After Irma handed her a printed invitation to save herself, they drove away, and she dropped the flyer in the paper recycling bin. There was nothing left to do, so she walked back to her tent in the corner of the fence, and then stood, gazing out through the chain-link fence.

A train thundered past on the tracks less than twenty yards away, shaking the ground. Its warning whistle drowned out even the thought of any other sound, and its line of open coal cars seemed to go on forever. *Clank-clank, clank-clank, clank-clank.* Headed for an export terminal across the border in British Columbia, she guessed. Years ago, the locals and the Lummi tribe had shut down a planned coal port north of Bellingham, but that didn't stop the trains passing through to Canada. How many more trains would thunder by tonight? Would she get any sleep?

After the train had passed, she heard faint music, accented

by an occasional yip or bark, playing from a small brewpub just beyond the Amtrak station. The brewpub welcomed dogs inside as well as in their fenced outside yard. Nancy had probably gone there. It was only a few minutes after eight o'clock, but with the overcast sky, the darkness was deepening. Nearby manufacturing and ship-repair businesses were shut down, and the gate had been lowered to close off traffic from Marine Park.

Life was so different on that side of the chain-link fence. Out there, people had money. They had friends. They had family. But she'd only had all of that for the summer she worked for Wilderness Challenge, and for a short time afterward when she went to community college. Other than those few months, her life had always been shit. And now she was back on this side of the fence. And on the wrong side of the tracks.

An older couple strolled down the sidewalk near the Bellingham Cruise Terminal, hand in hand, in and out of the shadows. In their fifties or sixties, maybe; they both had white hair. They seemed comfortable, happy. How long had they been together? Would she ever have anyone who loved her like that?

As the couple strolled out of sight toward the Fairhaven tourist area, a figure detached itself from the shadow of the ancient tree in front of the Amtrak station. Her breath caught in her throat at the familiar silhouette. *No.*

Eaze.

How could he be on the street, walking around like he hadn't done anything? Had the police let him go? Or had they never found him? Or maybe, and this seemed more likely, never even looked for him because they didn't believe her description of the break-in.

She couldn't see Eaze's face clearly, but she could tell from his posture that he'd spotted her. After stepping out of the pool of light under a streetlamp, he began to walk toward the tiny-home compound. *No.*

Her heart beating hard, she folded the fingers of her right hand, extending her middle finger, and then shook that gesture against the fence, clanking it. He stopped, frozen. She couldn't make out his face in the darkness, but she could see that he'd clenched his fists.

She quickly unzipped her tent and crawled in, stretching out on top of her sleeping bag. A minute later, her cell phone buzzed. I miss you.

The message tugged at her heart. To think that *anyone* missed her. But why did it have to be a sleazeball?

I forgive you.

Fury surged through her. She texted back, WTF? Ur the 1 that needs forgiveness!

You stabbed me!!

She considered several responses, but finally sent, I don't ever want to see you again.

After a brief pause, his next message was, I need you, Maya.

She deleted the conversation and lay in the darkness, listening to sounds from down the street. What was she supposed to do now, all by herself? She toyed with the idea of texting Sam or Blake. Maybe Katerina in New Mexico. No, none of them wanted to hear from her. Ever again. She wished she had some beer or wine or pills or something to quiet down her brain. Finally, she settled for searching through YouTube for videos of rescued animals.

Then a message bleeped in. Her cell phone bill was overdue. Her service would be cut off in two weeks if she didn't pay up.

Could life get any worse?

40

In the morning, Sam checked with Deputy Ortiz on whether any tips had come in to help identify the dead kids.

"One helpful citizen thought they might be the pair that's been breaking into cars at trailheads," he told her. "But we have no photos of that couple, and no way to check it out."

"So, our wolverine snatchers are still a mystery."

"Yep. All the cars uncovered have been matched to their owners, who are all accounted for, either dead or alive."

"All the cars have been dug out?" she asked.

"The parking lot has been uncovered. Six more dead. We think we've got them all now. But some cars may have been shoved over into a ravine, and the snowplows scraping the parking lot dumped tons of snow and ice in there. We might not find anything more until the snow melts."

"Shoot." She wanted to see for herself. "Is the road cleared now?"

"Mostly. But don't even think of going up there. They're only allowing authorized personnel in."

A thought occurred to her. "Can't you fingerprint those two?"

Bodies was the unspoken word that should have ended that sentence. She couldn't bring herself to utter it.

"We did. Thanks to the freeze and thaw cycles, the prints

are next to useless, but we got a few points and ran them through the system. No matches."

"Darn."

"Most teenagers are not yet hardened criminals, so they probably don't even have prints in the database," he reminded her. "And most haven't ever needed to pass a background check for a job, either."

As disappointing as that was, it made sense.

The volunteers Sam spoke to on Gina's team didn't have any insights into who the dead poachers might be, and they swore that they'd never give out the coordinates of the wildlife cameras that had captured footage of the wolverines. But after Becca Diehl told her that photos of all the team members were on the website, Sam perused the pictures there. The staff had been generous, listing even those who worked on the website and on data entry and such, as well as the "technical assistants," some of whom were probably Gina's "geek squad."

According to the Wolverine Project website, one Colin Neufeld connected solar panels to power the cameras so they could transmit data to cell phones when cloud and snow cover and satellite access allowed. She searched for that name on social media sites, got a hit on Instagram. According to his account, he worked at Best Buy for the actual Geek Squad company. Thankfully, the young man was big on selfies, and there were many photos of him with his mountain bike, his fiancée Sonya Latham, and his buddies on a soccer team. But no photos of Dead Poacher Kid.

Sam felt stymied. Another dead end.

The orchid was still on Chase's table when she walked into his room that afternoon. But now it had company, a totem pole about a foot tall, and a stone figure of a whale. She stroked a finger down the miniature totem. It was beautifully carved and painted in traditional northwest red, black, and white colors.

She recognized the stylized forms of an orca and a crow, wasn't quite sure what the other two were. The whale sculpture was of a greenish smooth rock that felt good in her hand.

An aide peeked in. Sam quickly checked her mask to be sure it covered her nose and put the whale back in place on the table.

The aide checked the water pitcher and the box of tissues on the bedside table, then nodded toward the totem pole and whale. "Those are from the healing ceremony."

"Healing ceremony?"

"Three elders were here this morning, chanting and praying over your fiancé. Lummi, Nooksack, Tulalip, coming together."

Chase had spent many months on Native American reservations over the last two years. Pandemic restrictions didn't stop crime from happening, and Chase was the FBI liaison for the tribes.

Three different tribes coming together had to be an honor. But what did it actually mean? His Native American heritage was another aspect of Chase's life that she couldn't share, along with his Hispanic heritage and all his FBI secrets. At times she felt like she lived a white-bread life, while everyone else was on the more interesting multigrain shelf.

She set the whale sculpture down on the table. "A healing ceremony like that sounds ... powerful," she said. "I thought only relatives were allowed to visit patients now."

"We make exceptions for clergy." His brow wrinkled. "Religious officials, I mean."

Sam studied the nurse's aide again. His build was stocky, and he had dark hair, olive skin. The name on his badge was Warbass.

"I'm Lummi," he answered to her unspoken question. "One elder was my uncle. That ceremony was a great honor. It shows that many tribes respect your man. He must be doing good work."

Her eyes swept over Chase. He didn't seem any different. "I hope the ceremony helps."

"His fever's going down, if that's an indication. But the docs say it's going to be a long haul. He's lucky to have you."

After Warbass left, Sam ran her fingers over Chase's cheek, along his arm. "I hear you had visitors this morning. A healing ceremony. Everyone wants you to heal." When there was no response, she left, trying to sort through her feelings. Envy or frustration about the Native American elders and their healing ceremony? How could the religion of Native Americans be any different from her father's beliefs, which hadn't saved her mother?

In the hall, an older woman pushed a wheelchair, keeping up a running patter with the bald man slumped in the seat. "It's a nice day, Frank. You're going to enjoy the sunshine on the deck. And I brought some of your favorite music for you to enjoy."

A string of drool dripped from one side of the man's mouth. His eyes were vacant. Stroke victim, probably. A vision of her mother gasping for breath rose up in Sam's imagination. Oh God, would Chase be like that? She couldn't handle it. No, Chase was not "lucky to have her."

When the woman smiled at her, Sam did her best to reflect the expression, but her face was stiff. She picked up her phone, pretending to study it.

The woman passed, and Sam watched her push her husband down the long hospital hallway, remembering similar scenes of her father caring for her mother. Those were not happy memories for her, and she suspected they weren't for her father, either.

She and Chase weren't married. They weren't even really engaged. She could just walk away.

A week had passed since the avalanche. Sam could no

longer sit still and wait for something, anything, to happen. Sitting in the hospital wasn't helping Chase right now. The cops didn't seem to be searching for Eaze or James, which made her worry each time she left the house. She didn't see how she could help Maya; the girl had to help herself. But maybe she could help find out who the two dead wolverine trappers were.

Identifying the poachers was not a priority for law enforcement. The kids had been killed by the avalanche, not through some sort of foul play. As for trapping the wolverine, the Fish and Wildlife Service had nobody to prosecute. The suspects were dead, as well as the victim. And nobody seemed to be missing any of them.

She went home to get her backpack and hiking boots, thinking about different ways she might be able to observe the cleanup efforts, see if the crew had overlooked any cars that might belong to the poachers.

Could she hike up to the wolverine site again, see if there were signs of other wolverines in the area? Ortiz had told her that only authorized personnel were allowed up at the end of the road. Did that mean there would be a barrier across the Mount Baker Highway? Many of the lower areas in the mountains were snow-free. The outdoorsy population of Whatcom County would expect to access those. So any barrier would probably be near the ski areas. She might be able to park below that barrier and then hike in. Doing anything would be better than doing nothing.

As she shoved a sandwich into her pack, she discovered she'd left Gina's damaged wildlife camera inside a side pocket. She needed to see what, if anything, might have registered on the memory card after the avalanche. She set the camera aside, determined to do that later.

She'd also neglected to give back another object: the deputy's cap with the Sheriff's Department emblem on it. That could be useful. She laid it on the passenger seat and started the ninety-minute drive to the mountain.

It was a typical April day, the sky spitting raindrops on the windshield off and on, with brief periods of sunshine between clouds. As the road increased in elevation, the clouds thickened, and a cold drizzle enclosed the mountaintops. The snow alongside the asphalt grew in height until she worried about an avalanche falling across the pavement, her anxiety increased by many small snow slides that had closed the inside lane. Just below the lower White Salmon Ski Area, a barrier blocked the road. A miserable-looking Forest Service ranger was hunched inside his SUV, next to an **Authorized Personnel Only** sign mounted on a sawhorse. Thank God it was a ranger and not a deputy on duty. The Whatcom County Sheriff's Office was probably small enough that everyone knew one another.

Sam pulled on the Sheriff's Office hat. When the USFS ranger slid out of his vehicle, she was relieved to see that he was young and wearing jeans under his USFS jacket. Maybe not an official ranger, then, or maybe a temp worker who'd been called up here on his day off. Sam gave him a two-fingered salute and a nod from behind her window glass.

The ranger nodded back and skidded the sawhorse out of the way. She drove through, feeling clever and only slightly guilty. She drove up the driveway to the White Salmon lot and parked near a line of portable toilets.

The huge parking lot at the White Salmon area served both the White Salmon Day Lodge and the smaller Raven Hut Lodge. Below the ruin of the Raven Hut Lodge, the road and adjacent part of the lot had been scraped clean of snow, but was now a beehive of heavy equipment activity. Containers of wreckage stood beside the snow cliff mounded by the plow, and a track hoe was moving back and forth over the snow from the collapsed hut to the container, carrying stacks of construction debris. Between the blaring of the back-up beeper warnings of the equipment, Sam heard shouting up the slope near the lodge wreckage. The air was thick with diesel exhaust. Today, this was not the quiet pristine area that she loved.

Aided by a smaller wrecker, a huge car hauler truck was loading vehicles that had been pushed to one side of the parking lot. Many of the vehicles were dented and smashed, and some had wheels splayed out from broken axles. It was hard not to imagine the chaos in the parking lot when the wave of snow had hit. Ortiz had said six more had been added to the death toll, but he hadn't said whether the victims had been inside their cars or running to them when they'd been entombed. Chase and Nicole and Daniel and Baby Emma were lucky to be alive.

Keeping the hat pulled low, Sam walked around the perimeter of the huge parking area, hoping she wouldn't be noticed. Across the lot, the main White Salmon Day Lodge appeared to be remarkably untouched, shielded by the same folds of the mountain that had funneled the avalanche down onto Raven Hut.

Ortiz had mentioned that some cars could have been shoved over the lip of the parking lot into the ravine below, and she studied it now. Filled with snow and blocks of ice shoved there by the plows clearing the lot, the place was no longer even recognizable as the deep cleft she knew it to be. If there were cars down there, they wouldn't be found before the thaw revealed them.

A worker in overalls and reflective vest emerged from a portable toilet, giving her a curious glance before shoving his hard hat on and striding toward the activity. Sam trotted back to her RAV4.

The road beyond the lower lot had been cleared, so she drove up toward the higher Heather Meadows Base Area and the large parking lot there, near the maintenance sheds, curious to see if the avalanche had damaged this area. The ski areas were shut down now and the jumps from the aerobatic competition had been taken down. This area had apparently not been affected by the avalanche. It was quiet here, peaceful enough that she heard the flap of wings overhead and the raucous cries of crows competing for space in the grove of trees nearby.

She decided to walk down to the dam to check out the conditions on the Bagley Lakes Loop, one of her favorite trails when the high-mountain paths were still snow-covered. It was more of a slide than a hike down from the parking lot, because the steep hillside was still buried under rotten wet snow. The need to balance on her heels and make one unplanned hop had her groaning; her ankle and ribs were not yet healed. She stood for a moment on the snow-covered dam, grasping the flimsy rail and listening to the water rushing beneath her.

A gray jay rushed past her head and then perched on a limb overhead, regarding her with a bright curious eye. It was soon joined by another of its kind. Hikers and snowshoers called these birds "camp robbers." She was always amazed that although they were wild birds, the jays acted as though they'd been trained to greet hikers.

"I know what you want," she told the bird. Pulling off her pack, she dug into her sandwich bag and tore off a piece of the bread crust. Breaking it into tiny pieces, she held it out on her open palm.

The jay fluttered down to light on her hand. She loved the feel of the bird's tiny feet grasping her finger. "This is probably not good for you, you know," she murmured. After picking up a piece of crust, the bird fluttered away, his position quickly occupied by the other jay. "At least it's multigrain."

She could have stayed for several hours, but the growl of heavy machinery called her back to her original mission for coming. Kicking steps into the snow, she worked her way back to the parking lot.

Several vehicles, probably belonging to the resort workers, were parked to the side of the lot, close to the equipment sheds. She'd parked alongside them, not wanting her SUV to stand out. She watched as one worker carried a coil of cable into a large maintenance garage. In a few minutes he strolled out carrying a giant wrench, hopped in a pickup and drove away. Like the employees in the lower lot, that worker wore a reflective safety vest. Sam felt conspicuous without one.

Across the lot, a storage container and an old blue Subaru were stationed beneath the vertical bank that separated the lot from the road to the summit. Snow had sloughed off the bank, partially covering the container and the hood of the car. Had that snow been there for a week?

She walked around the car, peering into windows. A potato chip bag lay on the floor in the back, and two Coke cans sat in a holder near the dashboard. She pulled on the door handles. All were locked.

There were no knobs that could be pulled up with a coat hanger. But levering up the inside door handles might open a locked door. That worked on her RAV4. She hoped the same was true for this Subaru.

She didn't have a coat hanger, but she did carry a spool of stiff wire in her cargo area, just in case she needed to make an emergency repair to gear in the field.

She unrolled about a yard of the stiff wire, straightened it as much as she could, and used the multitool gizmo in her glovebox to cut it free from the spool.

Maneuvering the wire between the rubber gasket and the window frame was a challenge, and she spent a lot of time twisting it and sliding it back and forth to get it where she needed it to go. The bent end of the wire was tickling the inside door handle, but still refusing to slide over it, when a loud voice made her nearly jump out of her skin.

"Hey! What are you doing here?"

Sam let go of the wire and turned. A female deputy—a real one—stood behind her, wearing the official jacket of the sheriff's department beneath a reflective vest. She stood a few feet away, her hands resting on her duty belt, her revolver in plain sight. The name GUNN was on the deputy's nametag. "Is that your car?"

Sam considered saying it was, but only for a second. "Uh, no."

The deputy scanned her from head to foot, then her gaze returned to the hat on Sam's head. "Is that your hat?"

Shit. "No," Sam jerked it from her head and pushed it into a pocket. "This hat belongs to Deputy Ortiz. I forgot to give it back to him."

"I see. And why are you wearing it now? What are you doing here?"

Sam gulped. Was she about to be arrested for impersonating an officer? She explained about trying to identify the dead wolverine poachers.

They both noticed a resort employee watching them from the doorway of a maintenance building. The deputy made a come-here gesture to the young man, who reluctantly walked in their direction. When he was close enough, Deputy Gunn asked, "Do you know whose car this is? It looks like it's been parked here a while."

"I don't know," the man responded. "It could be Syd's."

"Syd?"

"Sydney Schultz. She's still off on spring break."

"Would she leave it here while she was out of town?"

The man considered. "You know, that *would* be weird. I don't know why she'd do that. She lives in Maple Falls, I think."

Deputy Gunn thanked him and said he could get back to

work. She focused again on Sam. "Can I see your ID, please?"

"It's in my car," Sam explained. "The RAV4 there."

"Let's go." Gunn accompanied her to the vehicle and watched closely, her hand on her holster, as Sam opened the door and extracted her pack. Sam wanted to ask the deputy if she got any flack because of her name, but Gunn didn't seem too open to humor right now.

After checking Sam's ID, the deputy whipped out her cell phone and took a photo of it. "I'll be checking with Ortiz on this," she said.

Sam glanced toward the car. Her wire still extruded from the frame of the passenger door.

Gunn followed her gaze, sighed heavily, then said, "What the hell, I'll just check the registration, and then we'll lock it back up. Can you finish what you started?"

Sam hoped her cheeks weren't as red as they felt. "I hope so. I locked myself out of my old Civic once and managed to get in. But I'm not an expert."

Snaring the interior door release handle seemed even more difficult under the impatient scrutiny of the deputy, but when she finally pulled up on the wire, Sam heard a satisfying click. She reached for the door handle.

"Wait!" Gunn pulled her back, then extracted a pair of vinyl gloves from her duty belt and donned them. The door whined, partially frozen, as she jerked it open. Sliding into the passenger seat, she popped open the glove box door.

After pawing through a bunch of receipts, Gunn pulled out the car registration. "Gary Latham," she read. "Redmond."

"Definitely not Sydney Schultz from Maple Falls," Sam remarked.

"Not unless she was driving Latham's car." Gunn took a photo of the registration with her cell phone, then locked the car and took a photo of the car from the rear, displaying its license plate. Sam was glad she'd already taken her own photo. She wanted a photo of that registration, too, but was afraid to ask.

"I'll report all of this to Ortiz," Gunn told her. "And I'll take him back his hat." She held out her hand for it. Sam handed it over. "And you'll drive down the mountain. Now."

Sam nodded and then walked back to her RAV4. In her rearview mirror, Sam saw Gunn watching her drive out of the maintenance parking lot. The guard at the barrier gave her a peculiar look as he slid the sawhorse out of her way. She smiled and waved as she drove through.

Well, mission accomplished. Sort of. But she didn't have the opportunity to hike to the wolverine site, and she wouldn't get the credit for finding that car. It seemed more likely that she'd get a reprimand, and possibly even a fine, for wearing an official Sheriff's Office hat.

Latham. That name seemed familiar. Where had she seen it recently? She tried to sort that out as she drove down the snaking mountain road, stopping to stroll down a path to a platform on the Nooksack River. As she scanned the trees lining the banks of the river for bald eagles, the name clicked into her brain. Instagram. Not the geek crew volunteers she'd found online, but a connection there. The girlfriend?

When she reached home, she was relieved to see her cabin was unscathed, and Simon was snoozing in the sun on the back porch. No intruders, then.

She brought up the Instagram accounts again. Sonya Latham, girlfriend of Colin Neufeld. She found Sonya's account, scrolled through her photos. And there he was, Sonya's younger brother, Jackson Latham. The photos showed him with two dogs, one on either side. It was a silly photo. The dogs each held a toy in their mouths. Jackson faced the camera with a limp plastic duck in his, but his face was still recognizable. Dead

Wolverine Poacher Guy.

After locating a phone number for Gary and Cassandra Latham in Redmond in an online directory, Sam called and asked to speak to Jackson.

"He's off skiing in Idaho," a woman told him. "This is his mother. What's this about?"

"Jackson volunteered to help with a cleanup day in the city parks," Sam manufactured, "and we wanted to schedule him for that and be sure he had permission from his parents. Did he tell you about that?"

"I haven't talked to him since the group left a week ago. It's spring break, you know. He should be home tomorrow, though. He has to be back in class the day after that."

"I'll call back next week, then." Sam hung up before the woman could ask her name or a number to call for the Redmond Parks Department.

That poor mother. Father. Sister. Dogs. None of them knew that Jackson would come home in a coffin. Along with whoever the girl was.

Sam called Deputy Ortiz. "Still no news, Ms. Westin," he answered curtly. Apparently, Gunn hadn't called him yet.

"Another deputy, Gunn, is going to tell you that I found a car that I think belongs to the dead boy."

"What? Where?"

When she told him, there was a long silence on his end, and she wondered if he was angry that she'd gone up there. "The name on the car registration is Gary Latham, who lives in Redmond and has a son, Jackson, who is the right age for the dead wolverine poacher." She left out the details about wearing his hat, and she didn't volunteer all the social media research she'd done. Nor did she tell him about calling the Latham house. Law enforcement sometimes got a little hot under the collar about civilians doing that sort of thing.

"O-kay," he finally said, drawing out the word. "We'll check it out."

"You'll let me know?" she asked. "I'd like to talk to the family." She guessed that Jackson had found out about the location of the wildlife camera from Sonya's boyfriend, Colin Neufeld. But she still had no idea why he wanted to trap a wolverine.

Ortiz hesitated again before saying, "Only if you're right about this, and only if they want to talk to you."

"Also, I gave Deputy Gunn your hat to return to you." She ended the call, glad that she would not be the one to tell the family what had happened to Jackson. And to the dead girl.

Her cell phone chimed with an incoming text, and when she checked it, she found a text from Troy Johnson, Maya's old employer and owner of Wilderness Challenge. Saw Maya yesterday in the tiny-home village by the railroad tracks near Marine Park. Has she really sunk that low?

Sam sighed. So that's where Maya had vanished to. Was that an improvement over a tent in her backyard? Or was Maya, as Troy hinted, sinking to the bottom of the societal abyss?

The girl—Sam's protégé, her father had called her—was now living among homeless strangers. But she had chosen to be one of them.

Sam texted a response back to Troy. Maya's druggie friends trashed my house and shot at my cat. I told her she's no longer welcome in my backyard.

Even typing those words made Sam feel like an ogre, although she was also irritated. Her father said that it sounded like Maya was depressed and he hoped that she would get the help she needed. Hint, hint. Why did everyone assume it was Sam's job to take care of Maya? They weren't even related. Sam had, however, already cross-stitched in the trees on Maya's quilt square, covering the ugly stain.

She added a second, softer message to Troy. I'm sorry Maya ended up there. She needs to get a job and find a place to live.

A few minutes later, Troy texted back. Is Maya in danger?

Good question. Maya's friends, Eaze and James Winnow, were still in the wind, as far as Sam knew. She resolved to drive by the tiny-home village later and see if she could spot Maya or her criminal compatriots.

41

Maya and Nancy, with Piquant in tow, joined the throngs out for the monthly Art Walk evening in Fairhaven. The sun was setting, and crowds of people had come out to enjoy the clear evening. Like Nancy, Maya had made an effort to clean up and brush her hair so she would fit into the gatherings. Sometimes the galleries set out snacks and small glasses of wine or cider, and she wanted to take full advantage of the freebies. Not to mention that she had nothing else to do that evening.

In the first gallery, Nancy discussed something called pointillism with the owner while sipping a glass of chardonnay and gesturing to paintings. That left Maya to wander the room, feeling like an uninvited cousin as she sneaked two glasses of wine and three crackers from the table.

As they were exiting through the front door, the owner called out, "Au revoir, Nancy! I hope you and your granddaughter have a lovely evening. Enjoy the rest of art walk."

Nancy twitched a few fingers at the woman in an artsy goodbye, and they strolled up the street toward the next gallery on the map.

"Granddaughter, huh?" Maya grumbled.

"She assumed you were a college student here."

"Yeah, well." Maya didn't know what to say other than that. She changed tack, determined not to ask what the hell pointillism was. "Maybe the next place will have better snacks. They should at least set out *cheese* and crackers, not just crackers."

Without breaking her stride, Nancy abruptly said, "Cutting to the chase, Maya."

Maya gave her a sideways glance. "What?"

"This is said out of affection, dear," Nancy began.

That sounded ominous. "Yeah?" Maya said uncertainly.

"You're prettier than average, you seem competent enough, you're young and strong."

Maya started to thank the old woman for the compliments, but then Nancy continued, "Every business is looking for workers right now. So why are you on the street?"

Maya's first reaction was a desire to snarl, 'None of your fucking business!' But the words that came out of her mouth were "Why are *you*?"

Piquant stopped to sniff at a light pole, so Nancy paused there, too, her eyes now on her dog at the end of the leash. "I'm seventy-eight," she told Maya. "And I'm broke. And I'm stupid. I trusted my husband to take care of everything. And then he died, and I found out the shithead had gambled away all our savings." Her eyes met Maya's. "You think an old lady can come up with first and last and security deposit and pet deposit for an apartment?"

Nancy remained amazingly clear-eyed after this declaration, watching her, waiting for a response.

"Um," Maya stammered. "Like you said, everyone wants workers these days."

"I work," Nancy stated bluntly. "Three days a week, at the Visitor Information Center. It's the only place that would hire an old gal like me and let me bring Piquant."

The *only* place Nancy could work? "Lots of people are working from home, I think."

"Lots of people don't live in a tent. And I think you need a computer for that, which I don't have, and which I don't know how to use." Nancy's face crumpled then, and she summed up with a shrug. "Like I said, I'm stupid."

They stared at each other for a minute as the art walkers flowed around them. The silence seemed deafening. And then they both started talking at once, Nancy asking, "What's your excuse?" and Maya complaining, "Everybody died!"

At that, three women passing by stopped to gape. Pulling at Piquant's leash, Nancy walked forward again, gesturing at Maya to follow. It was easier to talk walking side by side. So, then it all spilled out: Her mother and father and three women she'd worked with. Brianna, her study buddy. And most painful, Jade, her half sister. Maya hated the whine in her voice when she ended with, "I never even got to meet her!"

"Is that it?"

What the hell did *that* mean, *Is that it?* Like everyone dying was nothing. Like Eaze trying to use her was nothing. Maya fumed.

Stopping in front of a shop, Nancy remarked, "This place always gives out dog biscuits. I'm going in." The older woman vanished through the open door.

Is that it? Just like Sam. And Blake. And Hannah. And Katerina Franco. And Troy Johnson at Wilderness Challenge. Nobody cared about how she'd suffered, and now even this homeless old lady wasn't sympathetic. Maya folded her arms across her chest, irate. *Fuck that. Fuck life.* It had certainly fucked her.

She was marching alone down the street to the next gallery when Eaze materialized in front of her, an unexpected solid obstacle forcing her to stop. The couple walking behind her nearly collided with her after the sudden halt.

"Baby." Eaze tried to smile, but his lower lip was split and bleeding, and the movement made a drop of blood roll off. He licked at it with his tongue, his gaze raking her face as he repeated, "Baby."

"Tired of hiding out with your friends?" She scanned the surroundings for James or other scumbags. Both of Eaze's eyes were ringed with dark bruises like a raccoon, and a huge red-and-black mark slashed across his left cheek and forehead. Had he been smashed with a brick? She didn't need to know. She didn't care. She held up a hand to stop him. "Leave me alone."

"What did you do with my gun?"

"The police have it," she lied.

"Maya!" He tried to grab her sleeve, but she stepped back out of reach.

"You'd better split, Eaze. The cops are looking for you."

His eyes flashed with anger as he pressed his lips together, running his tongue over his teeth. "Worse than cops, Maya." His expression softened. "They say they'll kill me."

"Oh, well, in that case . . ." She held out her hand, palm up, and he took a step forward. She didn't ask who "they" were. Thrusting out her index finger, she jabbed it into his chest with each word as she said, "I still don't care."

He grabbed at her sleeve again, but two men passing by stopped to stare pointedly in their direction. Catching Maya's eye, the blond one asked, "Is everything okay?"

Eaze held up both hands and backed away from her, muttering, "Just a misunderstanding, man." He soon vanished into the throng of tourists on the street.

Nancy rejoined her, a baggie of dog biscuits in her hand. Piquant trotting along beneath the treats, his nose in the air. Giving Maya a stern look, she said, "Now I see there's more to your story."

Her lips pressed tightly together, Maya glared at her.

"So people you cared about have died? Don't you think we all know what that feels like? I lost my husband. And you know that nice Troy Johnson, one of the volunteers that brings us dinner? His wife and daughter were murdered a couple of years ago."

Maya squirmed under her scrutiny. She studied the street for a minute. Rough cobblestones in this preserved section of town. "Someone told me there used to be streetcars here," she commented.

Not taking the detour, Nancy continued her lecture. "And more than a million people died from COVID. And that's only in *this* country."

The hand she placed on Maya's shoulder was soft, and her smile was wavering. "You've obviously flown through some storms, haven't you? I can tell your flight plan got wrecked. But when do you plan to pull out of that nose-dive?"

Narrowing her eyes at the old woman, Maya turned her back to Nancy and walked away.

"See you back at the village, Maya. Be careful."

After striding quickly to the next gallery, Maya pretended to admire the exquisite woodwork of the artists while helping herself to crackers and cheese and a tiny plastic glass of cheap sparkling wine that was supposed to pass for champagne.

Then she made sure she walked with other gallery visitors as far as she could before dashing across the railroad tracks back to the tiny-home village. As she trotted down the dark pavement, she mouthed Nancy's insults.

Is that it?

When do you plan to pull out of that nose-dive?

If Eaze had reappeared right then, Maya would have punched him right in the face.

42

Sam's cell phone sounded a wolf howl, startling her. An incoming call. An actual call, a human voice instead of a text. *St. Joseph Medical Center* was on the screen. With some trepidation, Sam answered.

"Mr. Perez's fever has responded to the antibiotics, and he's awake for short periods of time now," a nurse told her.

Finally, good news! Sam could hardly believe it. "Tell him I'm on my way."

When she entered his hospital room, she found Chase reclining in bed. Warbass was seated on the bed beside him, holding a mirror so Chase could shave himself. The razor he was using was electric instead of his usual blade, but she knew a shave would be the first thing her lover had asked for. She stepped in just as Chase finished. The aide took the razor and the mirror and left the room, a faint smile on his face.

Chase's cheeks were still flushed, and he stared at her for a long moment, during which a cold fist of fear gripped Sam. Did he not remember her? Did he have brain damage? She pulled off her mask.

Finally, he croaked, "Summer." And then, "What kept you?"

"Oh, thank God, Chase!" She rushed to him, throwing an arm across him and hugging him.

He groaned.

"Sorry!" She released him, backed away, took his hand instead. "How do you feel?"

"Like I've been run over by a steamroller."

"I guess you would."

"You're okay?" He coughed on the last word.

She poured him a cup of water. "Mostly. A little banged up."

"I'm glad you didn't get caught."

There would be time to tell him later about being buried by the avalanche.

"Nicole?"

"Torn-up ankle, and a scar on her head, but she's already out of the hospital."

He sighed. "She beats me at everything."

That sounded like the man she knew. Sam chuckled and squeezed his hand. "You'll catch up."

He snorted. "Long way to go."

"You'll be there in no time, Chase. And I'll be with you all the way."

He glanced toward the window. "Night outside?"

"After dark. And it's after visiting hours, but I had to see you. The nurses looked the other way."

As he turned his face back to her, he winced and moaned, squeezing his eyes shut for a moment.

"Are you in pain?" she asked. That was a stupid question. Of course he was. His insides had been ripped apart and stitched back together.

He grimaced, forced his eyes open again. "Drugs help."

"I hope so."

His eyelids fluttered. "Gotta go now. Sorry." Then his face went slack and his eyes closed.

She squeezed his hand, bent over and kissed his cheek. His skin felt much cooler now than it had on her previous visit. Sleeping, she reminded herself, not comatose. "I love you,

Chase," she told him before she left.

Happy now, she walked down the hall. She could do it. She *would* do it. Bring him home or move in with him, take care of him until he was healed. She wanted to do that.

In the parking lot, she stopped a moment in a shadow to survey the sky. The clouds had cleared, but the streetlights blotted out most of the stars. She needed to go camping soon, somewhere far from a city. She couldn't remember the last time she'd seen the Milky Way.

She yawned. It had been a long, long day. But a satisfying one. Now, to check up on Maya.

Hours after dark, Maya still couldn't fall asleep. Her brain was swirling with confusing thoughts of Eaze and Nancy's comments. It was only a few minutes after eleven when she unzipped her tent and climbed out.

Nancy's tent was vacant, and Maya briefly wondered if the old woman regretted saying all those nasty things. She was probably at the dog bar, spending some of her social security check or her earnings from the Visitors Center on another glass of wine. At least Nancy *had* a regular income.

Thanks to her, Maya couldn't get Kim and Kyla out of her head. She could still see Kim's face in the Wilderness Challenge office, still hear Kyla's laughter out on the trails. Damn Nancy, anyway, with her talk about a flight plan and a nose-dive.

Had she ever had a flight plan? Maya wasn't sure. More like a cruise plan, just riding the wind wherever it took her. How was anyone supposed to control the wind?

She walked over the railroad tracks and around the nighttime parking barrier to Marine Park, then strolled to the shore in the darkness. When she'd led groups in the mountains for Wilderness Challenge, she'd loved the stars overhead and the quiet at night. In her tent in Sam's backyard, she'd heard owls calling and the occasional soft footfalls of deer.

Now, sitting on a driftwood log, she listened to the soothing rhythmic rush of waves over the pebbled beach, trying to settle her jangled nerves. The moon was peeking over the Cascades in the east. Her shadow stretched out over the rocks at her feet.

"Maya."

The low murmur of her name gave her a jolt. Goosebumps rose up instantly beneath her jacket as she twisted around. Eaze loomed behind her, his long ominous shadow falling over hers in the dim evening light.

Was James with him? Her gaze searched the dark, vacant parking lot. "Go away," she hissed.

"I can't." He stepped over the log and slid down to sit beside her.

"Then I will." She stood up, but he grabbed her arm before she could leave.

He rose to his feet, his fingers still clenched around her forearm. "I need you to understand." His breath was foul, like he hadn't brushed his teeth for days.

"You're hurting me." She tried to pull away. She could already feel her flesh bruising beneath his iron grip. "Let me go!"

He pivoted so that he was halfway behind her, and wrapped his other arm around her shoulders, pinning her against his body. "I can't let you go. Maya, I told you, they'll kill me." Eaze's voice was a growl in her ear. "I don't want to hurt you."

"Then don't! Let go of me!" She struggled against him, trying to wrench herself free.

"You're the only thing I have that's worth anything." He made the words sound like a declaration of love, but his grip was punishing, and he forced her to take several steps toward the parking lot. "They're waiting."

She saw it then, the dark car idling just beyond the barrier that closed the park access. Her heart was pounding so hard that she was sure the beats could be heard for a mile. Who was in that car?

Eaze had been willing to trade her to James to get out of his debt, and now he'd said *they* were waiting. Was she going to end up a prisoner in some godawful brothel in Mexico or Belarus, drugged and raped by dozens of men every day?

She opened her mouth and drew in a breath to scream, but before she got out more than a squeak, Eaze's hand clamped over her lips, his forearm and wrist wrapping around her head so tightly that she was afraid her neck would snap. She tried to dig her heels into the ground so that Eaze couldn't force her forward.

He twisted around and began to drag her backward across the lawn toward the waiting car. Beneath his dirty hand, she was screaming as loudly as she could. The tiny-home village wasn't far away. People should be out walking their dogs. Why couldn't anyone hear her? Why couldn't anyone see this?

She tried to peel his hand away from her mouth with her free arm. He slid his hand down to her throat, his fingers clenching so tight she thought they might crush her windpipe.

"Stop it," he snarled. "Don't make me hurt you."

She clawed at his hand, unable to breathe. Wrestling her sideways, Eaze jerked his hand away and wrapped his arm around her neck in a chokehold and yanked her backward again. She didn't have time to suck in a breath. Grabbing a handful of his sleeve with her free hand, she tried to wrench his elbow away from her throat. Black dots were gathering, dancing in front of her eyes.

43

Sam cruised through town toward the tiny-home village near Marine Park. Up the street, lights were still on inside the dog bar, but the picnic tables in the outside area were deserted. A white-haired woman walked a little dog toward the dark park. That seemed a bit questionable to Sam, especially since Bellingham had recently experienced an uptick in crime. And now that she knew that Eaze and James Winnow were still out there somewhere in the darkness.

She turned off her car engine and studied the tiny-home village. No lights were on in the tiny-homes or in the few tents in the corner. All seemed quiet. She yawned. It was nearing midnight. She thought about texting Maya to ask whether she was okay, but then decided to wait until morning. Everyone was probably asleep inside the tall chain-link fence.

The dogwalker continued on the sidewalk toward the park. A long black car was parked in the shadows beside the barrier there, its engine idling. That seemed suspicious, especially when a passenger emerged from a door and vanished into the shadows beneath the trees. Maybe a drug deal going down in the park, or some sort of illicit sexual rendezvous? Sam watched from the safety of her car, concerned that the dogwalker was about to walk into trouble.

* * * * *

In her peripheral vision, Maya saw a silhouette slinking through the shadows toward her. James? No, too big, too bulky. Eaze was going to hand her over to the Incredible Hulk.

She tried again to twist away, struggled to get both feet under her for leverage. Eaze kneed her viciously in the backside, and she felt an answering clunk against her right hip. The pistol! Releasing Eaze's sleeve, she slapped her hand against her side, finally found the pocket zipper. Blackout was only seconds away. She finally managed to unzip, push her fingers inside.

Her vision was going black, the ringing in her ears intensified to a roar. The footsteps were coming close. She managed to thumb off the safety, pulled the pistol from her pocket and then, reaching over her shoulder, she slid it the barrel along the arm wrapped around her throat. Was it loaded? She wasn't sure. When she felt the cold metal of the grip graze her ear, she pulled the trigger.

The blast was deafening, an explosion of superheated air against her eardrum. Eaze dropped to the ground, his chokehold arm dragging her down with him. The loud ringing in her ears drowned out the sounds of her own gasps and coughs, but she sensed movements. Swishing through the grass, footsteps on pavement, running. Faint percussive sounds broke through the cacophony in her head. The slam of car doors?

Then only the ringing was left, a fire alarm in her head that wouldn't be silenced. There wasn't enough air; her lungs felt as if she were trying to inflate a beach ball using a drinking straw. Her chest rose with each of her own ragged breaths, but she couldn't hear her inhalations and exhalations.

There was no movement from the body beneath her. Wetness soaked the back of her head. Eaze's blood oozing through her hair. The globs on her scalp, his brains? She didn't need to look to know she'd killed him, ended the life of Ethan Zeran.

And now her life was over, too. She closed her eyes, ready. She welcomed the nothingness ahead, jail and then prison for sure, where all decisions would be made for her.

44

Sam startled as a loud bang suddenly resonated from the park. Unmistakably, a gunshot. Grabbing her cell phone, she dialed 9-1-1 and when the dispatcher answered, she reported, "Gunshot, Marine Park, Bellingham!"

The dispatcher was asking for her name and location, but then Sam saw the dogwalker dash toward the park instead of away from whatever was going on. What the hell?

Her cell phone still in hand, she jumped out of her SUV and ran after the woman. A door slammed shut on the waiting black car. As it shot past, Sam raised her cell phone and snapped a photo of the rear of the vehicle.

A police car, sirens echoing and lights flashing, slammed to a stop just behind Sam as she dashed into the shadows. "Stop! Police!" an officer yelled, running behind her.

He probably had his gun drawn. Sam stopped, held her hands up. The tableau in front of her was astounding. The white-haired woman, a gun in her hand, stood over Maya, who lay on the ground with a body beneath her. The small dog sniffed curiously at the man's face. With his jaw blown away, Sam couldn't be sure, but she thought it was Eaze.

* * * * *

The clanging in Maya's head diminished to a dense gray fog of white noise, as if her hearing was muffled by earphones. After a few seconds, she sensed someone kneeling beside her. Christ, they were back, the guys who Eaze was selling her to! But when the red and blue lights strobed over her and a hot, wet dog tongue licked her cheek, she was forced to open her eyes, Nancy stood beside her, holding the pistol Maya had dropped.

As two police officers approached, guns held out, Nancy laid the pistol in the grass and held up her own hands.

Flashlights blinded Maya, and she held up a hand to shield her eyes as she sat up. She still couldn't hear much except the loud ringing, but she thought she saw Nancy mouth the words, *I shot him. Self-defense.*

45

When she stopped at the hospital to see Chase, Sam was surprised to see that the bed he had occupied was empty, newly made up with crisp white sheets. The bedside table held only an unopened tissue box and an empty water jug.

The night had been impossibly long, and she'd spent most of it explaining to the police what she had witnessed. Maybe her brain was fuzzy. Had she stopped by the wrong room? She double-checked the door number. No, this was Chase's room. But his name had been erased from the board.

What the—? No. Sam clapped a hand over her mouth. She'd watched this scene in countless movies, the horrible twist where the main character believes her lover is going to be fine, but then something god-awful happens while she isn't there—a blood clot, a stroke, a heart attack—and he's suddenly gone.

The last words Chase had uttered before falling back to sleep had been, "Gotta go now. Sorry." A lump formed in her throat. Had Chase known he was dying?

The Lummi aide, Warbass, now in green scrubs, passed in the hall. Did the man never sleep? Spying her inside the doorway, he halted with a squeak of rubber soles on the tile floor, and actually backed up three paces instead of turning. "Chase has been transferred to rehab. Northern Rehabilitation Center, Sedro Woolley."

She let her hand drop back to her side. "Thank God! I thought—"

He smiled. "I could see what you thought by the expression on your face. A transport was going this morning for another patient. But then that patient wasn't released, and they decided to take Chase instead. Someone should have called you."

Got that right, she thought. *Way to put a woman into cardiac arrest*. She wasn't sure her heart had yet returned to its normal rhythm.

Warbass opened the drawer on the bedside table. "He had my uncle carve this for you." After pulling a sticky note from the object, he dropped a small wooden carving into her hands.

A wolverine.

"Good luck." He continued down the hallway.

The wolverine was carved of red cedar, its body and thick tail held low to the ground in hunting mode, its ears pricked and head thrust out, one paw outstretched as it moved intently forward.

So it was true, what they said. Even unconscious, Chase had heard her stories.

46

From afar, Sam found it easy to be angry about Jackson Latham and Alexis Eckhardt trapping and killing a wolverine. Now, in the sorrowful atmosphere of the Latham home, she was finding it difficult to maintain her righteous indignation. Jackson's sister Sonya was there as well as his parents. To make the situation doubly uncomfortable, the parents of Jackson's girlfriend, Alexis, were also present.

The house was clean but smelled a bit gamey. A cat had vanished around a corner as soon as they'd walked in, and Sam recognized the telltale scratches of dog toenails on the oak floor. If she wasn't imagining the sound, there were birds in a back room somewhere. Not squawking like Zeke, but softly chirruping. Maybe parakeets.

Jackson's father faced Adam as he said, "I just don't understand. As far as we knew, Jackson and Alexis were both on the spring break ski trip in Idaho with the rest of the high school kids. They were taking a few extra days, and we allowed that because, see, they were good students, seniors, and they were in love . . ." He shook his head and then put both his hands on his temples as if he had a massive headache.

From flanking easy chairs Tanner and Claire Eckhardt nodded sadly but said nothing. Claire sniffed and held a tissue to her eyes.

Adam, out of consideration for the grieving parents, was only doing an audio recording of the conversation at the time, but a video camera waited by his side on the couch. After seeming nonplussed for only a minute or two, Adam diplomatically replied, "Teenagers can be very secretive."

"The police said they weren't even at the ski resort. How did you know where to find them?" Cassandra Latham asked Sam for the second time. Clearly the distraught mother was having difficulty absorbing the information.

Sam explained again about the signal from the wolverine's radio collar and how she and Gina had gone to the camera location.

The mother wiped a tear from her cheek. "But how is that relevant? To anything? Jackson didn't care anything about wolves!"

"Wolverines," Sam corrected. "Actually, just one wolverine." She was irritated that neither the sheriff nor the forest service rangers had told the parents of the deceased what their kids had been up to. "She died, too, that wolverine."

"I just don't understand," Claire Eckhardt said. "None of this makes any sense."

"Does the name Anton Priest mean anything to any of you?" Sam asked.

Blank looks all around.

"Who is he?" asked Tanner Eckhardt.

"A taxidermist. He sells wolverine skins and uh, . . . preserved specimens of all types of animals," Sam explained, seeing jars of glass eyes in her memory.

Sonya, Jackson's sister, violently shook her head. "Jack would never hurt an animal. And he certainly would never kill one."

A dog, some sort of springer mix, came over to Sam and rested its head on her thigh, its soulful eyes searching her face.

She stroked a hand over its forehead.

"Rolf misses Jackson," Cassandra told Sam. "So does Midnight. And all his other animals. I don't know what we're going to do with all of them."

Oh God. Sam regarded the Lathams. "Do you know a boy named Colin Neufeld?"

From her position on a stool in back of the couch, Jackson's older sister Sonya volunteered, "That's my boyfriend."

Sam turned to look at her. "He's a geek type, isn't he?"

"Yeah, he likes to fool around with electronics."

"Well, he apparently wired this wildlife camera to a solar panel, so he knew about its location."

"Oh."

"And I guess Jackson must have gotten the location from Colin somehow."

Sonya squirmed. "Colin's sort of Jack's hero." Then she crossed her arms in front of her chest. "Was."

"And so he and Alexis went to that location to set up a trap and catch a wolverine," Sam concluded. "One detail I haven't worked out is how that trap got there, and when."

"I never saw Jackson with a trap," his father said. "He would think traps were cruel."

"So would Alexis," her father added.

"It wasn't one of those horrible steel-tooth traps," Sam told them. "It was more like a very small log cabin with a hinged lid."

Sonya clapped a hand to her mouth. Everyone pivoted to watch her. "Colin and Jack were building something like that a couple of weeks ago. They told me it was a house for some orphaned wolf pups at the wildlife rehab."

Gary exchanged glances with his wife. "Didn't Jackson go hiking with a couple of friends two weeks ago?"

She nodded. "I think that's right."

"Those were strong kids," Sam noted. "The site is miles

from the parking lot, and they would have been carrying heavy loads." The phrase "premeditated murder" sprang into her mind. But that thought was way too harsh to even ponder in front of these grieving families.

"The police are sure that it was them? Absolutely sure?" This came from Tanner Eckhardt.

"Yes," Sam answered. "The car left in the lot was registered to Gary Latham. And you identified them, correct?" She was careful not to say the word "body." Everyone in the room seemed to be avoiding that. She gazed from parent to parent. "And you were sure, right?"

Tanner Eckhardt glanced sideways at his wife. Tears dripped into her lap as she softly murmured, "I'm sure."

"Well, the public deserves to know about your children. We don't want them to be forgotten." Addressing Gary, Adam said, "I'd like you to tell me about Jackson. And you"—he turned to the Eckhardts—"about Alexis."

"Can we do Jackson first?" Again, Gary Latham addressed Adam. When Adam nodded, Jackson's father stood up and strode out of the room. In a moment, he was back, a scrapbook in his hands. He stepped between Sam and Adam. They made room for him to sit on the couch.

"Jackson was a good boy." The father flipped open the scrapbook, thumbed through a series of baby and little-kid photos to the pages near the end. "Here's Jackson. And that's Alexis." He pointed to a photo of the teens dressed in formal wear, Jackson in a blue tux, Alexis in a short purple dress. They each had one arm clasped around the other's waist. In their free hands were face masks that matched their clothes. "They were going to the Christmas Ball."

Clearing his throat, Adam picked up the video camera and flicked it on. "May I?"

The father nodded, and Adam focused the camera on the

scrapbook. "Is this a photo from this year?"

"Yeah, last December."

"That was a little crazy," Cassandra added. "The couples had to dance six feet apart from the others. They had their own little circles taped out on the floor." Then she glanced worriedly up at the camera. "And of course, they shouldn't have been together at all."

"The COVID restrictions were problematic for kids of all ages," Adam reassured them, standing up so he could more easily film.

"Nobody got sick." Claire Eckhardt sounded defensive. Adam raised the camera to film her face for a few seconds.

"Jackson has always loved animals of all kinds," his mother said.

"That's a bond he shared with Alexis." That came from Claire. "She has three cats at home." Her voice wobbled on the last word, and she sniffed.

"They both loved to be outdoors," Alexis's father said. "They hiked and snowshoed, canoed, skied . . ." He broke down at that point, no doubt remembering that they'd thought their daughter was still on a ski trip when she'd been dead for days.

"Alexis was working as a vet tech," her mother said.

If they'd used a tranquilizer on Feisty, that might explain where the drug had come from. Would a dart gun or a jab stick be revealed when the snow melted?

"Jackson wanted to study biology," his sister Sonya told Adam, staring straight at his camera lens. "He had every book ever written by an animal researcher. He was especially interested in animal intelligence." She inhaled shakily and continued, "My brother wanted to be an animal trainer. He taught his dogs and cats all kinds of tricks. And Alexis helped."

The black dog that had been lying in its bed in the corner padded around the couch to nudge Sonya with its nose. "How tall are you, Midnight?" she asked the dog.

With one piercing bark, the black dog rose to its hind legs and briefly pawed the air, then barked again before he sank back down onto all fours.

"See? Jack taught him that." Sonya rested her hand on the dog's head as she glanced at Sam and Adam, her eyes swimming with tears.

Sam nodded. She found it painful to be in the room with so much grief, especially since the dead kids might have been kindred spirits of hers if they'd lived. Adam was quietly filming all their tears and sobs.

Gary flipped through a few more pages of the album, and as Adam filmed, Sam witnessed photos of Jackson tying his shoes at a track meet, Jackson washing his car, Jackson dressed in uniform for a football game, his helmet under his arm. Then the father flipped to the last page, a photo of his son in ski gear. "This was the last one . . ."

Gary's voice broke, and his wife stood up and moved behind the couch to lay her hand on his back.

The father lifted both hands to cover his face. Sam took the scrapbook from his lap. She flipped back a page to the football photo. The team stood behind a kneeling group of girls in cheerleading uniforms.

"Alexis was a cheerleader," Claire commented. "The one in the center."

"The prettiest one." Sam hovered a finger above the girl's photo and nodded at her mother.

Jackson's uniform was red and gray. Embroidered across the front of the jersey was the word "Chiefs." An unusual team name these days. Sam asked, "So, the name of the football team was the Chiefs?"

"Yeah," the father murmured from behind his hands, inhaling jerkily. "Chiefs. Jackson was going to be quarterback next season. The 'chief Chief,' we used to joke."

"Except they weren't going to be the Chiefs next year," Cassandra told them. "They were changing the names, even though that meant we'd all have to spring for new uniforms."

A bell dinged in Sam's head. She looked up at Adam. After a brief dip of his chin in acknowledgement, he stepped back to focus the camera on both parents.

"What did the school pick as the new name for the football team?" Sam asked quietly, fearing that both she and Adam already knew the answer.

"They decided on the Wolverines," Cassandra said. "Even though it was a challenge to get so many letters on the shirts, and they were having problems finding a wolverine costume for the mascot."

She held up her hands. "Who makes wolverine costumes? I'm not even sure what a wolverine looks like."

"The Chiefs' biggest rivals are the Badgers, and that team actually has a live badger mascot that waddles out onto the field every game," Tanner Eckhardt contributed.

Jackson's father dropped his hands to his lap to grip both thighs. "Oh, my God." He grabbed the scrapbook from Sam, staring hard at the football photo. "Oh, son. You stupid boy, how could you?"

47

"The evidence was all there. Jackson had a book written by a wolverine researcher. It even had a diagram of the log trap he and Colin built, and they set it up there a week before the avalanche. Jackson apparently got the coordinates of the camera from Colin, and Alexis got the tranquilizer from the vet she worked for. Maybe a dart pistol or a jab stick, too. Unfortunately, their timing was perfect to trap Feisty. The young idiots planned to capture a wolverine and train it to be a mascot for their football team."

Sam had already told all this to Gina and Blake, and now she repeated the story for Chase.

"Unbelievable," he replied. He was sitting propped up in a reclining chair in his room at the rehab facility, a white blanket over his legs. His hair was combed and he was clean-shaven; he already appeared 500 percent better than he had when she'd seen him last in the Bellingham hospital. The orchid she'd bought for him sat on his bedside table between the whale sculpture and the miniature totem pole.

She'd decided to surprise him with this visit, and had washed and brushed her long blonde hair, put on her most flattering sweater and silver earrings that Chase had given her. But instead of being happy to see her, he seemed uncomfortable with her presence.

"They didn't just capture Feisty, they killed her," she continued. "And if she had kits like the researchers thought, they probably died, too. Stupid kids." Sam knew she was chattering, but she couldn't seem to stop. She wasn't comfortable in this environment, either. The hospital bed behind her had a trapeze device suspended from the ceiling over it, and a wheelchair lurked in the corner. A white folded cloth failed to disguise a bedpan on the table to the side. But Chase looked so much healthier, surely he wouldn't require any of this for very long.

"The last episode will be about the last two victims of the earthquake, a special feature after the news tonight. Adam is relishing the spotlight again. And he's including my discussion of wolverines and how they need to be protected." At least he'd said that he would; she hadn't seen the final edit.

Chase made a sour face. "Adam. Of course."

She had no idea what he meant by that, and for a second, considered throwing Nicole's name back in the same manner. She had a past with Adam; he had a past with Nicole. Not the same past, but—

"Well, it's done now," Chase said. "You can move on."

"I plan to hike up there again soon, destroy what's left of that trap."

"Please don't go up there alone, Summer."

That was a bit annoying, but she knew that her solitary hikes could be risky, especially this time of year with the lingering snow in the mountains, so she simply said, "Okay."

A beefy guy in scrubs walked in and announced to Chase, "Time for therapy."

"*Querida*," Chase said to Sam, "You've got to go."

She hadn't even been there half an hour, but Chase's tone insisted that she leave. She stood up. "When do you think you can come back home? I can either move in with you at your cabin, or you can move into mine."

His brow creased.

"Just temporarily, of course," she hastily added. "Just while you need help. While you're recovering."

Chase lifted his gaze from her to the worker. "Give us a moment, Grant?"

"Back in ten." Grant exited the room.

"Summer," Chase began, "You don't—"

She didn't want to hear about her deficiencies. "Chase, I mean it; you can stay with me. I'll take care of you." She tried not to focus on the details of what that actually meant—cooking and feeding him, helping him to the bathroom, taking him to physical therapy, helping him dress—and then, of course, she couldn't focus on anything else. Blake normally did most of the shopping and nearly all the cooking, but he'd just announced he was going to be gone for a month. How would she find time to travel to events and work and cook and take care of Chase?

Do you love him? She heard her father's voice in her head. *Then you'll do what you need to do. That's the way it works.*

Somehow, she'd make it work.

Chase shook his head. "I wouldn't do that to you."

Sam put a hand on his arm. "But I want to. I'm willing, Chase."

He regarded her, his brown eyes solemn. "I know you, Summer. I know all about your mother." He exhaled heavily. "I'd never do that to you, unless there was no other recourse." After another pause, he told her, "For now, I don't want you to come here unless I ask you to."

Her heart did a somersault in her chest. He didn't want to see her? Why would Chase say that? She searched his eyes, uncertain of the emotion there. Regret? Embarrassment? Was this goodbye? Was he finished with her? Finally, she dropped her gaze to the floor, uncertain of what to do next.

"I don't want you to see me like this, *mi amor*," he explained softly. "I'll be here for weeks, maybe even months, to get back on my feet. Insurance will pay the full bill."

Chase had effectively dismissed her from his life for now. But he'd also called her *querida* and *mi amor*. She rose and picked up her jacket, not knowing what to say, not knowing whether he'd welcome a hug or kiss now. "Can I at least call you?"

Then, unexpectedly, Chase broke into a grin. "Don't think for a moment you can get rid of me so easily. Of course you can call. And believe me, I'll be back as soon as I can. I have to take you horseback riding in British Columbia. And don't fix my broken porch step until I'm there to help."

Yes, Chase did know her.

"I'll see you later, *mi salsa picante*." Smiling, she leaned over to plant a kiss on his lips.

48

Gina unlocked her front door and limped into her house, then pivoted to help Sam bring in a sack of groceries.

"Sit," Sam ordered. "You're not supposed to carry anything. You're not even supposed to be back at home."

Her friend collapsed into a rocking recliner in the living area, wincing at even the slight motion the chair made as she sat. "I couldn't take it anymore, being treated like I'm an invalid."

Sam resisted the urge to respond with, "You *are* an invalid." Instead, she said, "I understand."

After setting down the groceries on the kitchen counter, Sam went back to the car and carried in the large canvas-covered cage from the cargo area. As soon as she whisked off the cover, Zeke began to squawk and bounce on his perch, shrieking *"Hello! Hello! Hello!"*

When the macaw spotted Gina, he switched to *Love, Love, Love! Gee-na, Gee-na!*

"I think he's excited to be back." Sam grinned.

Gina grimaced. "I can tell. How're you doing, Zeke?"

"Gee-na! Love! Alexa!" the macaw squawked. *"Good orning!"*

The Echo Dot on the kitchen counter began to speak, saying something about this day in history.

"Alexa, stop!" Gina commanded. The device lapsed into silence.

Zeke made a strange noise that sounded eerily similar to Simon's meow. Then he uttered in a sing-song voice, *"Dunk-en sai-la, dunk-en sai-la!"*

"Oh, happy days. New tricks," the older woman commented drolly from her chair.

Sam observed her friend carefully. "Will you be okay here on your own?"

"I am *so* ready. I'll be slow, but I'll be fine. I have Zeke for company."

"Me-yow!" They both stared at Zeke, who bobbed his head excitedly, then followed up with a somewhat strangled but still recognizable owl hoot.

"You have a cat," Gina stated. "And an owl?"

Sam laughed. "My cat, Simon, kept watch on Zeke for hours every day. They definitely made an impression on each other. The owl is Blake's cell phone ringtone." She moved to the kitchen and began to put away the groceries.

Gina raised an eyebrow. "You seem excessively cheerful for a woman who's been visiting the parents of dead kids."

"You forgot the shooting and attempted kidnapping in Marine Park," Sam put a half gallon of milk into the refrigerator, then filled Gina in on the latest news.

Both Maya and Nancy had been released from custody while the events were investigated farther. The pistol had yielded fingerprints from both Maya and Nancy, and Ethan Zeran's were on the bullets inside. Along with their testimony, Sam's photo of the license plate on the escaping car had led to the arrest of a man the police had long sought for human trafficking. And although James Winnow had not yet been arrested, witnesses to his drug deals and connections to prostitution were slinking out from the shadows, and his future as a free man did not look promising.

Gina snorted. "Your life is so much more exciting than mine."

"It's going to be a lot less exciting for a while," Sam responded. "Chase will be in rehab for a month to six weeks, and Blake is taking a month-long absence to babysit some gorillas in Evansburg."

"Gorillas?"

"Signing gorillas." Sam grabbed an orange that had escaped to the bottom of the cloth grocery bag and stuffed it back into its original plastic bag. "There was an article about them in a magazine. It described how difficult it was to get anyone to care for intelligent apes in the rural area they live in, so Blake emailed the gorilla owner and offered to come for a month. He left yesterday. God only knows what they'll learn from each other. Blake's been practicing sign language for two weeks now."

She spun the bag of oranges, then closed it with a twist tie. "This doesn't seem like Blake's thing, but I think he wants to do something totally different for a while." Gina didn't know about Blake and Claude, and that wasn't Sam's tale to tell. "I wish I could go, too, but someone's got to hold down the fort here. And feed the cat."

Unfortunately for now, James Winnow was still in the wind, and he knew where she lived. Sam told Gina about a few disturbing slow cruises past her house. Black or gray vehicles, all after sunset. One massive pickup had stopped in her driveway, switched on its hunting spotlights and scanned the yard. "I suspect they're looking for Maya."

"Gawd. Aren't you scared?"

Sam hesitated. Of course, she was frightened. Every single time any car slowed past her house. She had even constructed an escape hatch for Simon, with a narrow cat ramp zigzagging up the walls and a cat door high in the utility room, where no human could go. She couldn't stand the thought of her pet being trapped inside if the house was invaded again.

"Before Blake left town, he helped me install security cameras and an alarm system." She shrugged. "I hate that thing, and I've accidentally set the alarm off twice already, but what else can I do? I'm not going to let a bunch of thugs drive me from my house. And hey—I clawed my way out of an avalanche! I'll handle whatever comes up."

"Do you think that dead guy's friends are out for revenge?" Gina raised a hand to her mouth. "Isn't Maya worried?"

Sam met her gaze. "Blake took Maya with him. But that's only for your ears."

Gina pinched her fingers together and made a zipping motion across her lips.

"Maya's got PTSD, according to her counselor."

"Blowing someone's head off will do that to a girl," Gina commented.

Sam winced. "Yeah. Even if Eaze deserved it. She's got to come back for a hearing in four weeks, but until then, she will be taking care of the gorillas with Blake. I think a change of scene and routine will do them both good."

Maya had extracted a tentative promise from Troy Johnson that if she got her act together, stayed drug free, and was found innocent of all charges, she could work at Wilderness Challenge again. Sam had placed the repaired quilt square in Maya's suitcase for her to find.

In a completely unexpected move, Troy had hired Nancy to watch over the office and answer phones. She cooked in the employee lounge and slept on a cot in the equipment storeroom, and Piquant had his own bed there, too. Nancy was also required to attend the upcoming hearing, where Sam fully expected her to claim again that she had fired the fatal shot to save Maya, keeping the police confused about who had fired the gun that night.

"Me-ow! Dunk-en sai-la!"

Gina groaned. "Zeke will motivate me to get back out installing wildlife cameras in no time."

Sam pulled her cell phone from her jacket pocket. "Speaking of wildlife cameras ... Remember that I told you I picked up the camera at the wolverine site? It's in the shop to get the screen replaced right now. But I took the memory card out first."

Sam held her phone in front of Gina and swiped with her finger through the photos. They had been captured through the dirty lens and were a bit blurry, but the image could be identified. A wolverine, her fur dark and matted around the snout and shoulders, carrying a dingy white snowball in her mouth.

"Is that—?" Gina's mouth fell open in astonishment.

"Feisty," Sam confirmed. "Bloody but unbowed. Not only did she escape from the carrier, she broke out of her collar."

"Unbelievable." Gina grabbed the phone, used her fingers to enlarge the image, focused on the small, blurry brownish-white snowball sandwiched between the wolverine's jaws. "Is that—?"

"Yes. She's carrying a kit." Sam swiped to the next photo. "And here's another one. This baby is a little darker than the other one. I'll send these to your new cell."

"I've never seen a baby skunk bear before, not even on a camera." Gina's face was beaming. "Never underestimate a wolverine."

"I'm definitely going to add one to my quilt," Sam said.

Gina's brow crinkled. "What?"

"Never mind." Sam waved a hand in the air. "Just thinking out loud. I'm making a story quilt, with squares that represent important moments in my life."

"Seeing a wolverine definitely qualifies as one of those." Gina smiled at the cell phone as if it were her best friend, but then reluctantly handed it back. "Thanks, Sam. For everything." Gina held out a fist.

Sam bumped Gina's fist with her own. "Meet you in the mountains."

Books by
Pamela Beason

The Sam Westin Wilderness Mysteries
Endangered
Bear Bait
Undercurrents
Backcountry
Borderland
Cascade

The Neema the Gorilla Mysteries
The Only Witness
The Only Clue
The Only One Left

Romantic Suspense
Shaken
Again
Call of the Jaguar

The Run for Your Life
Adventure/Suspense Trilogy
Race with Danger
Race to Truth
Race for Justice

Nonfiction E-books
So You Want to Be a PI?
Traditional vs Indie Publishing: What to Expect
Save Your Money, Your Sanity, and Our Planet

Keep up with Pam on https://pamelabeason.com

About the Author

Pamela Beason is the author of the Sam Westin Wilderness Mysteries, the Neema the Gorilla Mysteries, and the Run for Your Life Adventure Trilogy, as well as several romantic suspense and nonfiction books. She has received the Daphne du Maurier Award and two Chanticleer Book Reviews Grand Prizes for her writing, as well as an award from Library Journal and other romance and mystery awards. Pam is a former private investigator and freelance writer who lives in the Pacific Northwest, where she escapes into the wilderness whenever she can to hike and kayak and scuba dive.

https://pamelabeason.com